Felt

Felt

Mark Blagrave

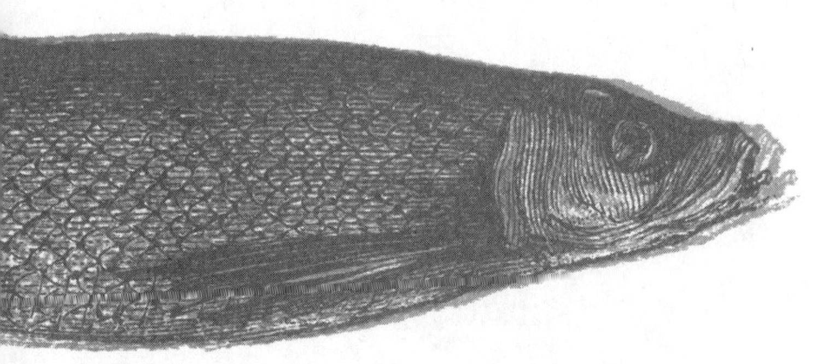

Cormorant Books

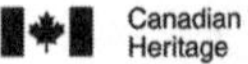

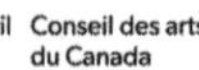

We acknowledge financial support for our publishing activities: the Government of Canada, through the Canada Book Fund and The Canada Council for the Arts; the Government of Ontario, through the Ontario Arts Council, Ontario Creates, and the Ontario Book Publishing Tax Credit.

LIBRARY AND ARCHIVES CANADA CATALOGUING IN PUBLICATION

Title: Felt : a novel / Mark Blagrave.
Names: Blagrave, Mark, 1956- author.
Identifiers: Canadiana (print) 2024032756x | Canadiana (ebook) 20240327586 | ISBN 9781770867567 (softcover) | ISBN 9781770867574 (EPUB)
Subjects: LCGFT: Novels.
Classification: LCC PS8603.L296 F45 2024 | DDC C813/.6—dc23

United States Library of Congress Control Number: 2024930589

Cover and interior design: Marijke Friesen
Author photo: Sheila Blagrave
Manufactured by Friesens in Altona, Manitoba in June 2024.

Printed using paper from a responsible and sustainable resource, including a mix of virgin fibres and recycled materials.

Printed and bound in Canada.

CORMORANT BOOKS INC.
260 ISHPADINAA (SPADINA) AVENUE, SUITE 502,
TKARONTO (TORONTO), ON M5T 2E4

SUITE 110, 7068 PORTAL WAY, FERNDALE, WA 98248, USA

www.cormorantbooks.com

JBB (1923–2022)
and Grat, David, and Tim

"History issues from geography in the same way that water issues from a spring: unpredictably but site specifically."
— Robert Macfarlane, *The Old Ways*

"It is an assistance to the memory if places are stamped upon the mind ... For when we return to a place after a considerable absence, we not merely recognize the place itself, but remember things that we did there, and recall the persons whom we met and even the unuttered thoughts which passed through our minds when we were there before."
— Quintilian, *Institutio Oratoria* XI, ii, 17–22,
trans. H.E. Butler

"Memory runs her needle in and out, up and down, hither and thither. We know not what comes next, or what follows after."
— Virginia Woolf, *Orlando*

Lookout

WHEN SHE REACHES the top of the mountain she finds she cannot recall getting there. Obviously, she has parked by the inn (must have parked, must have driven, though she remembers doing neither). And she would have swished through the long grasses past the peeling carriage house before beginning the actual ascent. The trail — cut for horse-drawn picnic wagons a century before and rimmed with massive, reassuring retaining walls of quarried granite — would have crunched and crackled under foot. It is autumn and most of the leaves are down. She would have paused at the lookout point a little more than halfway up, what was left of her breath taken away momentarily by the view across Chamcook Harbour to Ministers Island. The final scramble over the grey skull of rock to the summit would have set her hips complaining. All of this she can conjure up from the scores of times she has made the climb. But she cannot swear that any of it happened today.

She knows this is not necessarily uncommon, reminds herself it is not. How often, driving along a highway, do you suddenly focus on a feature of the landscape and then realize you can't recall anything about travelling the past twenty miles? Or fail to be sure you have locked the door or run the dishwasher? But this is different. She knows it is, at the same time that she knows there is not a thing she can do about it.

The air is crisp — *an odd expression*, she thinks. Perhaps that is not the right word. A better word for bedsheets. Or people. Or the leaves she cannot recall tromping over to get here. The air doesn't need a word, she decides, any more than the colour of the sky, which is the colour of the water anyway. Or is it the other way around?

She sits on the rock, checking first that it has been warmed by the sun, and runs her fingers over the initials carved into it. These are recent inscriptions; she knows that. The really old ones — some of them well over a hundred — were sandblasted away by one of the fools who has owned the inn in more recent years. Hers are gone along with them. That used to upset her. Now she finds she no longer minds. You have to pick your battles. That much she has learned. *And can still remember*, she thinks ruefully. She wonders whether her mother ever carved her initials on the rock — her mother and who, she wonders, wishes she had asked her, and then is glad she didn't. Less to regret losing. If she were inclined to regret. Matt has admitted lately to having brought girls up here, times when he had begged her to borrow the car to drive to St. Stephen or St. George, not willing to divulge his real purpose of getting to whatever base it was with whichever young woman of the moment. She has scanned the rock in vain for his initials, supposes he was wary of leaving any trace.

When she feels in her coat pocket for the sandwich she planned to eat, there is only a forlorn tissue — crusty, but no substitute for a crust of bread. The sandwich will have been put somewhere odd. She knows that much still, and can still be amused by the behaviour. She will find it later in a sweater drawer or in the microwave. If she made it. If that wasn't some other day.

"Fuck," Penelope whispers. Then louder: "Fuck!" There is nobody around to offend. Not that she has ever understood why people get offended by some words and not by others. Or why some words that are acceptable for use by men are apparently not for women. In her mother's house there were no such prejudices, of course, but a person had to live in the world too. And the world had problems with certain words. Especially, it seemed sometimes, the world of Charlotte County. She taught Matt her entire expressive vocabulary, encouraged him to use it with gusto, and then sent him away to school, to protect him from the pettier attitudes of the town. She wonders how Matt is doing at that school, thinks she must write him a letter, then remembers that he is a grown man — a fully grown man, nearer retirement than graduation. She could still write him a letter.

Perhaps her mother will have packed a lunch, she thinks. It won't be fish. Thora hates fish. Not all fish. Just proper fish, not shellfish. As a small child, Penelope ate lobster and scallops for years before she even knew mackerel and herring existed. She realizes that to some this might look like privilege. In fact, it was only her mother's history.

Looking down at her hands, stubbier than Thora's and broader — her father's hands, George Arnold's hands, she has been told — she is appalled by the liver spots, the ropey blue veins. They are the hands of a very old woman. What does that make her mother? Dead, of course. Penelope laughs. Laughing is what she does when she has these sudden and increasingly frequent epiphanies that people have died, many of them years ago. She's not laughing at them being dead — what would be funny about that? — just at herself for mixing things up.

Giving up hope of food, she stands and makes her way to the south slope, pausing to read strangers' initials on the way, plotting each step carefully so as not to get her foot caught in a crevice and twist an ankle. Who would give little Matt his supper?

Coming around a contorted cedar, she encounters the skunky smell that her neighbour has told her is marijuana, wonders why anyone would want to inhale that stink right into their lungs. Before she can see the source of the odour she hears a scrabble of small stones and a rustling of branches that means somebody has retreated into the scrubby spruces that fringe the mountain. Giggling. Two people. She imagines the man in uniform, the woman with her stockings rolled down, then realizes that is not right. The smell would be rum or whisky, not this wretched skunk. And she would not be the wizened old hag she once again realizes that she is.

Leave them be. That is what she will do. Just drink in the view she came for. The harbour, the town, the bay, the island, and the coast of Maine all lie below, exactly as she has captured them again and again in her work — a scene you couldn't design if you tried, but once seen could never forget. She gazes on it for a full two minutes, stores it up, and then shuts her eyes and imagines that couple in the trees, allowing the two forms of desire to become for a moment one.

When she reaches the inn at the bottom of the mountain her car is nowhere to be seen. She must have walked. It is quite a long way back to town but she knows the route like ... what is it! She knows the route.

Tiny Perfect Town

THE IDEA FOR the Model Villages exhibition was Jennifer's. A few years earlier, they had been in Bergen, admiring the paintbox gable ends of the Bryggen district. Matt had said they reminded him of Water Street in his hometown. They had gotten into a debate about whether the best streetscapes are those you plan or the ones that just happen over time. She had argued for chance and he for design. As her *coup de grâce* she had trotted out Prince Charles's pet project, Poundbury, once described, she reminded him, as "a Thomas Hardy theme park for slow learners." In defence, Matt produced the model industrial villages of the nineteenth century. There was a long list of them, and he struggled with a few: Saltaire, Akroydon, Copley, Bournville, and (his favourite) Port Sunlight, built by Lever Brothers and named for their famous soap. Jennifer had countered with Shaw's fictional village in *Major Barbara*, designed by the arms manufacturer Andrew Undershaft to ensure the creature comforts of the very same workers who produced the means to annihilate all creatures and their comforts. Perivale-Something-or-other.

Not long after the fiasco at the museum, Jennifer had recalled this conversation word for word (her memory was always much better than his) and that was when she had the idea: Matt needed a new project to work on. He should do something on model villages. He could start with a visit home, a return to the tiny perfect town laid out by the United Empire Loyalists on the shores of Passamaquoddy Bay. Champlain's doomed French settlement on Saint Croix Island was there too, just up the river. And wasn't there a model village that had been built at Chamcook for the workers at the sardine factory? It would give him a chance to check up on his mother after the unsettling call from Bernadette, and — although Jennifer didn't say this, didn't need to say this — to have some time away from her, and she from him.

Matt supposed he shouldn't have been surprised that The Director instantly supported the idea, even though the proposal, in Matt's view, was full of holes. The Director appeared to want him out of the city nearly as much as his wife did. Although the potential shitstorm around Matt's faux pas with the artifact had been contained, as had Matt's near ruin of his marriage, time and distance could only help heal both wounds. And so he phoned his mother and asked if he could come and spend some time. She paused before saying yes. He knew how much she valued her space. In the next breath she was all for picking him up at the airport. He said he didn't think she should make the hour's drive. He didn't add how he didn't think she should still be driving at all, even just around the town itself. There were dozens worse than she, he knew. After a stony silence on her end, he finally managed to persuade her to bring Bernadette along to the airport for company. He knew Bernie would insist on driving and they stood a chance of arriving in one piece. Bernie was probably only fifteen or sixteen years younger than his mother, but — at what he suspected was a shade under eighty — she was the safest bet he could think of. He would drive back, of course. Penelope always let him drive her. *I suppose you'll want to drive. I wouldn't dream of undermining your male pride*, she would say, but he knew she actually liked his driving.

He had purchased only the flight out. These days, there was no advantage in buying round-trip. No monetary advantage. There was, of course, the assurance of knowing you were indeed going to return. When he had raised that point, Jennifer had only smiled and rumpled what was left of his hair. *It's only 1,100 kilometres. You could walk it in ten days*. He doubted that, but she showed him on Google Maps. They looked together at the blue dots stretching through Maine and Québec from New Brunswick to Toronto. The math was impossible, he knew, the formula misconceived somehow. Who could walk 110 kilometres a day? But the unbroken line of dots was reassuring, a pathway of perfect stepping stones linking the two places. And he really didn't know exactly how long his research would take him or exactly what his mother might need.

Packing was a challenge for an open return trip east this time of year. Any time of year. He would not need summer gear, but everything else was on the table, even if he stayed only the month he had planned notionally. His mother's house was never warm. That was normal in a town where most of the houses were either over two hundred years old or built for summer people. The wind off the water blew right through. You wore sweaters. His mother, and his grandmother before her, had made use of that fact of Maritime life to organize the county's knitters to produce acres of woolens that they then sold in their shop on Water Street. Matt knew that there would still be piles of unsold Fair Isle sweaters in the house should he need an extra layer. In the end, he managed to fit everything into a carry-on, reasoning that the dollars saved on checking a bag could buy him a parka and boots at a thrift store if necessary. Jennifer laughed but didn't try to talk him out of it.

They said goodbye at home. The drive to the airport was something they had always found too stressful, and a solo drive back would be an absolute nightmare for her. Jennifer offered to accompany him on the UP Express, but he knew the offer was half-hearted so he told her to save the hit on her Presto card. "And buy myself a parka?" she had quipped. He started into the now familiar formula of asking for forgiveness, but she squeezed his arm and pushed him out onto the street. On the walk down to Dundas he paused to wonder whether she had a lover coming in the back door. No. She was not the eye-for-an-eye type.

Two a.m.

PENELOPE SELDOM GOES into Matt's room anymore. It isn't respect for his privacy — though that was once an issue, God knows — or a fear of ghosts. She has simply gotten out of the habit. It is a big house. You didn't need to go into every room every day. And once you stopped, it became normal not to think about some of them. The bathrooms were the easiest to forget, and the most rewarding. Who needed to clean three toilets when there was only one set of buttocks in the house? The place has effectively shrunk to four rooms: her bed, her bath, the kitchen, and that room with the wood stove and her wingback chair.

When Matt announced he was coming to stay (*had he phoned or written?*), she had immediately written herself a note. She writes a lot of notes these days, sometimes notes about checking the other notes. "Matt's sheets," this one says. *What about them?* she wonders. Presumably, she had wanted them to be fresh. The problem now is determining beyond any doubt that they are. Because doubt is a problem these days. There are sheets on the bed. Have they been there since his last visit, whenever that was? If so, dirty or clean? She used to wash sheets as soon as visitors were out the door, but that may have stopped. She thinks it has.

Has she read the note before — it looks familiar, but then she uses the same pad of paper for all her notes — and already changed the sheets? She doesn't mind running them through the machine again, but she doesn't want to be doing that time after time forever and ever. Perhaps if she washes and dries them and leaves them folded on top of the quilt for Matt to make up for himself ... Or she could make up the bed and attach a note. Destroying the original note once that's done would also be a good idea.

She stoops to sniff at the sheets. If they smell of lemons (or is it lavender in her detergent now?) they are probably fresh. Unless Matt wears scent to bed. Or that wife of his. Penelope wonders whether she was here on Matt's last visit but can't picture her. It's natural for daughters-in-law to be uncomfortable around mothers-in-law, but she can't recall many occasions when the girl has even given herself that opportunity. She herself was spared the experience of a mother-in-law, but Thora had some stories of her first few years of marriage. Penelope was too young when her grandmother died to remember much of anything about her, let alone recall witnessing the strife between her and Thora. All she had in place of memories of her own were Thora's horror stories of her in-laws. Her father would never have been able to produce competing stories about his in-laws. Thora appeared to have sprung from the earth. That's what people used to say. Sometimes it was with admiration.

Of course, everyone knew that Thora had come not from the earth but from Norway, which was almost as mythic. Many of the details were not for public consumption, but Penelope learned to repeat her mother's story at a very early age.

Mamma sailed from Bergen with about a hundred other Norwegian girls who were answering an advertisement for sardine packers at a new plant about to open in Canada. *Weren't you frightened coming all that way by yourself?* Penelope always asked this even though she knew the answer. It was a way of keeping the story fresh. *No, Mamma wasn't frightened.* She had travelled with her brother Nils. Mamma's parents were apparently very strict and would never have allowed her to travel without a chaperone. The young Penelope loved that word *chaperone.* It sounded so worldly, so sophisticated, which helped cancel out the sardine-packing part of the history. She quickly learned not to ask about brother Nils. He vanished from the story not long after they arrived. The sardine part actually cancelled itself out pretty quickly too as the saga followed Mamma through the founding of Handworks — it was called something else at first — and then, four or five years later, with the marriage to one of her new town's princes (this was Penelope's father, whom she could barely remember). The story always concluded — if it didn't end — with the birth of Princess Penelope. That was her favourite part.

She imagines her mother, an immigrant, cast among the descendants of the town's Loyalists (themselves immigrants, though they never would admit to that), and can't decide whether that would have been harder or easier than breaking into the society of the summer people, who had only recently begun to build their shingled palaces. Penelope's experience had been that the summer-people nut was the harder one to crack, but then, of course, thanks to her father, she had Loyalist blood in her veins, and that bought her a little access to the townspeople, regardless of how some continued to see her mother.

The country women — the ones who knitted and wove and hooked and felted for her — loved Thora. There was no question of that. The enterprise they called her *smokeless factory* had seen them through many hard times when the crops were bad (most years) or the price for pork dropped or the herring stopped running or there were no boats to build or summer people to hire their families on as help. After she took over the business from

Thora, Penelope was never sure whether the women loved her for herself or because she was Thora's daughter. In the end, it didn't really matter. She had taken the business that her mother had founded and run for thirty years, and she had kept it going for a further forty. *That was a lot harder to do in the last forty than in the first thirty*, she thinks.

She is glad Matt had those early years with his grandmother. Glad too that she had Thora to help her raise him through his first decade. People, usually summer people — summer women — often made a fuss over how remarkable it was that Penelope could both run the business and raise a child by herself. She usually smiled and nodded and said, *You do what you have to*. Almost never did she give any of the credit to her mother. She doesn't feel guilty about this. They had agreed that if the myth of the single mother helped sales — and it did — then there was no harm in it. In private, Penelope showed her mother how grateful she was every day. She thinks she did. Hopes she did.

She looks at the clutter of objects on the shelf above Matt's desk. He was always untidy after Thora died. She supposes he was untidy before, and that Thora simply kept him in line. There are commemorative Coke cans (*what an idea*), a menagerie of impossible pottery animals, an RAF epaulette he found somewhere, and a battered tin cup brimming with defunct ballpoint pens. She knows they are defunct because she has tried every one of them but has not had the heart to throw them out.

She must get at it, she thinks, must gather these things up for the scrap drive. The cans and the tin cup can be melted down, the epaulette sorted with other unused woolens lying about the house and bagged. She is not sure whether the war effort has any use for pottery animals, whole or broken. Perhaps they could go with the bones she has been saving. They say they make them into glue for building airplanes to fight the Nazis.

Something about airplanes. Matt is coming home. He should have clean sheets. She gets up off the bed (*when did she sit down?*) and begins stripping it. She will have to hurry. Her watch says it is two o'clock. Why, then, is it pitch black outside?

Baggage

THE FLIGHT WAS less than half full, although there was still barely enough room for his carry-on. Matt and Jennifer had a theory that every night, while the airplanes slept, someone came in and performed a kind of grim avionic proctologic surgery that made their insides less functional: adding seats, subtracting bins. In the stark tarmac-level waiting room that was always assigned to the Saint John flight, Matt had overheard someone say they'd heard the airlines might be about to start charging for carry-on bags instead of the checked ones. Maybe they'd bring back free meals while they were at it.

He knew he should worry that the flight was so undersubscribed. At what point would the airline simply suspend the service? If they did, how would he get to his mother in a hurry if there were an emergency? The luxury of having a whole row of seats to himself calmed those concerns for now, though.

Matt saw Bernadette first, waiting at the gate. A little more wizened, perhaps stooped by an additional degree or two since he last saw her, but still the same Bernadette who had helped out in his mother's shop from a time before Matt could remember right through until the day the business closed. She had always been a mystery to him: a pretty enough woman with yards of personality and a razor-sharp mind who chose a lifetime of (apparent) celibacy as a shop clerk in a marginal enterprise. He knew that view made him all kinds of things ending in *ist*, but still, he couldn't help the wondering.

"Your mother's gone to the loo," Bernadette announced to the entire assembly in Arrivals as she beetled over to give him a hug. "It's a long drive back, you know." Matt knew it really wasn't. An hour and a bit. But he nodded and said he thought that was a good idea. "We'll wait for your bags, shall we?" She tugged him in the direction of the carousel like he was still a little boy.

"This is it. Just my carry-on."

"Your mother packed more than that for the car." He had never once heard Bernadette call his mother Penelope. She was always *your mother* to him and *the boss* to anyone else, even now. "There she is now."

Matt watched the bent but determined old woman as she emerged from the bathroom and looked about her before making a beeline for the gate. He tried waving from beside the carousel but she had set her course, no doubt with eyes only for Bernadette where she had left her beside the arrivals gate. It took only a few long strides to cut her off. "Mamma," he said, wincing at the sound of it from a grown man's mouth, wanting to explain to bystanders that he was speaking Norwegian, not baby talk. Her face lit up and he stopped caring what other people might think.

"Matthew. Darling. You look so ..." She trailed off, leaving him to insert the adjective: *good*? *tired*? *old*? "Where's Bernadette?"

Bernadette tore herself away from watching strangers' bags go around the carousel. "We'd better get going. The boss put the meter on a pretty strict diet. It will be hungry by now and those commissionaires are vultures."

"Where are your bags?"

"This is it. He travels light."

"I doubt it." His mother chuckled.

The Volvo was nosed crookedly into the angled parking space. Even Bernie's skills were obviously fading. When he was a boy, Matt had seen her back one-ton trucks into the narrow laneways between buildings on Water Street in a single try. His mother would have been barking instructions then too. Not that Penelope had ever been an authority on operating a motor vehicle. She blamed that on having been born the year before New Brunswick switched to driving on the right-hand side, claimed she had been oriented in the womb to driving on the left, and if she was sometimes in the middle of the road, that was probably a reasonable compromise.

Matt threw his bag into the trunk, running his fingers over the bandages of duct tape that were holding even more of the rear bumper together than at his last visit. He decided he would ask about these later, make a thorough inspection of the body when his mother was not around.

"I suppose you'd like to drive," she said and made quite a show of trudging around the front of the car from driver's side to passenger's, as if she and not Bernie was the one who would otherwise take the wheel.

"Well, if you don't mind," he said, folding himself into the seat and adjusting the mirrors. Bernie smiled at him from the rear seat.

"Can you navigate from the back seat, Bernadette?" his mother asked. "Bernadette did a wonderful job of navigating on the way up. I'd never have found the place."

Matt checked the mirror to see Bernie shaking her head, pointing to herself, and making the universal sign for driving. His relief that Bernie had in fact done the driving was instantly eclipsed by the realization that his mother didn't seem to remember.

"I think I can find the way," he joked.

"There are a lot of new roads."

"They were all here the last time, Mamma."

"Oh."

He had expected an argument, was disappointed, even though he knew he was right. Her *oh* seemed less a concession, though, than simply bemusement.

The airport was on the far side of the city, which you could now bypass completely thanks to an added spine road, or arterial, or something else anatomical. Matt knew that this was one of the innovations his mother was warning him about. It made her nervous, he knew, and so, in deference, he remained silent for the first ten minutes as he pretended to be giving the drive his undivided attention. Once they were on the highway proper, although still east of Saint John, he turned to speak to his mother, only to discover she was fast asleep. A glance in the mirror revealed that Bernadette was in the same state. Matt took a deep breath, couldn't detect any carbon monoxide (*was it a thing you could smell?*), but went for the button to crack his window anyway. Nothing happened. He would get that looked at. And hope in the meantime that it was age and not air quality that had prompted the naps.

On the Harbour Bridge, his mother's head snapped up. "Do you have twenty-five cents? Bernie, do you have a quarter for the toll? Bernie? My God, has she fallen asleep? Typical."

"They took the toll off, Mamma. The bridge was paid for."

"How will they afford the upkeep?"

Matt was relieved. How indeed? The old sharp-minded Penelope was still in there after all.

Bernadette was awake now and asked after Jennifer.

"She's fine." It was neither a lie nor the whole truth. "Very busy with classes and her research. She sends her love." Jennifer could never remember Bernadette's name, called her Fredette, which was preposterous and a little perverse, Matt always thought.

"What is it she teaches again?" Bernadette asked this every time, as if in instinctive retaliation for Jennifer's muddling her name.

"English literature!" Penelope called out. Matt had thought she had fallen back to sleep. "Contemporary," she added with disdain. "I have an essay due next week."

"What?"

"The essay, for Professor Tweedie, it's due next week. I'll have to go to the library."

"We'll see that you get to the library, boss," Bernadette crooned from the rear seat, slipping her hand between the headrest and the seat to rub Penelope's shoulder. She shot Matt a look in the rear-view that said to leave it alone for now; they could talk later. Clearly, he had a lot of catching up to do.

At Lepreau, bored by the utter monotony of the divided highway and disoriented by the absence of any recognizable landmarks, he took the ramp for the old road that hugged the coast. Expecting praise for this decision from the two old souls, he was disappointed when neither of them spoke. "I thought this would be nice. You know. For old time's sake." Still silence. Then he realized that only by staying on the new main road would he have gotten a reaction from them. What he had done was just what they thought came naturally.

The road was even more deserted than the highway and Matt started to question the validity of his memories of endless vistas of the bay, or — failing that, and at least equally frequently — of the fog that advertised the bay was right there. There was a little glimpse near the provincial park and then a quite splendid stretch in Pocologan, but much less than he remembered. He was on the verge of asking if the road had somehow changed its course but then thought better of it. He knew it had not.

"Get back on the highway here," Bernadette whispered over his shoulder. "Your mother doesn't like to go by Pennfield Ridge anymore." So they rejoined the characterless dual carriageway until the exit for St. Andrews wound them in through Bocabec and Chamcook and finally down the hill and into town. He took the long route around the point to drop Bernadette in front of the laundromat where she rented the upper apartment.

"Nice outing, boss. I'm glad you're home, Matt. Call me."

"Are you opening tomorrow, Bernadette, or am I? I want to get those new sweaters out," his mother said to the closed window. Bernadette smiled, gave a cheery wave, and was gone.

The weeds in the driveway were nearly a foot high and the dried-out front lawn was a leaf-covered mess, but the house looked like it had been freshly stained. "My son usually does the grass," Penelope began to apologize and then caught herself. "Shit. There I go again. Sorry, Mattie." She had never called him Mattie. And he had never cut the lawn.

He offered to make supper.

"I don't know what I have in the house. I meant to go to the market."

The fridge was full, including a nice piece of haddock that smelled fresh enough. On the shelf, between the fish and a tub of margarine, was Penelope's calendar. Most of the entries were in a hand too neat to be his mother's. He recognized it instantly as Bernadette's. Bernadette had done all the tags and signage at the shop. No cursive loops and dips for her. It was all caps, perfectly proportioned, like you might see on an architectural drawing. Matt found the entry for his arrival, and then an appointment with a gerontologist in Saint John for two days later.

When he asked his mother about it, she laughed apologetically. "That was something Bernie arranged, I think. You know how she loves to interfere."

Procedural

THE DOCTOR ASKS Matt to leave them alone for a few minutes. Penelope supposes he wants to examine her down there although she had not thought he was that kind of doctor. Matt has tried to explain what sort of doctor he is. Maybe he was embarrassed to mention this part. She looks around for the table, the stirrups, sees neither.

"He's very nice, your son."

Is the meeting about Matt then?

"He lives in Toronto, is that what he said?"

"Yes, Toronto."

"And what does he do there?" She wonders whether the doctor is interested in Matt that way, the way men are sometimes interested in other men. "Can you tell me what he does?"

"He works in a museum. He's a curator. He was always interested in history."

"I suppose that makes sense. Growing up in St. Andrews."

She wants to tell him how it was only quite recently that the town reinvented itself as a historical site, but intuits that this conversation is not about that.

"And what about you? Are you interested in history?"

"Up to a point."

"Can you tell me who was the prime minister during the war?"

"Which war?"

"Either one."

"Of Canada? Mackenzie King."

"Excellent."

"He wasn't really."

"No. Your answer. And who is the prime minister now?"

"Trudeau. The second one."

"Joseph."

"Yes, that's right."

"And what year is this?"

"The year of the rooster."

"Fair enough. Can you put a number on it?"

She knows she is ninety-six and was born in '21. She hates that she will have to carry the one. "2017?"

"Thank you."

Did he actually not know?

"I am going to show you some pictures and ask you to remember some things about them. Okay?"

She wishes now it *was* just the stirrups. "I suppose."

They are all people she has never seen before. He tells her a story about some, and the names of others. There seem to be a lot. Then they chat about other things: the weather (*ye gods*), and the highway between St. Andrews and Saint John and how easy it makes the trip to the big hospital (she guesses he is a Conservative).

When he shows her the pictures again, she has no trouble telling him which person operates the bakery and which one is a potter. She wonders whether he knows about the pottery she ran for all those years, is about to tell him, but he moves on so quickly. When she insists that he tell her again about the photos that she hasn't been able to recall, he shows her one he says is

Mr. Baker and another that is Mrs. Potter. It seems like a dirty trick, but she doesn't tell him so.

Matt is asked to join them in a room that looks like a kitchen. A crummy kitchen, quite unlike hers at home, but with the basic appliances so you know what it is meant to be.

The doctor asks her to make them some tea. Her mother would have had something to say about that. Thora believed that women waiting on men was nearly as bad as fucking a sheep. That's what she actually used to say. She had nothing against sheep — had for many years depended on their fleeces for her living — but she maintained that some things just were not right. Penelope had spent much of her early childhood wondering whether the father she barely remembered had perhaps absconded with a sheep. The image — even though she did not have many of the anatomical features correct — fed her nightmares until she was twelve. She thinks better of telling the doctor any of this. Matt has already heard most of it, except the part about her nightmares. Instead, she fills the kettle and plugs it in.

"Mamma, that's milk," says Matt.

"Oh. So it is. I'm sorry." She pours the kettle out, goes to rinse it out at the tap, dying to tell him *make your own fucking tea*, but knowing that will not be the right thing to say in this whatever-this-is. Instead, she says, "I can replace the kettle if the milk has ruined it."

The doctor says he is sure it will be fine, not to worry. She wonders whether he tricks all the old people into pouring milk into his kettle. He probably keeps another one somewhere else to make tea properly for himself. Matt knows his way around a kitchen. She should tell the doctor that. He seemed interested in Matt.

"Mamma?"

"Yes?"

"Can you do that?"

"What?"

"The doctor was asking you to show us how you take a shower."

"I'm to get undressed?" She'd rather die.

"No, Mamma. Just pretend. With all your clothes on. He wants you to show us, to show us how you would ... bathe."

How has she raised such a prude? "You want to know where I would put the soap?"

"Yes, please," simpers the doctor.

"I'll warn you, I used to be in the community players." She wasn't, but she doesn't think Matt will contradict her. She begins with an elaborate mime of turning on the shower and checking the temperature. Then she steps under the imaginary stream and lets it run down her, wetting her all over. The performance is obviously convincing because now the doctor passes her a cake of soap — an actual cake of soap — which she thinks is spoiling the artfulness of the whole exercise, but she takes it anyway and begins rubbing it on her shoulders, moving down her arms and then to her armpits. For a minute she wonders when she last shaved them, then remembers it doesn't matter because she is not naked. As she is running the cake of soap over her belly, it slips from her hand. She sees Matt go for it and the doctor wave him off. Obviously, she has to show them how she does things for herself. Either that, or the doctor has those prison-shower fantasies she has read about in movie reviews. With her knees and lower back screaming a little, she retrieves the soap and begins rubbing it on her shoulders, then her armpits, wondering when she last shaved them.

"Everything all right?" asks the man sitting beside Matt.

"Fine," she says, and is proud of herself for remembering to reach over and turn off the imaginary shower as she announces she is all through.

On the way home, Matt announces he wants to stop in Pennfield for blueberries.

"They'll be frozen." She knows what time of year it is, whatever that cocky doctor might think.

"Frozen is good. Maybe I'll get a pie, too."

She says she'll wait in the car. Her mother would not approve of her being here.

Base

MOST OF THE townspeople have been suspicious of the air base since that poor girl was murdered a couple of years back, in '42. Penelope has been prepared to remind Thora that the murder did not actually happen on the base. Bernice Connors had been lured to a field near the Deadman's Harbour Road by a man she had met at a dance in Blacks Harbour. There, when she resisted his overtures (that is what everyone supposed), he had battered her with a rock, raped her, and then — later, it appeared, after she was dead — cut her throat before burying her naked under a thin blanket of moss. That the murderer happened to be an RAF sergeant armourer was incidental. He only needed to be a man. He might have been any man. And it was all two years ago. Sergeant Hutchings had been found guilty and hanged behind the county jail in St. Andrews. The Connors family was devastated, but fish had gone on being canned under their family name just the same. Miss Shaughnessy and her sister, Mrs. Redmond, had started up the Mercury Club in St. Andrews to give the personnel at the base an alternative to the community hall dances (and the bootleggers) of Blacks Harbour. Thora was not at home when Penelope slipped out of the house, so she has not had to explain herself or defend her destination.

The Mercury Club was where Penelope met Captain Reade. Miss Shaughnessy (they call her the Honourable because apparently that is what she is, being the daughter of a baronet or something) arranges a roster of local young women to assist at the club. In Penelope's case — probably because she has her mother's Norwegian good looks and her father's Loyalist name — *assisting* is more in the French sense of *attending* rather than the more mundane English sense that might include changing the bed linens and cleaning the toilets. Those jobs are for other girls, ones who might have performed similar duties at the Algonquin Hotel before it announced it was closing for the duration of the war. The Honourable has something quite different in mind for Penelope. What that is, is never spoken about directly. Penelope does not think it amounts to prostitution per se. More like prostitution without the sex. But with the promise of sex. The important thing is that the men from the air base who spend their forty-eight-hour leaves at the Mercury Club should be shown a good time and distracted from drinking too heavily. That means table tennis and dancing and quite a lot of flirting. Where the flirting leads, that is up to each individual young woman to determine — to the extent that it is under her control.

Captain Reade is very good-looking, Penelope thinks, like Gary Cooper only with a little RAF moustache and a beautiful English accent. He is not very good at table tennis, very good at dancing, and so-so in the flirting department, which is just about the ideal combination. She does not have to push herself very hard to be nice to him, which you do with a lot of the other fellows. She doesn't mind pushing herself a bit, and does it readily when the Honourable is watching, but with Captain Reade it is just easy. *Jonathan*, he has said, *call me Jonathan.*

They have talked about everything, but especially books. He has made the predictable joke about his name — *Reade by name, reader by nature* — and they have compared notes on Dickens and Austen and Wodehouse and even Rider Haggard. He has read Ibsen, in the Archer translation, which would please Thora if Penelope ever decides to introduce them. Rather than make fun of her for her degree in English Literature, he claims to be jealous. He did Maths at Cambridge, but he really loves literature. Some men might say something like that to try to get into a girl's knickers — and it might work — but in Jonathan's case she is sure the interest is unfeigned and without an agenda.

On their second day together (Penelope had traded shifts and the Honourable, who usually discourages such shenanigans, turned a blind eye) she asked him what exactly he did at the base. She knew the broad outlines, of course. Everyone knew those. How the British Commonwealth Air Training Plan had been set up to train RAF and RCAF pilots and crews for deployment overseas. How Dexter Construction had carved the field and built the base in record time, unequalled since the building of the old sardine plant in Chamcook before the first war. How the RAF training unit at Pennfield (Number Thirty-Four) had been transferred there from Greenock in Scotland. What she wanted was something not in general knowledge, something just her own, perhaps with a whiff of enemy fire and death, a little secret, a little dangerous. He had said it might be better to show her than tell her. Although it wasn't really allowed for civilians to visit the base, he thought he could arrange a limited tour. She said he must be quite important, which she suspected was what he wanted to hear, and she didn't jump back when the back of his left hand brushed a little too slowly across her right breast when they kissed goodbye.

So here she is, standing in front of what is easily the most ungainly looking aircraft imaginable. Its short, squat body features curved undersides that sweep up to its twin tails. Penelope thinks of Mrs. Sutherland, who taught her English in the tenth grade: the swoop of her belly, her sticklike legs, and her impossibly high bottom. Like an awkward bird.

"This is a Ventura. It's modelled on a civilian aircraft, the Lockheed Lodestar Model 18. You might have flown in one of those."

Penelope does not want to admit to never having been in any airplane, Lockheed or no, so she asks a question: "How fast does it go?" Men can be distracted by such things.

"We can get her up to 312 miles per hour. She has a range of about 950 miles."

"Goodness." She has no idea whether either of those numbers is actually impressive.

"She has a Pratt & Whitney engine. Eighteen-fifty horsepower. Eighteen cylinder."

"Heavens." She can tell that those are large numbers, certainly compared to a horse or a motorbike. What she really wants to ask him about are the guns, the bombs.

"Maybe you'd like to go up one day?"

Penelope is shocked by the proposal. Surely the military can't be giving joyrides to civilians — *even pretty ones*, she adds to herself. Then she thinks of how the trainees love to buzz the town, driving some of the older residents to distraction. She supposes that practice is not strictly by the book either. "Maybe." She gives her response the exact inflection that the Honourable has trained them to use at the Mercury Club. Jonathan blushes.

A young man in coveralls interrupts whatever this is by suddenly tumbling out of the plane. He springs to attention, cracking a tiny smile at Penelope in the split second before he salutes Captain Reade.

"At ease. This is Nielsen. He is training with us from the Royal Norwegian Naval Air Services. Nielsen, this is Miss Arnold, from St. Andrews." Despite the tea-party tone with which Jonathan has made the introduction, neither Nielsen nor Penelope knows the etiquette for what to do next. She extends her right hand and he goes to take it, then pulls back, holding aloft a blackened palm. They laugh. He has beautiful teeth. He runs his left hand — which she hopes is cleaner than his right — through his blond hair and says he is pleased to meet her. His English is near perfect though heavily accented. She wonders about saying one of the five or six things her mother has taught her to say in Norwegian but realizes more than half of them would be inappropriate. She shouldn't curse in front of a stranger.

"You must miss home," she starts, then realizes that Norway is occupied, so this may be a stupid thing to say.

"Some things here remind me of it. The coastline mainly. Some of the people too."

Penelope looks at Jonathan to see how he will react to this obvious allusion to her appearance, but he seems oblivious. "My mother came from Bergen."

"Nearly time for mess, Nielsen. Better get cleaned up."

The man snaps to attention again, turns, and is gone. Captain Reade continues the tour of the aircraft, pointing out that she can carry a 2,500-pound bomb load, and showing Penelope where the eight .303 machine guns are located. She no longer cares about the weaponry. She is thinking about the smile of the Norwegian airman named Nielsen.

Steeped

MATT WAS NOT surprised by his mother's silence in the car. If he was exhausted by the appointment, he couldn't imagine how tiring it all must have been for her. She did seem to perk up a little after the stop in Pennfield, which he thought was odd because she was so obviously against the idea when he proposed it. The pamphlet he had glanced at quickly in the waiting room while she was in alone with the doctor mentioned this kind of mood swing. Or was that just confirmation bias? Like when you buy a new car and suddenly it's the only model you see on the road.

He made tea, orange pekoe steeped ten whole minutes in the old brown pot, the inside of which was tarred a quarter of an inch thick with decades of tannin. It had been his grandmother's pot; he thought that was the story, thought he could maybe remember her pouring from it when he was a child. When he took the tray to his mother's bedroom, she appeared to be searching for something. She was shuttling from dresser to cedar chest and back, muttering words he could not make out.

"Mamma, have a cup of tea."

"Matt?"

"I made tea."

"Did you steep it long enough?"

"You could stand a spoon up in it."

"Good boy." She looked around. "I don't want tea in my bedroom."

"Let's go into the sitting room. What were you looking for?"

"Looking for? Let's have our tea. Did you steep it long enough?"

He had to move a stack of newspapers to find a place to perch, but the sitting room, for all its clutter, always had an instantly calming effect. It had not changed in its essentials in the more than fifty years that he could remember it. That had taken some effort. Finding matching chintz when the chairs had needed re-covering had been the biggest challenge, but he had gotten someone at the museum to help source the fabric. And he had rewired the ancient trilights on visits home and rotated the carpet, so that the worst worn sections ended up under the couch and beneath the coffee table that sat in front of it. There were rings on the tabletop in the few places that were clear of junk. These had not been there on his last visit, but he could see where someone had tried rubbing lemon oil into them, leaving a shiny aura, a slick that he would clean up later.

"Now, what is it that Jennifer is doing?"

"Still teaching. In Toronto."

"She likes the children."

"University. She teaches at the university, Mamma."

"Does she miss the children?"

Jennifer had never taught children. Matt thought for a moment how that would have turned out. Then he recalled some more advice from the pamphlet in the doctor's office: avoid contradiction. "Yes. But she likes what she's doing now."

"She has lovely hair."

"I'll tell her."

"Will you be seeing her?"

"When I talk to her, I'll tell her." He should have added *if I talk to her*, but decided that was not for his mother to worry about. Eventually, they would talk.

"The tea is good. What kind is it?"

"The usual. The kind you always have."

"It tastes different."

"I steeped it good and long. I warmed the pot. And the spout."

"Should we have a biscuit?"

"I couldn't find any."

"That's right, of course. When the war is over, then perhaps."

After he had rinsed the cups, he went to find her to tell her he was going for a walk. She was back in her bedroom, once again shuttling back and forth. He offered to help her look for whatever it was, but she said she was fine, he should enjoy his walk.

There was an old Fair Isle sweater in the dresser in his room. He shrugged it on, gagging at the thick sheep smell, and left by the front door. Standing on the step in the late November sunlight, he hesitated for a moment over which way to go. Then he set off west for Joe's Point. He was less likely to encounter other walkers that way.

It always took several minutes of walking for the aches and stiffnesses to retreat and his mind to clear. He didn't mind, having learned to respect each ache as the memory of a particular past event. The body archive. That was what Ingrid had called it. Feeling instantly disloyal, he tried to think of Jennifer instead of Ingrid: Jennifer, who would be wrapping up her seminar about now (it was Tuesday) and going home to an empty house and a half-empty gin bottle. He should have left her with a backup. That was silly. She knew how to buy gin. She knew how to do everything, really, needed him not at all if he was honest about it.

But she had seemed devastated when she found out about Ingrid.

The relationship started through work. Ingrid Haakonson and her Canadian collaborator, Gina Snell, had a Canada Council grant to collaborate on a dance piece. The project had to do with memory. That was why it had occurred to them to approach the museum.

Ingrid and Gina proposed working with a group of people from the community, eliciting their memories, and then re-presenting them through movement and words. They would meet with the group every Saturday for six weeks and then produce a kind of performance, which they described as echoes of the memories they had gathered. What their grant proposal said was that the material from the participants' *body-archives* would be absorbed by the dancers' *archive-bodies* and then re-presented for an audience. They hoped the museum could provide the space they needed. The Director decided that the exhibition gallery that was usually devoted to travelling shows could be kept vacant for the performance date. It would accommodate about sixty people once enough space was carved off for the dancers. He apologized for the small size, but Gina and Ingrid assured him that an audience of sixty would be a very gratifying outcome indeed.

Matt had only recently put the finishing touches on an exhibition on the art of medieval and Renaissance memory systems. He had been working on the project for two years and all signs were that he was heading into the slump that always followed an opening. The Director evidently thought this dance project might perk him up. He asked Matt to meet with the women. *Someone has to protect the museum's interests*, he said. The institution would need to know what kinds of memories were being solicited. The sharing of certain kinds of memories could be fraught, obviously, as could the presentation of them — no matter how distant the echo. Not that the museum was necessarily closed to the airing of challenging issues, but, at the very least, trigger warnings might have to be devised. Matt told Gina and Ingrid he would need to review the paperwork that participants would be asked to fill out to cover confidentiality and the assignment of rights to their stories.

Ingrid and Gina were like salt and pepper. Gina was short and powerfully built. Her cropped hair always looked unwashed, her breath carried a tang of sinus infection, and she evidently did not pay any attention to cleaning her armpits. Matt had a hard time keeping his nickname for her from slipping from his lips. *Snell* and *Smell* were so similar sounding. Ingrid, on the other hand, was taller than Matt by an inch or even two; stronger too, he imagined, when he first shook her hand in the Director's office. She always smelled of lemon shampoo.

Ingrid brought the draft forms to his office two days after their first meeting.

"Thanks. You could have emailed them."

"I like paper so much better. Something I can hold in my hand, wave around, riffle, dog-ear."

"Me too. But we have printers in the office here."

"I thought we could review them together. That way I get your response ... unmediated." She produced a blue ballpoint pen and aimed herself at his worktable. As she sat down, she slowly unwound the turquoise scarf that was looped four or five times around her long neck and let it drop to the floor.

Nothing leapt off the page as either deficient or overdone, but Matt finally had to admit that he would need to run the forms by the museum's ethics committee. He apologized for her wasted trip to meet with a person who didn't actually have the final say.

"Not wasted at all. It was nice to see you again." After she had rewound her scarf, she touched his forearm for a second — one last scent of citrus — before wafting out of the office.

The ethics committee had no trouble with the draft forms when he passed them along. Matt wished then that he had simply told Ingrid when they met that everything was fine. He needn't have revealed his lack of control over the matter. The committee did, however, have questions about the methodology for actually gathering the material. The project, the members felt, qualified as research with human subjects and they wanted to see what they called *the instrument*. When Matt conveyed this directive to Ingrid and Gina via email, Ingrid immediately responded with several bright smiley faces, followed by the statement that each participant would simply be asked to begin to talk about whatever came to mind. Their first words, in every case, were to be: *I remember* ... That was all she could say about it at this point. Everything happened in the room, she said. Everything and anything. They were making art, not writing an article. When Matt met with the committee again to read them this response, he expected the project would be nixed. And so before he really knew what he was doing he undertook to attend every session and to report back to the committee on any methodology that might raise concerns. He was shocked when they agreed.

Ingrid was in his office less than an hour after he emailed the news. Gina was not with her. "This is a wonderful development. And very generous of you."

He had already started to wonder to what degree generosity entered into it and how much it was something else altogether.

"It will be such a help to the project, having you there, listening, watching."

"I am not really very artistic. My mother and grandmother, on the other hand, were both." He fiddled with the half-dozen pens on his desk, lining them up and scattering them once again.

"It is very hard to avoid shaping the memories. You can help us with that."

"The shaping or the avoiding?"

"Certain prompts will trigger certain memories, or kinds of memories, privilege them over others, and that can distort the result. Gina and I are very careful, but now you can be on the lookout too." She leaned a little across his desk.

"You are talking about suggestibility."

"I think so. But also, do you know what Derrida said?"

Matt was about to tell her he knew quite a lot of what Derrida said, though he didn't always completely understand it.

"The archivization produces the event as much as it documents it."

"You could just embrace that, foreground the problem, even. Couldn't you?"

"I am not sure your ethics committee would find that an acceptable approach, would they?"

Matt supposed maybe not. And he chose not to think about the ethics of agreeing right then to go for a drink with Ingrid Haakonson.

THE SWEATER HAD begun to be itchy around the collar by the time Matt had walked as far as the golf course out on the point, but he was sure he would be too cold if he took it off. He had never been comfortable with wool next to the skin, which seemed perverse given how he had been raised, and what had put food on the table and paid for his schooling. When he had finally confessed his wool problem to Jennifer on their twentieth anniversary, she had bought him a brushed acrylic vest from L.L. Bean that had propelled his mother into a rant against *so-called fleecies* (and Jennifer) that he had never completely forgiven. He wished now he had brought the fleecy with him.

Last-Minute

PENELOPE SHAKES OUT the sweater and folds it again. It is one of the green Fair Isles her mother started the women working on just when the war seemed like it would never end. From the beginning, her mother has insisted that all of their yarns must reflect some colour that can be found in the landscape around them. There are blues and greys for skies, and some others for water, rusts for rocks, and charcoals too, lavenders and yellows for flowers that grow wild — even a valiant effort to match the elusive iodine shades of the knotted wrack that festoons the shoreline, tracing the high tide. This particular green was at once an echo of the thick spruce forests and an invitation to hope. They had scoured and dried and dyed the wool in the early summer of 1944. By Christmas, it had been carded and twisted into rovings, spun, and then knitted into caps and scarves and sweaters like this one. She remembers the display in the tiny hole-in-the-wall shop on Water Street that year. Thora made an ingenious rendition of a Christmas tree from the new stock. That funny little girl, Bernadette, came by that December every day after school to admire the pyramid of green wool that she insisted looked so much more interesting than any real tree. Sometimes Penelope gave her a nickel to mind the shop while she slipped out for a bit. *Not a word to the boss, mind.*

She is still getting used to the new shop, so much larger and brighter than the wartime location. When her mother announced she wanted Penelope to take over the business, Penelope had to come up with a deferral strategy. After all, her mother was only fifty-two and fitter than most twenty-year-olds. Thora loved running Handworks. It was hard to imagine her doing anything else. So Penelope said she couldn't possibly work with the tiny, dark space on the main street.

She had not adequately reckoned with her mother's famous determination. Within two weeks of her daughter's erecting this obstacle, Thora announced she had purchased the empty warehouse on Market Square and had already arranged for renovations and an addition. With the war just ended, building supplies were scarce, but Thora had sorted out that problem too. Many of the buildings on the base at Pennfield Ridge were being sold off to anyone who was willing to remove them whole or demolish them for parts.

At first, Penelope was troubled by the knowledge that she was looking out a window that had once been part of the base, a window Jonathan — or that Norwegian airman, Nielsen — might have looked out time and again. But she reminded herself that everything has a history. This was not really different from the hooked rugs with which her mother had founded the business. For the rugs, it was strips of what had once been clothing pushed and pulled through holes in what had once been burlap sacks. For the shop, it was lumber and glass from a defunct air base tacked on to an old lobster plant.

The sun pours in on the harbour side of the new showroom, picking up highlights in the wool that you can't see otherwise. Imperfections, she knows them to be — fibres where the dye did not take properly, or flecks of seaweed that were not carded out

— but they are what gives life to almost everything in the shop. Her mother explained that irony to her when she was barely old enough to understand the words. It has taken her until now to understand the implications. In turn, she has tried to make little Bernadette understand this too. More and more, the child hangs around the shop. Penelope has come to accept this, even thinks it is not too bad that she is there. The girl is too old to be her daughter, but having a child around the place kindles something in her that she would not want to be without just now — even if she is a constant reminder of the wedding that took place the summer they dyed this green wool.

When Penelope and her mother asked Bernadette to serve as flower girl, she accepted immediately. They did not explain how it was all very much a last-minute thing. She was too young to understand — should have been too young to understand.

Penelope had not seen Jonathan since the unit at Pennfield Ridge was disbanded the previous month. The whole training program was winding down anyway, but the Pennfield operation was the earliest to be terminated, having been pronounced by Air Command to be the least successful of all the training units. Problems servicing the aircraft, frequent fog, and an inadequate number of qualified instructors were all listed as factors. Penelope thought all of these might have been foreseeable. Jonathan, transferred temporarily to Manitoba, had arranged three days of leave in St. Andrews before he assumed his next responsibilities. These were to take him to the Pacific theatre where he was to be assigned as an observer with the U.S. Air Force. Observing what, he was not allowed to say, but she hoped it would help take from his mouth the bitter taste of the last days at Pennfield Ridge.

Problems with publishing banns were easily gotten around with wartime weddings. The haste, the inattention to detail, and the modesty of ceremony had all become commonplace by 1944.

Thora said Penelope should be grateful for that. It was the only remotely sharp thing her mother ever said to her throughout those difficult months. Penelope doubted she really meant it. She thought her mother was actually a little grateful. She could not imagine Thora planning and hosting a large, extravagant wedding. The wedding dress, which Thora fitted and sewed herself — staying up night after night beading it — was about the only concession to tradition. That and the last-minute idea of a flower girl.

Jonathan was spared the morning suit he might have worn in other times, appearing instead in his dress uniform. Penelope thought how beautiful he looked, standing at the front of the mostly empty church. He had arranged for a captain from Camp Utopia — a man he barely knew and Penelope had never met — to stand beside him. For a moment she wondered whether he had deliberately chosen the least prepossessing officer he could find within a thousand-mile radius. But why would he feel that need? He must be used to being the handsomest man in nearly every room.

Thora did double duty, both *giving this woman to be married to this man* and standing as matron of honour. The rector objected at first, insisting that even in wartime some lines must be drawn, but Thora had talked him round; they are old friends. Penelope hoped the conversation had not included arguments about fucking sheep.

There was champagne afterward at Birch Hall. Penelope found it amusing that Jonathan was so delighted by the fact that she was raised in a house that had a name. It is by any standards a nice brick Georgian (unusual for the town), and, despite Thora's best intentions and direst threats, it still has a lot of mahogany and plasterwork that would not feel out of place in England. She supposed he had written to his family that he would be marrying a girl whose great-great-great grandparents had fled the United States out of loyalty to the Crown and then built themselves a fine solid mansion in the English style, even if on colonial shores. *Ceremony from the Book of Common Prayer with reception to follow at the bride's home, Birch Hall*, he would have said. With these parent-pleasing details he might have easily filled a sheet of paper, relieving him of the need to include any of the other — much less parent-pleasing — details of the impending marriage.

Penelope's Nordic frame and Thora's tailoring skills meant that none but the two of them and the groom knew there was more behind the haste of the ceremony than the very real threats of war and the uncertainty of Jonathan's future. Bernadette's mother, beaming with pride over how sweet her daughter looked in the church, and flushed with champagne, took Penelope into the back garden to give her a little womanly advice.

"It hurts less after a few dozen times, though you'll likely never figure out why they like it so much. I haven't. Sooner have an enema, myself. Don't be frightened by the blood. It's normal. Oh, and they like a little noise." She demonstrated.

Penelope bit the insides of her cheeks and thanked her for the warning. Later, she thought, she would tell Jonathan about it, putting on the woman's voice and exaggerating the moans. She thought he would find it funny, though he could be a bit stickish. Maybe better to keep it to herself. Or tell only her mother. Thora would laugh, she was sure.

In fact, that first time with Jonathan, in the tiny single bed at the Mercury Club on his second visit there, had been far less painful than she had been led to expect by all the talk she had heard. And soon she had found there was no need to perform the noises. They came quite naturally — too naturally for the furtive circumstances of their next few fucks. Jonathan winced when she said that word, preferred to call it *cuddling*, which had led her to an ill-advised comment about his nanny that had at first caused him to sulk but later, she was sure, had made him harder than ever.

As it turned out, there was no cuddling on the wedding night, which was a waste of the soft double bed in the best guest room at Birch Hall. Jonathan had drunk too much champagne. He said he was nervous about making love to her with a baby already growing up there. She told him that was nonsense, reminded him they didn't know when they would be together again. He said then that was the problem: not knowing what would become of him. She was more inclined to credit this, though she still blamed too much champagne as she fondled him to no effect. Then, as if to illustrate the vagaries of war — even behind the lines — he told her about Nielsen.

"You might remember meeting him. Norwegian fellow," he said.

"I do," she replied. *Did it sound too tentative?*

"Nice fellow. Damn good-looking."

"If you say so. I don't remember very clearly."

"He came with us to Manitoba, of course, to continue his training."

"Oh." *As if she did not know this.*

"We'd taken the old Venturas out there, did I tell you, even though they were mostly using Mosquitos?"

"You did."

"Anyway, poor bugger went up one day in a Ventura. In the bomber's position, you know. Routine run. Next thing we know, he's falling out of the sky. Like Icarus. Poor bastard. Had to be scraped off the field."

Only a very drunk Jonathan would talk like this in front of a woman, she thought. She kissed him on the forehead and rolled away with her back to him, pretending to go to sleep. He was snoring within a minute. *Good.* He would not hear her sobbing.

She shakes out the spruce-green sweater again, folds it, and sets it with the others on the shelf.

The Lodge

THERE ARE THREE *kinds of felt. Unless you count the past tense of feel. Then there are four.* Matt's grandmother would tell this joke weekly when he was a little boy. It was the only joke he could recall her telling. His mother had assured him over and over that Gran was actually a very funny woman. He never saw it. Perhaps it was because she was Norwegian. Or because she had died in their house when Matt was ten and that final leave-taking coloured all of his other memories of her.

Thora was only seventy when she died. It had been an awful shock for Penelope, although lots of people died at seventy and his grandmother had been referring to herself as old for years. Matt wondered what his mother must feel now that she had bettered her mother's three score and ten by a whole quarter of a century.

It was Jennifer who suggested he pay a visit to the Lodge. He had telephoned her, unsure that she would even pick up. There was no one else he could think of to tell about what he had discovered since he'd arrived home. Her first response was to ask how he could possibly have missed the cues in all those weekly telephone calls with his mother. She seemed to stop just short of accusing him of negligence, even elder abuse. He shot back that the gerontologist had reassured him that often in the very old the onset may be so gradual as to be almost unnoticeable. We put the odd confusion and all the repetitions down to "senior's moments" over months, even years, until one day in all the wandering, a threshold is crossed. The onset can seem to have been so sudden then, but it's only the diagnosis that has come suddenly; the disease has been there, hiding, biding its time. Talented actors, he said, can sometimes fool people successfully for years, so polished and habitual is their performance of familiar social roles and small talk. You might notice their memory slipping a little (whose doesn't?), but unless you are around them every hour of every day you would have no way of knowing how far the disease has progressed. After that, Jennifer listened quietly — twice he had to ask whether she was still on the line — and even made some sympathetic noises near the end of his litany. Then she had said (quite coldly, he thought), "You'll have to find a place for her. The doctor will get a social worker involved. There will have to be a care plan."

Matt wondered how she knew so much about these matters. Her own parents had died in a car crash when she was twenty-five. "She loves this house. I can't imagine her anywhere else."

"Are you planning to stay there, then?"

"Of course not." He nearly asked her whether that was what she wanted, but thought better of it. This was about Penelope.

He wondered whether he could ask Bernadette to go with him to see the place. She might ask better questions, notice things he missed. Having known his mother longer than he had, she might have some special insights into what would or wouldn't work out. Then he realized this was not, unfortunately, like picking out a pair of shoes or a winter coat. It was about the much more basic question of having shoes or coat at all. Besides, Bernie might appear to the staff as the potential inmate. She would hate that.

It took several calls to arrange the tour. Not the best advertisement for the place. On his first two attempts no one answered the phone at all. On the third, the harried voice said it thought the RN/administrator would be in on Tuesday. He should be able to come by for a tour then. Should he have an appointment time? *No.* Any time was fine. *But maybe avoid mealtimes.*

He walked there. Covering the distance between Penelope's house and the Lodge on foot somehow seemed to minimize it. You could drive it in fewer than five minutes, it was true, but it was also true that once you got into a car you could drive just about anywhere on the continent. Being able to walk it in fifteen minutes underlined how close it really was. Not that his mother would be walking the distance — though she could still easily manage much longer walks than that — but he thought it would help to comfort her that she would only be moving a fifteen-minute walk away.

A fifteen-minute walk and a whole world. The Lodge stood on a height. Between the trees you could see out across Passamaquoddy Bay toward St. George and, farther to the right, Deer Island. Standing on the front porch you knew exactly where you were: on the northerly side of the peninsula looking east-northeast. Once you went in through the doors, though, all bets were off.

The building was an untouched monument to 1970s institutional design. The historian and curator in Matt recognized that, even appreciated it. The concrete-block walls just inside the main door were painted two shades of ochre, darker below lighter. There was genuine linoleum tile on the foyer floor. Perhaps it cheered the old people with its familiarity. A water-stained sign (he thought it was water) instructed visitors to buzz for admission after seven p.m. and to push the green button to the right of the door during normal visiting hours. Matt pushed the button, instinctively taking a step back, expecting the powerful sweep of an automatic door. There was only a click and he realized too late that he was to pull the door himself. Pushing the button a second time, he grabbed the door as soon as he heard the click and tugged it open just enough to slide in sideways. Already he was falling in with the atmosphere of maximized security.

There were three wheelchairs parked between him and the hand-sanitizer dispenser. He hadn't until that moment expected he would want the cold alcohol goo, but now having clean hands was the only thing he could think about. Three sagging faces were turned toward him while three pairs of clawed hands stood perched atop the chairs' wheels, ready to spin their owners into retreat if necessary. He tried too hard to smile, then decided a warm, compassionate look was more appropriate. But compassion for what, he wondered. None of the three appeared to be begging to be let out, unless it was out of their skin. They were all nicely dressed and clean. The hallway smelled a little of urine if you breathed in deeply, but he did not think any of this greeting party was directly responsible.

He was wondering how inappropriate it would be to ask them to take him to their Leader when Crystal Donovan RN appeared from a doorway on the left, leading with the left breast that bore her large-print nameplate.

"May I help you?"

"I phoned. About my mother. About seeing the place. They, someone, said it was okay just to come by. But if I should make an appointment ..."

"Mum is failing a bit, is she?" asked Nurse Donovan in a placating tone that suggested that he was the enfeebled one. He wished he had brought Bernadette along.

"It's just that ... well, yes. And I live quite far away."

"But mum lives in St. Andrews, does she? Or the county at least?"

He wondered how many people would try to wheedle a place here for their loved one if they weren't local. Or why it would matter. It wasn't like it was the poorhouse. Penelope wasn't threatening to be "on the parish" like some pathetic figure from a nineteenth-century novel. "St. Andrews. All her life." He knew at this point he should volunteer his mother's name. If the woman had lived here any length of time she would surely recognize it. But it felt like a betrayal.

"Well, let's have a look around, shall we? Have you visited many special-care homes?"

He knew there was no right answer to this. If he said no, he might appear not to be taking his research seriously enough. He might look like the kind of son who simply stuffs his mother into the nearest nursing home and runs for cover. Or he might seem like a rube, someone on whom she could easily put something over, though what there was to put over he was not sure. On the other hand, if he said yes, she would almost certainly catch him out very quickly in the lie. "I have heard very good things about this place," he said.

"As you can see, this is the main entrance. The door is locked at all times. That's for the safety of some of our patients, who do wander. Is mum quite mobile?"

"She is. Very. But she doesn't wander off. Hasn't." Matt wondered whether this was actually true. How would he have known?

"We do insist that visitors buzz in after seven, and that they are careful when coming in that nobody goes out. To exit the building when your visit is done, there is a keypad. Four digits. Just the current year." That she made this announcement without any effort to whisper surprised Matt, but if the information made any impression on the three inmates — who had now backed up their chairs by several feet — Matt could not detect it. Either they were content not to bolt, or they were deaf, or they had no idea what year it was. There was no way of knowing which of the three things it was.

"On the right here is the common room, the living room." She beckoned Matt to crane his neck around a doorframe.

A quartet of wheelchairs was pointed at a large-screen television tuned to the classic movies station. From the angles of their heads, Matt could tell that none of the occupants was watching. *Too bad*, he thought. *Sunset Boulevard* was one of his own favourites.

"We do programming in there a couple of times a week."

"Programming? Of the patients?" The words were out before Matt had even considered them.

Nurse Donovan hesitated and then chose to laugh. Fortunately. "Local schools and church groups put on programming for our clients."

"Religious programming?"

"Only for those who want it."

Matt wondered how you would be able to tell who wanted it. "The schoolchildren sing, I suppose." He thought about how his mother hated bad music. And children.

"Sometimes. And they do crafts. Simple things they can manage."

He did not ask whether *they* meant the schoolchildren or the old people.

"And down the hall this way is the dining room. One of them. We have two small dining rooms. We want our clients to feel as much as possible that they are at home. A large dining room can really spoil that for some. How's mum's appetite?"

Unable to answer that question, Matt asked one of his own: "How many patients do you have?"

"Thirty-five."

"Are there more tables in the other dining room?" There were three small tables in the room in which they stood, with settings for only a total of eight people.

"Some of our patients prefer to eat in their rooms. We respect that."

Again, Matt wondered how you would be able to tell. He figured that some had to mean about fifty per cent. "It smells very good, the food." It did, in fact, in a Chef Boyardee way. Comforting. Not what Penelope would cook, but what lots of people eat. "Can I ... can I see a ... room?" Matt was suddenly a stammering teenager at the Redclyffe motel in Robbinston while Amanda Williams waited in the car, her red-nailed bare feet planted confidently on the dashboard of his Cortina.

Nurse Donovan was apparently more perplexed than the motel keeper had been all those years ago, although surely the request was more natural under these circumstances than under those. *More natural and less natural*, Matt reflected. "I've been off for a few days," she said. "I'll have to find out what we can look at."

To find out whether anyone had died, Matt supposed.

"No. I know. We can ask Ruthie. It's just that we try to respect the clients' privacy. We like them to feel the room is their own."

"Are they single rooms?"

"We do have a few single rooms. The rest are shared. Ruthie won't mind, and the other bed in her room is empty right now."

Someone had died.

"So what are the chances of a patient getting a single room?"

"Lots don't want them. They like the company."

Matt tried to imagine the quality of company. "But if they want one?" He knew he wanted one. Visiting his mother with a roommate present would tip purgatory into hell.

"We have a waiting list and a lottery. Everyone starts out in a shared room. Pretty much. Usually, they find they like that just fine. Let's go have a look."

Ruthie-who-won't-mind was parked in her doorway. Matt recognized her immediately through the sunken cheeks and hooded eyes. "Hello, Mrs. MacHattie."

"Hello, dearie."

"Hello, Ruthie," cooed Nurse Donovan. "Is it all right if we have a look in your room? This gentleman would like to see."

"Are you police?" the old soul asked, and then cracked a toothless smile and let loose a laugh that Matt recognized from her days at the box office at the Marina Theatre.

"Cheese it, it's the cops," he growled and she laughed again until she was choking. Nurse Donovan seemed unfazed by the fit, simply pushing the wheelchair a little way into the room so she and Matt could pass in too.

"Ruthie's done a lovely job with this room, haven't you, dear? All the photos. Her son came and hung them. And you might have noticed the glass cases outside each of the rooms. That's where our clients can put special things, things they treasure, that tell people who they really are."

There was one window on the wall between the two hospital beds. The view was of the parking lot. Each patient obviously had a regulation metal wardrobe and a regulation chest of drawers. There were two tubular-steel chairs; for visitors, he supposed, since everyone he had seen so far was confined to a wheelchair. "Are they all this size?" he asked.

"They are all pretty much the same, yes. The privates are smaller."

Matt's own privates were feeling smaller. "Thank you, Mrs. MacHattie." He leaned down to take her hand.

"Say hello to your father, dear."

He didn't bother to correct her, wouldn't have known where to start.

"This has been great," he bubbled to Nurse Donovan at the

door, hating himself for the hypocrisy. "Given me lots to think about."

"I have some literature for you."

"Literature?"

"There's a guide the province puts out. And some information on the Lodge. And an application form." She was holding out a fat manila envelope, which he took reflexively. "It's all quite overwhelming, I know. You'll get through it."

Matt doubted she had any idea who she was talking to. Out in the parking lot, he realized that was literally true. He had managed not to reveal his identity or his mother's. And he was quite sure that Mrs. MacHattie would not be able to rat him out.

Humane

MATT REALIZED TOO late that he had not thought carefully enough about his decision to feed lobster to Penelope and Bernadette. He knew he wanted something special (at least to him) and that it should be something neither of them would feel they needed to help with, or would be likely to cook for themselves. The season was open and there were live canners to be had at the wharf for a price that bit its thumbs at Toronto rates — even cheaper when the lobstermen discovered who he was. Everyone on the wharf had fond memories of Penelope and many could remember their parents speaking admiringly of Thora.

Late November, though, is a less accommodating time than late July for a lobster boil. There would be no problem with the cooking itself. That didn't have to be done outside, although it added charm when it was. Penelope had a pot easily large enough for three canners and it would fit perfectly on the stovetop. It was the cutting and the eating he wished he had thought through. No matter how much you shake the lobsters out over the pot after cooking, there is always a gush of water when you plunge the knife in to open up the tail and body. The claws are often full too. Outdoors, none of this presents a problem, but in Penelope's kitchen — forget the dining room — there was certain to be quite a mess.

As they were having their drinks and chatting, watching the trio of lobsters crawl around on the painted pine floor and waiting for the water to boil, he began to apprehend additional, more philosophical, problems with his choice.

"I heard on the CBC the other day that the Swiss have banned the boiling of live lobsters." It wasn't Bernadette's fault. She couldn't have foreseen how this piece of small talk would ultimately deliver them into discussions of pain, damaged brains, and death.

"Imagine that," said Penelope, taking a long draught of her neat gin. "How would they police it? Surprise inspections?"

"Surveys? I don't know." Bernadette mimed filling out a questionnaire with a clawed hand.

"Are they advocating eating them uncooked? I don't understand."

"They say there are alternatives. The people the CBC interviewed. More humane alternatives."

"Lobsters have feelings now?"

"Something like that, boss."

"But it's all rubbish, all that nonsense you used to hear about them screaming when they went in the pot. Just air escaping or something. What alternatives were they talking about?"

"They can stun them with an electric shock."

"How is that more humane? The humane thing would be not to eat them at all." She took another swig of her gin.

Matt wondered whether his mother was cooling to the idea of supper.

"I suppose you're right," said Bernadette, eyeing the largest lobster, which was climbing over the other two. He looked like he might be heading for the back door.

"But I love lobster," said Penelope. "I can't imagine giving it up. My mother used to hold them upside down." With this, she picked the largest off the smaller and held it by the tail with its head toward the floor. "Then she stroked them. She said that put them to sleep."

"I don't think —"

"She made it up to make me feel better. I've always known that. As a very little girl I used to ask a lot of questions. About death and things. She made up a lot of stories."

"A man on the radio — it was that call-in, what-do-you-call-it — said he believed in inserting a very thin, very sharp blade into the brain. He said that kills them instantly and then you can boil them."

"What if you miss the brain, though? It's not very large. Or what if you just nick it, make it go haywire? Where does that leave the poor lobster? Demented. Nope. I say just drop them in the boiling water. It's a quick death. And, for all we know, painless."

"Matt, the pot's boiling over!"

He grabbed the lid, burned himself, swore, and scooped up a dirty dishtowel to protect his hand for a second try.

Penelope was still holding the lobster. She brought it very close to her face and whispered, "Would you like a last cigarette?"

Bernadette growled, in what Matt supposed must be her most lobsterish voice, "No thanks, I'm trying to cut down."

Both women laughed until their faces were wet while Matt plunged the three crustaceans into the pot. They didn't make a sound.

He had made potato salad and bean salad. Bernadette had brought rolls made by the new bakery on Water Street (they still called it new after ten years). It was a meal the three of them had shared dozens of times, but not for many years. Matt wondered whether the Lodge ever served lobster. Probably not. As he shuffled the salads from counter to table, he apologized for having to eat in the kitchen. He had chosen the deepest-rimmed plates he could find. "All the water, you know."

"I'll show you a trick," Bernadette said, "when they are done. You hold them over the sink and twist the tail until it comes free of the body. Then you dump both sides out. It doesn't look as nice on the plate, of course, but you're going to take it apart anyway."

"The claws are still a problem," Penelope said.

"When are they not?" Bernadette yowled and hissed like a cat. And again, the two women dissolved in laughter.

After Matt had twisted and dumped and snipped and cracked, he lit the candelabra he'd brought in from the dining room. Penelope asked whose birthday it was, and he wasn't sure whether it was a joke so he pretended not to hear as he made a note to himself to polish the silver one day soon. It was Grandfather Arnold's. He knew that some of it, but not these candlesticks, had been brought from the States when the family fled. It had been in Birch Hall, always gleaming, when he was a little boy. He supposed that his grandmother must have maintained it, though she had never struck him as a silver polishing kind of person. They certainly didn't have a maid. When Penelope had to sell Birch Hall and move into this house, she had let a lot of the Loyalist furniture go to the province, but she had kept the silverware and china and everything from the dining room. He supposed he should have it revalued. There might not be anyone local, but he could ask one of his colleagues at the museum for a name. If the house was going to sit unoccupied for any length of time, he'd have to see about updating the insurance. Not that anyone even locked their doors.

The meat was perfect: enough salt and fishiness that you knew it came from the ocean, but still mild, and well on the soft side of rubbery. Penelope began by sucking on each tiny leg, using her front teeth to squeeze the meat through the thin tubes. She had always eaten lobster this way. It had frustrated Matt as a child. He would have completely finished his claws and tail while she was still fussing about getting meat from all the less giving places before going on to tackle the main parts. Now, it reassured him that she had not changed in this small way at least.

"Tell us about your research project, Matt." Bernadette had a tiny bit of coral stuck to her right cheek. She was the only one of the three of them who liked the eggs.

"Model villages," he said through a mouthful of potato salad.

"You're going to build some?"

"Possibly. To scale. Study them anyway, gather documents and visuals. Try to put together something for an exhibition. It will be a mix of some UK and some Canadian examples, I expect."

"Successful and failed?"

"Well, yes."

"They all failed in the end, didn't they?"

He had not thought Penelope was following the conversation. "Well, yes, Mamma, I suppose in the end they all —"

"So you're looking at Saint Croix Island," said Bernadette, understanding dawning in her now.

"And even St. Andrews itself. The town plat. The Loyalists' dream, all of that."

"No Vikings, though. They left without a trace."

"What Vikings, Mamma?"

But Penelope apparently did not hear. "And Chamcook," she said. "He's looking at the Sardine Town."

"Not much to look at, is there?" Bernadette cracked her final claw. "After the fire and the blowing up."

"Fire?" Matt had known that the army had blown up what remained of the sardine plant to make room for real estate development in the eighties. He had made his mother send him clippings. "I don't remember anything about a fire."

"It was a long time ago. Before you were born. Your gran was still working sometimes in the shop, when we could get her to; '52, I think, or '53. No, '53 was the coronation. York House burned to the ground."

"York House?"

"One of the dormitories. Hasn't your mother told you about the dormitories? They were quite amazing. Almost like little hotels. They looked a bit like the old pictures of the Algonquin, how it looked before it had its own fire in '14. Mansard roofs and dormers, all of that. Quite attractive."

"I've seen a photo."

"Then you'll know what I mean. Burned right to the ground. They never found out why. Nobody was hurt, of course. There was a family living in one of the company houses at that point, but they weren't in any danger. Anyway, it was one less thing for the bulldozers and dynamite thirty years later — more than thirty years. And that demolition was thirty years ago, a little more than, too. *Tempus fugit.*"

Penelope had eaten both claws, but appeared to have given up on the rest of her lobster.

"Shall I put it in the fridge for your lunch, Mamma?"

"You eat it, dear. You're a growing boy."

"You might feel more like it tomorrow."

"Yes, it was quite a place, I guess, the old Sardine Town. They had electric lighting on the streets, which was really something in 1913. And a movie house and bowling alley, houses for managers, and cottages for married workers and dormitories for the unmarried. There were stores, too. And their very own jail. There must be lots about it in the county archives," Bernadette said, eyeing the uneaten lobster meat on Penelope's plate. "Your gran would have lived in one of the dormitories, I suppose."

"Gran?"

"Sure, when she came out to pack sardines," said Bernadette.

"She was a sardine packer? Mamma, you never told me about that."

"Did I not? I must have."

"I wouldn't have forgotten." He regretted the choice of word the instant it was out but he knew it was true. He had grown up on stories of the founding of Handworks and the marriage to Grandpa Arnold not long after the Armistice. The fable was always that Thora was an established businesswoman well before she married into the town's elite. But now he realized there was never any mention of how Thora got to New Brunswick in the first place or where her nest egg came from. He had never thought to ask.

"It was York House. She lived in York House. She wasn't very happy there."

"You should run up to Blacks Harbour, too, Matt," chirped Bernadette. "It might not fit your mould exactly, though Connors Brothers did its best. And you should look into the Quaker Pennfield colony. Maybe it's Beaver Harbour. First place in British North America to ban slavery. 1784. That's a kind of model community too, isn't it?"

Matt had stopped listening. He was too busy revising so much of what he had thought he knew about his grandmother.

The Art of Memory

MATT'S FIRST DRINK with Ingrid Haakonson could plausibly have been described as purely collegial. They walked from the museum to a bar nearby, sat across a table from one another, and would have happily welcomed anyone from the dance or museum communities to join them. Ingrid had surprised him by ordering bourbon. He had been tempted by the bourbon but settled on a pint of Guinness. It lent a vaguely tweedy academic air to the proceedings, he thought; it said *this is a working drink with a colleague.*

She had quizzed him about the exhibition he had running at the museum. When she seemed genuinely interested, he found himself prattling like a child. *Or a pedant. Both, really.*

"Everyone, every one of the ancients anyway, tells the same story. Simonides discovered the Art of Memory. He was at a dinner party, apparently, and went outside for some reason. Probably not a cigarette."

She laughed. He thought the response was genuine.

"While he was outside, the roof of the building collapsed, killing everyone inside. The damage was so significant that when they went to retrieve the bodies, they were unidentifiable."

"Their faces had been so smashed up by the falling roof?" Ingrid's brow was furrowed.

"That is the story."

"Were they all looking upwards at the time?"

"Not part of the story. I'd never thought about it that way."

"Sorry."

"Anyway, Simonides was able to remember where everyone had been sitting when he had left the room. And thus, they were able to identify each of the dead by where they found them. And so place and person became the two fundamentals of the art of memory."

"Where does Cicero come in?"

Matt began to think Ingrid might know more about the subject than she had at first let on. That, he reflected, was perfectly natural. She was, after all, an artist with a particular interest in memory. That was the reason they had gone for a drink. "Cicero was important, of course. But even more than Cicero, an anonymous tract that everyone used to think was by Cicero. Something called the *Rhetorica ad Herennium*." He hoped this arcane factoid might restore him as resident expert. "The tract laid out instructions for choosing the most effective architectural settings to stock your memory. They had to be large enough to afford several *loci* (places, so to speak), and the *loci* needed to be different enough from one another to avoid confusion."

"Variety is the spice, and so forth. Not too many niches that look alike. Wise."

He agreed, although later he thought she might have been talking in some kind of code. "The *ad Herennium* also set criteria for the kinds of images to place in those locales in order to remember the things you wanted to. The images had to be vivid, active — even grotesque; anything that would make them stick out. Writers on memory stole passages from *ad Herennium* well into the Middle Ages."

"So they thought up images that would remind them of the things they wanted to be reminded of."

"Yes."

"And then they set them, in their minds, in alcoves, or windows, or between pillars in a remembered building."

"Something like that. When you say it out loud it sounds a bit —"

"If I want to remember you, then, I should memorize what you look like and then picture you sitting here in this bar. I'm not certain that's a world-changing system, Matt, the way you describe it. It seems rather obvious. I think I am up to the task without any artificial aids. And how would it help me to memorize a speech, for example, or remember a concept?"

"Nobody really understands. There are all kinds of theories, of course, having to do with correspondences and cues and even visual puns, like rebus puzzles, you know. But what was really interesting about the system, for my purposes, is actually some of the visual imagery it produced, and all the crazy things the Renaissance did with what the ancients left them. The category of places could include actual buildings (theatres became very popular) but the boundaries were later expanded to include the seven planets, or the twelve signs of the zodiac, or any other system you had for understanding your universe. And so you get these marvelous sixteenth-century prints of staircases where the individual steps are labelled from the top: god, the angels, the planets, man, animals, plants, flowers, stones. That's the kind of thing we put into our exhibition. And we added some reproductions of the more sophisticated Renaissance memory wheels, where all of human knowledge was plotted, in note form, on concentric circles, or sometimes squares within circles."

"Like a mind map."

"Exactly. Sorry. I am boring you."

"Not at all. I would love to see the exhibit. Would you give me a personal tour sometime?"

This was not a request Matt was used to receiving at all, let alone from a woman whose resemblance to Greta Garbo was uncanny. Ingrid, of course, was Norwegian and not Swedish; he knew that. "Of course. Any time."

It was after that tour that they had their second drink. Although they could easily have returned to the bar on Bloor Street, she suggested a place quite far west along Dundas, a new place that was too cool to even have a sign outside. She gave him the address, said she would meet him there after she did a couple of things. He called Jennifer and left a message that he would be working late.

"And now I have an image of you here to remember," Ingrid said after they were sitting in front of their bourbons in the bar-without-a-sign. "I wonder whether it will become confused with the memory of you in the other bar. Which will I remember? The first because it was the first, or this, because it is most recent? Thank you again for the tour."

"It is very interesting, isn't it? Visually. Even if you forget the memory stuff — set it aside, I mean."

"But I won't forget it. I can tell you exactly where each piece was in the room, every panel."

Matt laughed. He wasn't sure whether she was being funny or not. There was an earnest note in her voice that never completely went away. You had to read her eyes.

"I liked very much how you placed Dante. *Inferno* as a memory system is a brilliant idea: all those circles, all those punishments to fit the sin."

"It's not an original idea, I am afraid."

"Is there such a thing? Original sin, on the other hand: '*Nel mezzo del cammin di nostra vita*' ... Midway in the journey of our life ... *'Mi ritrovai per una selva oscura ché la diritta via era smarrita.'*"

"I found myself in a dark wood where I could not find my way," Matt translated automatically. When he looked down at the table, he realized he was holding her hand.

His phone rang.

"Go ahead and answer it."

Jennifer. He let it go to voicemail but made his excuses ten minutes later. Ingrid walked him up to the subway where they said an awkward goodbye.

THE SATURDAY SESSIONS began.

On the first day, Gina gathered the ten participants — the body-archives — into a circle. She invited Matt to join but he shook his head, pleaded his special observer status.

"Please. It is better for the work at this early stage if everyone shares equally in it."

Ingrid dropped the hand of the person to her right and held hers out for Matt.

They worked their way around the circle, each person providing their first name, where they were born, and the name of their favourite movie. Matt overthought the latter, finally settling on *Memento*, which was just silly in the circumstances. Then Gina passed a small wooden box around. It was a rich brown, maybe mahogany, Matt thought, and inlaid with brass and ivory. There was a tiny brass clasp that Gina forbade the participants to open. "Tell us what is in the box," she said.

The answers ranged from wittily evasive to excruciatingly confessional. Matt had been all set to say *Pandora*, but a short sweaty man with large plastic glasses beat him to it. So he said *Schrödinger's cat*, which, he decided, was even cleverer. One of the confessors had wanted him to explain, but Gina reminded them of the ground rule that nobody had to explain or defend their contribution. Later, at the coffee break, he heard plastic glasses explain superposition and how "everything existed in multiple states until it was actually observed, like a cat in a box that was both alive and dead until the box was opened." Matt thought about blowing the whistle on the guy but supposed the ground rules about no explanations did not extend to coffee time.

When they reconvened, Gina told him to just sit to the side for the rest of the morning session. She explained to the group that Matt worked for the museum and was there more or less to observe. He thought she made it sound like he was a cross between a voyeur and a prison guard.

"Matt is helping us develop the project," Ingrid added. "It is important to have another pair of eyes and ears. It lets Gina and me work more closely with all of you." She shot him a smile and missed Gina's glare.

The types of memories that were shared that day followed a similar pattern to the what's-in-the-box exercise. Matt listened to recollections of childhood birthday parties, vacations, concerts, the smells of grandparents. One young man began to recount his first sexual encounter — with a schoolteacher, he said — but he broke down before getting into any details, which was a relief. Matt made a note to review his concerns around that one with Ingrid and Gina.

"Are you hungry?"

Matt was packing his notebook into his briefcase. Ingrid smelled of patchouli under the lemon shampoo. He looked at his watch.

"I am asking your stomach, not your watch."

He was. He suggested the bar on Bloor. She said she had some scallops that needed eating and he was welcome to come to the place she was renting to help her.

"I liked your Schrödinger answer," she said as they sat together on the subway.

"Gina didn't."

"Gina doesn't judge."

"It was pretentious, obnoxious. I'm sorry."

"No, I think it was perfectly appropriate. It reminded me somehow of something of Bergson's I read the other day. Something about how, at each moment, time splits into a present that passes and a past that is preserved. It's a little like superposition, don't you think? A kind of temporal polyphony."

Not since he and Jennifer were graduate students had Matt had such a serious intellectual conversation on the subway. He looked around to see if anyone was listening.

Ingrid's flat was furnished entirely from Ikea. Matt was not sure whether to make a joke of that or not. He didn't need to think about it for long. Five minutes after they were in the door, they were naked beneath the Skogsnarv sheets. He knew those sheets from other beds. Ingrid, on the other hand, was a revelation.

Life Drawing

THE PICTURE WAS never a very good likeness, Thora said, when Penelope first brought it home that summer. The mid-1950s it must have been, when she fluttered around the edges of the artist colony. Not long before Matt was born. The painter (what was his name? something to do with birds) was more interested in showing off his technique than capturing his sitter's essence. That was how her mother had put the matter. Penelope was crushed. Only Thora could manage to ruin something like that. Robin (that was it) had said so many flattering things, so many loving things, as the summer wore on, that she had come to believe he knew her better than she knew herself. He had a special way of working. He said it was inspired by late-career Degas — in fact, the blind Degas. He ran his fingers all over her face, discovering the planes and dips, tickling the fine hairs, waking the skin from its long sleep since Jonathan. Only after he had memorized her in that way did he pick up a brush and actually look. Late in August, after they had become lovers, Robin persuaded Penelope to let him paint her nude. She did not bring those canvases home, not because she thought her mother would be shocked (nothing shocked Thora) but because Robin had insisted on keeping them.

Penelope, it seemed, would have to make do with the memory of his hands as they learned her collarbones and armpits, breasts and belly and bottom.

Just as well, she thinks, as she stares at the portrait hanging above the mantelpiece. It is hard enough to look at that young face. To be reminded of the rest of the youthful body would be too awful. She could hardly have hung Robin's full-length portraits, in any case. What would Matt have thought when he grew old enough to notice and ask questions? What would she have risked by telling him about the man who had painted her?

She knows she came into the living room to do something. Only it isn't the right living room. It is too small, though brighter. And the portrait should be behind the door, not above the fire. There is a musty smell, a summerhouse, wooden house smell that doesn't belong to Birch Hall. She should find her mother.

THORA IS IN the kitchen. She has finished separating the cloth for the scrap drive. There isn't much. They use most of it in their rug hooking. Penelope has wondered whether keeping it back from the war effort for their art is treasonous, but Thora argues that soon the war will end and people will want their rugs. People need cheering up now too, even while the war grinds on. And she always makes sure to donate a bit, in the hope that will appease the scrap-drive gods.

"You should be resting."

"I hate lying there. It makes it all worse. I can't stop thinking. I need something to do."

"Thinking about it is part of it, part of the recovery, I am afraid. You can help me with this, though, if you like." Thora pushes a high stool up to the large stone sink. "You'll have to lean over a bit, but at least you can sit. It will just be your shoulders taking the strain."

Penelope perches on the stool and looks down at the carefully arranged wool rovings awash in the soapy water. She rolls up the sleeves of her cardigan. She has known how to do this since her hands were big enough to work the wool. Before that even, since she had started watching her mother make felt around the same time she had learned to walk. Having her do something familiar is part of her mother's remedy, she supposes, as she plunges her hands into the sudsy fleece. The aroma of mutton along with a sharp overlay of what can only be described as sheep piss rises up from the sink. She knows it is not urine, sheep's or otherwise, though it is something equally natural, earthy. When she used to complain about it as a little girl, her mother would simply remind her that a sheep's wool was a kind of record, a memorial to everywhere it had been and everything it had done and that was something to respect, wasn't it, not wrinkle your nose at.

The warmth of the water rises up her arms. She pictures mercury rising in a thermometer the way it does in montages in the movies. The idea of the soap — even if its fragrance is overpowered by the reek of sheep — makes her feel clean. Feeling anything has been a challenge since the thing happened. All that blood. She thought it would never stop. A blighted ovum. It sounded so accusatory, so cold. The Latin word for sheep is *ovis*. Not that far off. She begins to work the mass in the sink, patting it with flattened palms, turning, and repeating. She grates in some more soap as she feels the fibres forming a mat. Then she starts kneading it as she would dough, cajoling the scales on the wool fibres to seek one another out and bond.

"You will have another one, you know, a proper baby."

"How do you know that, Mamma?"

"I had you, didn't I?"

It has never occurred to Penelope that her mother might have had miscarriages, though as she thinks now about the two whole years between her parents' wedding and her birth, she realizes she should have guessed. She had supposed that her parents had just enjoyed the luxury of being able to wait to introduce a baby into the marriage. She and Jonathan have really done the opposite: introduced a marriage into the having of the baby. But now she hasn't had it. An empty sac was how they had explained it. All the covering up and rushing and worry over what turned out to be an empty sac. She turns the mat over in the sink, inspects her progress.

"You need to write to Jonathan."

"I don't know where he is."

"The air force knows where he is. You don't want to worry him, but he would want to know. It's natural to be afraid of how disappointed he will be."

"What if he is not? Disappointed? What if he is relieved?"

"Jonathan is a good man."

"What if he feels this lets him off the hook? Like he was lured into marriage under false pretenses?"

"You were pregnant. Nobody made that up. Jonathan loves you. You will be pregnant again."

"I don't even know when I will see him again. If I will."

But she is talking to no one. Thora has vanished the way she does quite often now, and Penelope is in a different kitchen, the newer one, sitting at the large pine table, examining a hooked mat she has spread out on her lap. The design doesn't interest her, the pastoral scene like so many she and her mother produced after the war. She is focused on the rags she is worrying between thumb and forefinger, telling them off one by one, beads on a soft rosary that has no obvious beginning or end. She can still identify each piece of clothing that went into this rug all those decades ago. The sky and the water are the easiest. A pair of Jonathan's service dress trousers had ripped and so they joined a frayed uniform shirt in Penelope's bag of scraps. This had been when he finally returned in 1946 on the long-awaited leave that he ended up cutting short. She runs her fingers over the cliffs, a red-brown dress she had sewn herself to welcome her returning warrior home. It was not a colour she would normally wear, didn't really suit her skin or hair, though it did provide a vivid contrast with her eyes. She had chosen it because it complemented the coffee-coloured camisole and drawers that she had found on sale at Scovil's and immediately knew she had to have for the homecoming. Jonathan had demonstrated no interest in helping her out of the dress and had not even seemed to notice the underthings. She had kept them folded in a drawer for six months after he left, and then she had worked them into this rug. The camisole had proven much more effective employed as the pale-coloured rocks at the base of a sandstone cliff than it had been as a mender of a marriage.

"Mamma, what happened to the portrait in the living room?" Matt starts the question in the dining room but is in the kitchen before he finishes. She doesn't think he sees her startle at the sound of his voice. *When did he get home?* She can't ask him straight out.

"Matt. It is so nice to have you here. She must be missing you though."

"Jennifer is all right. She wants me to be here with you."

Not much to go on there. He hasn't arrived just this minute. That much is clear. But how long will he stay? There is something about some research. On the sardine town. Thora has been out there. Came back reeking of smoke. When was that? She went as soon as she heard about the fire. That must be right. Maybe she took Matt. But no, the fire was before he was born. Thora was very agitated, not herself at all, though she did calm down a month or two after the fire.

"Your grandmother loves to have you visit."

He puts his hand on her shoulder, rubs.

Shit. She has done it again. "I mean she loved having you in the house as a small child." *Does he even remember her? How old was he when she died? Ten*, Penelope thinks. *That's old enough.*

"Mamma, the portrait? You didn't sell it, I hope."

She wants to ask him what business that is of his. It is her portrait, hers to do with whatever she likes. Instead, she says, "I think I must have taken it down. It was hidden hanging there behind the door."

"You've had it over the mantel since the day you moved into this house."

"It was never a very good likeness," she pronounces, hoping to put an end to the conversation.

The Old Reptilian Brain

WHEN BERNADETTE SUGGESTED coffee, Matt leapt at the offer.

The fancier café, the one that did lattes and advertised themed and seasonal coffees, had posted a sign announcing that it was closed for renovations. That usually meant a quick lick of paint for the walls and a much longer winter holiday for the owners. So they met at the "new" bakery. There was just one kind of coffee, brewed on an ancient Bunn, but Matt didn't care. It was the conversation he wanted, the counsel.

Bernadette was the nearest thing to family Matt and Penelope had. Matt couldn't remember a time when she had not been around. Jennifer was convinced that Bernadette had been in love with Penelope. She even wondered aloud occasionally whether the two had consummated that attraction back when Matt was away at school. Matt thought this was mostly to tease him. When he reacted, Jennifer would accuse him of all kinds of prejudices. He didn't think that was fair. Nobody wants to picture his mother having sex, no matter with whom.

He arrived early, but Bernadette was already there with two cups of coffee in front of her.

"Didn't we say ten? It's five minutes to. I wanted to buy yours."

"The tables fill up. Especially with the other place closed. It's been a long time since I treated you, Matt."

"Let me get some muffins."

"I shouldn't."

Looking at Bernadette, he saw the slim form of a lizard, the hollow bones of a bird. She had always been thin, but age had made her truly gaunt. "You think you shouldn't. But you will." It was he who shouldn't, but he did too.

"Your mother. It's not your fault, Matt," she began as he slathered butter on his plump blueberry muffin.

"How could I not have known?"

"She was always a very good actress. There is no way you could have known just from talking to her on the phone how she was getting, how she had been getting for quite a while, I suppose."

Matt nearly asked why Bernadette didn't call him sooner. But his mother was not Bernadette's responsibility. She was his.

"So many of their social skills they hang onto, the ones like your mother. They can fake attention and find the right conversational formulas to get by. For years."

"She would repeat things. I noticed that. But she's ninety-six. Much younger people repeat themselves."

"I find it helps to think of it as tangled skeins of wool. The disease, I mean. An appropriate thing for her, don't you think?"

"But she's still so agile. Physically. I think she's in better shape than I am."

"Thora raised her well. She has always been active. The way that woman can walk is amazing."

"Gran certainly didn't do herself any favours, being active. Her heart."

"She put in her three score and ten. That was enough for her."

Matt knew that Bernadette had worked at the shop for his mother from the time she took over the business. She must have known his grandmother for at least twenty years. "Enough for her?"

"We are all different. Some people need longer than others. The problem is we can't see around corners. Your mother and I used to trade elaborate plans for how we'd end it all when we'd had enough, when what we saw in front of us was not worth living for. Hers usually involved rocks in her pockets, a bottle of gin, and the bay. I hate the cold, so mine centred on a sealed garage and a running car. The problem for me was I didn't have a car, or a garage. And your mother had you. And, anyway, you make these plans and tell yourself you'll know when it's time, but you go beyond somehow, without noticing. And then the old reptilian brain kicks in and you just keep on keeping on."

Matt could remember his mother joking that there were two alternative endings to everyone's story — the Lodge or the Bay. When he had told Jennifer about it she had been appalled. Jennifer had never tried to understand his mother, had never got her sense of humour — if that's what it was.

"A doctor gravely tells her patient that he has cancer. The patient says *oh dear*. Then the doctor says *but I am afraid I have more bad news. You also have Alzheimer's disease*. The patient smiles and says *well, at least I don't have cancer.*" Bernadette stirred her coffee, looked straight at Matt. "Have you been to see the Lodge?"

He nodded. "I never once regretted being an only child until now."

"Misery wants company I suppose."

"I was thinking two heads are better than one."

"Not really. Not in cases like this. They usually just drag things out before arriving at the same solution."

It was true that Matt had not regretted being an only child. But he had often wondered how it had come about. On the rare occasions he had screwed up the courage to ask his mother or his grandmother about it, their story had always been the same. After the war, Matt's father had worked in military intelligence. His duties took him all over the world, sometimes for periods of months that extended into years. He had met Matt's mother in St. Andrews during the war but had only been back there twice — once for their wedding and once in 1946. After that, Penelope had had to make do with visiting him when and where he was available, usually between assignments. When Matt was old enough to know about such things, he had been able to infer that on one of these occasions, about ten years into the marriage, conditions must have conspired favourably for the conception of a child — him. The story didn't have a happy ending. Between Penelope's last visit with Papa and Matt's birth, they told him, Papa had been killed in the line of duty. At a certain age, Matt had become obsessed by the espionage overtones in the story. It seemed to him now that his mother had intentionally catered to that interest, embellishing the story here and there with details she couldn't possibly have known. Thora was dead by then, so there was no other version to compare.

"Did you know my father well?" he asked Bernadette now. He knew she had been the flower girl at his parents' wedding. There was, in a box somewhere, a grainy photo taken in front of the church. Even as a little girl, Bernadette was unmistakably Bernadette.

"Your father?"

"You were their flower girl."

"That. I was. I met Jonathan on the day of their wedding. *Captain Reade* I had to call him. Things were different in those days. He was on leave. He didn't have very long, so nobody saw him or your mother for two days after the wedding." Bernadette sniggered. "And then he was gone."

"And only back once."

"Was it only once? Yes, perhaps. It probably was only once. It was a long time ago." Bernadette pulled at the cap of her muffin. She had pushed the bottom, still in its paper panties, across to Matt.

"There aren't many pictures. All of them are from the wedding. You'd think he would have sent her some more pictures at least, over the years. You'd think she would have asked for more. They must have taken snapshots together when they met up. What couple doesn't do that? There should be some from that last visit they had, in Halifax." Matt supposed that what he wanted to see was the beginnings of himself in the glint in his father's eye.

"People have different ways of recording memories. Your mother was never one for photos."

"But it is odd, don't you agree?"

"You'd have to ask your mother."

"I wish I had seen him. Even once. So I would have something to remember."

"Childhood memory is notoriously unreliable. You know that. We hear stories over and over and we grow to believe that they happened to us and, worse, that we can remember them happening to us. I'm not sure I can tell the difference between what I actually recall about my father when I was a girl and what I have manufactured over the years in between."

Matt knew she was trying to be consoling, but he resented her response nevertheless. He knew that if he had seen his father, experienced his father, he would have remembered every detail accurately forever. To suggest that his memories would only end by being false anyway was not a remedy for his having been robbed of the chance to make them in the first place. He took a long sip of coffee, swirling the cup and staring at its dwindled contents.

"Your mother always loved you enough for two parents. Hell, for twenty-two parents." Bernadette fluttered her papery, ridged claw over Matt's free hand and gave it a squeeze. "I know that makes it even harder now."

"They are going to say she is not safe in the house, aren't they?"

"You know she is not."

"But ..." He wouldn't say this to anyone but Bernie, he thought. "But what if that is okay? What if something happens at home that, you know, takes her off. Is that so bad? Wouldn't it be better for her to die at home from some mishap than to put her into that place? She's going to hate it. And she could go on there for years. What you said about the old reptilian brain —"

"They won't let you leave her in the house. Think about it. There could be a fire. That would endanger other people. Or she could fall but not on her head and then the result would be the same, only she wouldn't be able to move around. Once the social worker gets that doctor's report, they won't let you leave her alone at the mercy of chance — or the chance of mercy."

"I suppose I should thank you for making the appointment."

"Me? I had nothing to do with it. Your mother did that on her own."

Matt wished that information made the whole thing easier.

He had come to coffee prepared to ask Bernadette whether she would ever consider moving in with Penelope. Like she had in the seventies — or was it later? Not that he thought that Social Development (who had cooked up that name?) would go for it. If they were sisters, perhaps, but the idea of an eighty-year-old looking after someone sixteen years older was not likely to fly.

"I'm too old, Matt." She had always had a knack for reading his mind. "I wish I weren't, but I am. And I don't think she'd want me anyway."

"She loves you."

"But not underfoot, not every minute of the day. And it would have to be every minute of the day and night."

He knew this was true. He looked into Bernadette's sad, cloudy eyes and wondered who would look after *her* when the time came. "It's not that bad, the Lodge, really. You'd visit her, wouldn't you?"

"As long as they don't try to hang on to *me*," she laughed. And then, "Of course. Every day. There are a few others I know up there too. I could pop in on them at the same time."

Matt knew what it cost her to pretend that Penelope was just one among many old souls to be popped in on.

Foreign Bodies

PENELOPE'S INFORMATION CAME from a conversation she overheard in the shop. She learns lots that way, has come to see it as one of the advantages of holding on to some shifts for herself. God knows, Bernadette would be happy to sit behind the till every day of the week, but Penelope pleads poverty sometimes, or good labour practices, and so manages one day in every seven when she is all alone. And all ears.

They were college girls. You could tell that right away. She had them pegged for New Englanders up from Bowdoin until she heard the conversation. Then, from some of the references, she realized they must be from Mount Allison. But she didn't raise her own alumni connection, didn't quiz them on how the place had changed in the decade since she had left. That would have seemed too forward, too presumptuous. Thinking afterward about the intimate nature of the conversation she had overheard, she wondered why she had felt any such qualms.

The girls were whispering, which always made her want to listen more. One was holding up a knitting needle and waving it around, and they both made faces and groaned.

"Can you imagine?" hissed the taller of the two. She might have been pretty with less makeup, Penelope thought. "But she swears that's what they used to do."

"Jesus." The shorter girl wore a sweater that was two sizes too small, and a push-up bra that offered her breasts up to heaven. "But your aunt didn't, she didn't ..."

"I don't think so. Maybe. She always tells the story like it was about another girl. You know: my friend this, my friend that."

"Well, just don't mention any of this to Emily. Not until it's all over, anyway. It won't be like that, though, will it? I mean, they must have modern procedures, techniques now."

"She'll be able to tell us all about it. Not that we need to know, but you know Emily. She'll want to share. 'A lot less fun getting it out than putting it in.' That's what my aunt always says when she tells the story. That's enough detail for me." She put the knitting needle back on the shelf.

"She should be in Halifax right now." The short one looked at her watch. "If it was today. I think it was today. She was taking the train down and going straight to the ... the place. It's not far from the station. Apparently, it's behind a hairdresser's. In a backroom. Can you imagine?"

The girls went on to discuss how foolish Emily was to get pregnant in this day and age — as if the day and age made any difference — and how they were glad that their own boyfriends (possibly fictional) never pushed them past second base. Penelope lost interest, struck as she was to learn that an abortion could be had behind a hairdresser's shop near the train station in Halifax.

Now, as the train chugs eastbound out of Moncton, she is beginning to doubt her initial conviction about the significance of the girls' conversation. It made so much sense at the time to believe that she was meant to overhear it, that it was predestined, part of a supernatural communication plan designed just for her.

As she draws closer to Halifax, fate seems to be both less and more at work.

She has borrowed money from the shoebox she and Thora keep stuffed in the back of the pantry, behind the jars of preserved rhubarb. Borrowed is probably not the right word since she does not know how she will ever pay it back. The procedure is not an investment that will yield dividends over time in any of the usual ways. She has told herself, though, that it is a kind of investment in her future power to earn a living. How could she go on running the business, keep it thriving, with a baby hanging off her breast? Her mother will understand. She hopes a hundred dollars will be enough. Her information is not that complete, she reflects. She also hopes she will be able to find the right hairdressers' shop near the train station, although she supposes there can hardly be a wrong one — only ones that just do hairdressing. Eventually, she will rule out all but the one. Unless they all do abortions, which will deliver the same result.

At Sackville, two groups of university students board and seat themselves in her car. There are four girls in a cluster and three men in a line. If this were Noah's ark, Penelope muses, somebody would be out of luck. As the train begins to slither across the marsh, the women become more voluble while the men stop talking altogether. She cannot decide whether the men are theologues or engineers. The women, she can tell after two minutes, are fine arts students. They are going to paint *en plein air* on the Halifax waterfront (if that counts as *plein air*). Longshoremen. Whores too, they hope. Penelope wonders whether their fathers and mothers know, and what the school can be thinking. Their errand is far more dangerous than hers. She feels quite sure of that.

Her own mother doesn't need to worry about her. Thora is used to Penelope's sudden excursions. She understands that her daughter needs a change of scene, a larger canvas, every now and then. Penelope is all the more grateful for her understanding since she knows her mother has not travelled more than a hundred miles in any direction since she landed in St. Andrews more than forty years ago. Thora always asks where Penelope is going, but never why. This time, Penelope came very close to telling her anyway, but something stopped her, though neither the reason for the errand nor the errand itself would faze Thora.

At school, and later when she was in university, Penelope's friends had all envied her for her mother. She is so liberal, they would say, never dreaming that Penelope sometimes wished she were less laissez-faire. Later, one of them pronounced Thora of the earth, earthy. It was meant kindly, an appreciation of her salty tongue and her willingness to talk frankly about sex. None of the other girls had mothers like that. Or fathers. By the time Thora's unflappability was being put to its toughest tests, the friends had all fallen off or moved away. None of them was around to witness the equanimity with which she took Penelope's wartime pregnancy and rushed wedding, or the subsequent miscarriage and desertion. Nor were they there this past summer when Thora encouraged her daughter to get involved with the artists' colony.

One of the things "the colony" did endlessly was to debate whether it should really be called a colony. The term sounded so artificial, some argued; it undercut the organic spontaneity with which it had all begun. Others looked to precedent — and were jeered by their friends for being too rooted in the past. A few said the word *colony* made them uncomfortable for its political connotations and historical baggage, but the majority said they really didn't see why people had to mix up politics and art. Penelope tried to stay out of these navel-gazing sessions. She preferred to meet one or two for coffee and talk about pigments, or to lounge with a cigarette while one or another poet intoned her work, which was always footnoted with the words "in progress." She had spirited conversations with the photographer about leaving space for the viewer, weighing the relative merits of his Verichrome prints against the felted seascapes she was herself making this summer.

And then there was sitting for Robin. He didn't mind that she talked half the time or that she would suddenly leap up and run off, having remembered she had to mind the shop. Her accounts of the business that her mother started and she now ran seemed genuinely of interest to him. When she recounted how her mother had preached to the women who knitted and wove and hooked for her, exhorting them to look for inspiration in the simple life and glorious scenery around them, he seemed impressed. And he nodded appreciatively when she explained that Thora had studied at the Statens høgskole for kunsthåndverk og design in Bergen. As if he, or anyone, had heard of it. He laughed when Penelope told him how her mother had to change the name of the business almost right away from *Håndverket* to *Handworks* for the benefit of people who didn't know the difference between Norwegian and German, or that Norway was neutral in the first war.

Thora didn't say a word when Penelope and Robin began making love at Birch Hall, though she did start sleeping downstairs. Penelope explained to her mother that Robin said he'd rather not do it in the studio he was borrowing. He said he didn't like to confuse aspects of his life, but Penelope thinks he was afraid of getting caught. She supposes that Thora was happy for her. Since Jonathan's brief last visit (can it really have been eight years ago?) there have been no men. And Thora would be the last person to raise the objection that, technically at least, Penelope is still a married woman.

Seeking a divorce has never seemed important, even if she could locate Jonathan. At first, she thought he might come back, though she doesn't know what she would have done if he had.

Then it became easy to let people suppose his duties to king and country kept him away. Nobody knew about the miscarriage, just as they had not suspected the pregnancy, but there was enough sympathy to go around for the lonely young wife whose dashing RAF officer was off making the world a safer place. She and Thora started having fun spinning the story. Captain Reade had risen very high in military intelligence. They couldn't really talk about it in detail, they said (and that was true), but his work took him all over the globe. It was as dangerous as it was secret — also true since the secrecy was a complete fabrication. It was Thora who had come up with the idea of explaining Penelope's periodic escapes from St. Andrews as clandestine reunions with her secret-agent husband.

The girls on the train have moved from discussing specific plans for painting on the docks to more general concerns about representation itself. Penelope remembers these debates from her own undergraduate years, but also the renewal of them at the colony. One young woman, with a voice that might as easily be nails drawn across a chalkboard, insists on the emphasis of form over content. She argues, as Penelope had done herself little more than a month ago, that "in an age of mechanical reproduction the only true work of art is one that is unique, one that expresses its maker as much as it demonstrates its subject."

Penelope is struck by the term "mechanical reproduction." Is that what she and Robin have enacted? There is, of course, no pinpointing the moment of conception, no certain singling out of one act of lovemaking in a series that lasted nearly two weeks. She would like to think that the sperm found the egg their first time, which was, contrary to her previous experience, their most satisfying encounter. But it could as easily have been one of the last three or four times, when neither she nor Robin did much more than go through the motions. It wasn't a cooling of their love;

she did not think that. Rather, it was the spectre of separation. Knowing they would soon be apart, they were already as good as separated in bed.

A second girl, with the overdeveloped shoulders of a swimmer or a sculptor (maybe both) is talking about what you leave unsaid, unshown. "Representation is not reproduction," she says. The engineers or theologues look up when they hear the word *reproduction* for the second time in five minutes. "Representation is about capturing the experience, the feeling, and transmitting it so another can share it. That means the person looking at a piece of art has to be enlisted, engaged." She goes on to talk about *the invisible complement*, which Penelope thinks she may not be applying entirely accurately. But still, she understands the girl's drift.

She tries to picture the invisible mass of cells forming, the unseen presence inside her. And then she thinks of Robin. She has not told him, of course. She has been on that route before. While Robin is a hundred degrees less conventional than Jonathan, he might nevertheless feel manipulated, trapped; and she knows how that ends up. The circumstances are different this time — she knows that — especially in their essentials, but she is still afraid of stepping into the same river twice, no matter that those ancient Greeks thought you couldn't. The last thing she wants is for someone to think they need to make a so-called *honest woman* of her. She wishes now that she had invited her mother along on the journey for company, for advice. Thora knows a thing or two about miserable marriages, though not how to avoid one in the first place. She also knows what it is to raise a child without a man around, interfering — a joy she has never tired of describing to Penelope.

From her purse, she takes the embroidered cambric handkerchief, checking before she does that the knots are still tight. She does not want her precious collection rolling around on the train's grimy floor. Placing the package on her lap, she carefully pinches at one knotted corner, tugging cloth through cloth until she has an opening large enough to admit two fingers. *The pearls are at their best this way*, she thinks, *felt but not seen*. She worries one between her fingertips, marvelling, as she does every time, at the creamy smoothness. To look at, scallop pearls are not as beautiful as oyster ones, of course. The iridescence is missing. But when rolled between your fingers they feel the same.

She cannot recall a time when she didn't have at least two of the magical spheres to roll together. Her mother started her on the scallop pearl collection before she can remember. "Any mollusc can produce a pearl." Thora has said this each time she has added one to the group. "It's simply the way they deal with irritation, a means of dealing with invasion, foreign bodies. Nobody cares much about any of those pearls, though, except the ones made by oysters. It's not hard to see why with mussels. Those calcified stones can break a tooth. What makes the scallop pearls special," Thora says, "is that they are usually overlooked. You have to shuck scallops right on the boat, as soon as they are up from the bottom. That means you are always in a hurry and you don't watch very carefully what you are doing. So, when you do actually notice a pearl in all that rush, it is something to celebrate." As she thinks back over the occasions when she can remember Thora giving her a pearl, Penelope cannot discern a pattern. They came with sorrow, they came with joy, and sometimes they came on a day when she felt nothing at all. For a long time, Penelope planned to do something with her scallop pearls, to make something with them. Now, she knows they are best left loose, to be brought out and rearranged or worried between trembling fingers in a knotted hankie on an eastbound train.

At the Truro station stop, she begins rehearsing the story of her absence. Not for her mother — who understands — but to distract herself, and for the craftswomen who will ask, for the neighbours. This will be another installment of the spy saga she and her mother have created, she decides. Jonathan had a brief layover in Halifax, she will say, and she went to be with him. *Yes, it is a shame he can never manage to get back to St. Andrews, but at least they can arrange these … reunions*. She will say the word *reunions* with a bit of a giggle to cater to her audience's prurient interests, she thinks. And that is when she has the idea. She will return the hundred dollars to the shoebox after all.

WHEN SHE LOOKS down at her lap for her handkerchief, she sees her withered hands are clamped instead onto a tiny paperbound photo album. It is one of those you used to get with your developed prints: golden embossed paper with an aluminum two-pronged clip that holds the three-by-five memories together. The train is gone; her coachmates, she supposes, graduated and married and with children of their own, grandchildren even. She opens the album, loving the way the scalloped edges of the prints tickle her fingers. Every picture is of a baby, some baby who looks much like any other baby, sleeping, startling, snuggling, smiling. Matt.

Tin Cans

MATT LEFT A long voicemail message for Jennifer. He had deliberately called at a time he knew she would be in class. Every word was rehearsed in front of the mahogany-framed mirror in the bathroom. It was the same mirror he had used as a teenager to practice his bedroom eyes.

"Hi. It's me. I … I forgot that you still had … that classes were still on. This must be the last week though? And then there will be all the marking. At least you can spread out the marking all over the house if you want. Nobody to get in your way. So, about that: I think I'm going to have to stay on here through January. There's a lot to do. There are meetings with civil servants who are apparently too important to do anything in December. There's getting the house organized, getting Mamma set. And I've done almost nothing on the model villages yet. So there's that, too. I'm really sorry. I know you won't want to come out here for Christmas, and neither of us is that nuts about Christmas anyway. And you're never all that … all that … happy here. I should be able to wrap everything up by mid-January, I think. Anyway, I'll miss you. I'll email later. And call anytime, of course, I don't want to disturb the marking. Sorry again that I only got the machine."

They had always had a pact that neither would sign off a voicemail with anything lovey-dovey. That had been Jennifer's idea. She said she hated the thought of playing the message with somebody else in the room. Or, what if the intended recipient died and a stranger picked up the hugs and kisses and love-yas? He was glad of this arrangement now. Nothing could be read into the way his message ended. Everything was as usual. Except that he couldn't face a live conversation with his wife, and that he was going to spend Christmas without her.

He found Penelope in the kitchen, trying to jam a baking sheet into the drawer under the stove. When he leaned in to help her, she jumped.

"Matt! I didn't know you were here. Did I? I can't get this damn thing to fit. It's never been a problem before."

"May I have a look?"

"Fill your boots."

Matt set the offending sheet on the table and knelt before the drawer. Under a pizza pan covered in cheese-crusted tinfoil he found the portrait of his mother that had gone missing. *Missing portrait, missing mother*, he thought.

"Now how the hell did that get there?" A week ago she might have laughed.

"One smart cookie with the cookie sheets?" He knew it was feeble. "I'll just put it back over the mantel."

"Behind the door."

"I'll make tea."

"I know how to make tea."

"I'll hang the picture." There was some consolation in the notion that she probably wouldn't notice where he put it.

When he returned to the kitchen, she was struggling again with the baking-sheet drawer. She had all the contents out on the table. The kettle was cold and empty.

As he began to run the water, the air was suddenly sliced by the whoop of a siren. The firehall was only a couple of hundred yards away, up and around the corner on the way out of town. Ten-year-old Matt had seen this as one of the house's key selling features when they moved here from Birch Hall. He stepped closer to the window to have a look. Only an ambulance, he saw, and wondered which of the town's old souls had fallen or clotted or infarcted.

"Where is your grandmother? Has she come back from Chamcook?"

"Yes." *Just not lately.*

"She'll be back out there tomorrow, sifting through the ruins."

"York House?"

"I tell her to let the past alone. Whatever it is."

"She lived there when she first came out from Norway. That's what you said the night we were having lobsters. You'd never mentioned it before."

"She didn't live there at first. At first, they put them up in an old clam factory in town. The dormitories weren't finished. They converted the upper floors for sleeping. Lots of partitions. There was a large dining room in the bottom. I expect it was pretty rough."

"And she really came out to pack sardines?"

"More than a hundred of them came, none any more than a mere girl. Can you imagine? Packed like sardines themselves. Worse. Sardines don't care about privacy. The men were put up at Kennedy's, so at least there was none of *that*."

"The men came to pack too?"

"Mostly the men came to accompany the women, but they did a lot of the other work. Men's hands are not as good for the packing. They were hired to make the tins and work the fryers and stoke the smoking shed. But mainly they were husbands or chaperones, like her brother Nils."

It was the first Matt had heard of a great-uncle and he wanted to stop her there, to probe about his grandmother's brother, but did not want to threaten whatever spell had been woven.

"The men made more trouble than they made tins or packing crates. Not that it was their fault. The factory wasn't ready, and they were sent to work on construction jobs that they hadn't signed on for, and couldn't do. They were forced to work alongside the Italian crews that had been brought up from the States to build the factory and the town. They were a rough bunch, constantly striking for more pay or one thing or another, brawling, whoring, shooting off guns even. The Norwegian consul had to be called in several times. The men complained the company was trying to get rid of them, that they only wanted the women, which was true. Some of them were deported."

"Your uncle Nils?"

"She never said. Maybe she did. Things settled down a bit when the plant was finished, although the fish never really ran as expected."

"They canned clams instead." Matt had managed that much research.

"Until there was a surplus on the market. And beans and brown bread. It was ingenious. There was a partition in the tin, like the bedrooms in an old clam factory."

"Did she ever think of going back? Gran. To Bergen?"

"She never talked about Bergen. This was her home."

"But when the sardine factory closed? It must have been hard."

"She got by. Your grandmother was very ..." Penelope smiled, "resourceful."

"She never talked to me about the sardine factory."

"Are you sure? Perhaps you've forgotten. You were very young."

"I was ten when she died. You never talked about it either. The other night was the first I had ever heard of it."

"It was state of the art. Nothing like the thrown-together places along the Maine coast. It was all hard surfaces, and there were no square corners, no place where anything could catch or gather and grow germs, no pores to capture smells."

"You saw it, then?"

"She used to say it was a place without a memory. All glass and porcelain tile that you could hose down. No traces left. A blank slate every day. She said she loved that about it, though not much else."

"Gran liked things clean and neat."

"I think she also hated it a little too, the forgetfulness. Or envied it. Her fingers were never free of the smell of herring, she said. Or her hair."

"And the model village? The dormitory — York House?"

"She never spoke of them."

"Not even after the fire?"

"Not even then. But she kept going back out there for weeks after it burned. I don't know. I suppose there was something that drew her, something she wanted to make sure of, make her peace with. Mamma liked things to have tidy endings."

The siren whooped by on its return trip. Something urgent, then. Matt hoped whoever it was would keep for the hour's drive to Saint John.

"Has she been out there again, my mother?"

"I think she has stopped." It was true. And a harmless thing to say. In fact, the right response, according to the pamphlet in the doctor's office. *No reason to contradict them*, advised the several books he has since consulted. But Matt wondered, as he abetted his mother's increasingly frequent time slips, what that might bode for his own grasp on reality.

Folds and Shadows

THE SPEED WITH which Gina and Ingrid's memory project started to take on a definite shape had surprised Matt. The shape itself surprised him even more.

He went to the second workshop prepared to cringe at a series of lurid confessions, which he expected he would have to flag as problematic for the museum. Gina's opening exercise did little to calm his fears. She had the participants stand in a circle again, but all facing away from the centre this time. Each was asked to recall a smell that they associated with a powerful memory. Even though his place as observer outside the circle was now established, he thought of what he would choose. There was the scent of lemon shampoo, of course. But that was too fresh, dangerous, and Ingrid was there in the flesh — well, not as entirely in the flesh as a week ago — just twenty feet from him. There was the tang of the intertidal mud of home, that bouquet of salty farts with a tint of iodine. Or wool, with its cocktail of ammonia and lanolin. But there were too many memories there to disentangle, he thought.

The participants' responses formed a series of unwitting homages to Proust: smells of baking, and soap, and tea, and associated instances of states of innocence, and guilt, and indifference. Matt winced at the mention of Clorox, but the memory actually turned out to be about cleaning. After they had gone around the circle once, Gina asked everyone to repeat the exercise, only this time they were to use the smell that had been identified by the person to their left in the first round. In about half of the cases, the memory that was evoked was uncannily close in narrative shape and details to what had been shared by the original rememberer. In the rest, the adopted smell triggered something completely new. Unfailingly in those cases, the rememberers stated how surprised they were, how the memory that was evoked was something they had not thought about for years. Some shed tears of relief at having recovered what they described as repressed memories.

Matt was impressed by how deftly Gina Smell used these results to direct the conversation toward the act of remembering itself, challenging the group to think about what it all meant. She guided them gently but unwaveringly to conclusions about suggestibility and fabrication. She encouraged them, too, to think about how there is no memory without a correspondence in the present, that memory may be more properly recognition rather than recollection. Some of the discussion went too fast, Matt thought — the leaps were too great — but she managed to keep all but a few of the group engaged and in agreement. Ingrid then took over and talked about Surrealism, losing the interest of a further one or two participants, but plunging on regardless. The unusual objects in a Surrealist work, she told them, were designed to open up a slit in time, to allow current lives, former lives, and future lives to melt into one another. Recognizing that ability for blurring and overlapping was crucial to understanding the nature of memory, she said, and it would be very important for the project. No memory is unalloyed, untouched by time. She finished with a line from Pinter's play *Old Times*: "There are things I remember that may never have happened, but as I recall them so they take place."

Matt wondered whether she had actually read the play or just found the snippet online.

By the end of the second afternoon, Gina and Ingrid had managed to prompt the group to decide that the project would be as much about recollection in general as about individual memories. They had also decided that everyone would participate in the final performance.

Matt had told Jennifer he had a work thing all evening following the workshop. She had not asked what could possibly be happening on a Saturday night. He had no idea, in fact, whether Ingrid would invite him again, but he wanted to be ready.

"Gina and I would like to invite you for a drink. To compare notes."

"Um, sure." Matt tried, and failed, to mask his disappointment.

They went to the bar on Bloor where he had had his first drink with Ingrid, sat at the same table. He would have made a comment on memory and persons and *loci* but he didn't know whether Gina knew about that first occasion. He also doubted that she had seen *The Art of Memory* exhibit, so it would have seemed like an in-joke anyway, and he was determined to deny Gina any whiff of the fact that he and Ingrid already shared a special past. The women ordered white wine, debating the relative merits of Pinot Grigios and Chardonnays before settling on a Sauvignon Blanc. He opted for Guinness, hoping the taste would restore, however secretly, some of the aura of the earlier encounter. He found he was dying to discuss all of this with Ingrid: how subsequent events had coloured his memory of that first drink, imbued it with a mystery and excitement it probably did not have at the time.

"So, what do you think? Are we going to be all right? Are we passing inspection, boss?" Gina meant him. She had a knack for putting herself in the subservient role. He chose not to take it personally. He was relieved that he could truthfully report he was very pleased with the direction. And then, to try to wriggle out of the overseer position, he lavished praise for how she had managed the group.

"It was Ingrid's idea," Gina said. "To steer it more in the direction of being about the nature of memory itself, I mean. It gets us out of that bind we were worried about: you know, that the framing of every question biases the response and therefore constrains the narrative."

"Or if it doesn't get us out of it, it at least gets it out on the table. Well, the floor, I guess." Ingrid smiled at Matt and took a long sip of her wine.

"And it helps with so-called recovered memories. In case somebody comes out with something truly horrible as a result of our workshops."

Matt thought of the young man who broke down at the first session, and of those who had been reduced to tears by other people's memories of smells.

"We can respect the memory without validating it." Gina sucked her mouthful of wine between her molars. "We can problematize it. Ingrid thinks that any truly traumatic thing that we think we have forgotten or repressed has nothing to do with memory per se and everything to do with the original circumstances of the event. A blow to the head, too much booze, blanking out — they all interfere with the ability to store a memory in the first place. So it's a storage problem and not a retrieval problem. Something like that."

"Something like that," murmured Ingrid.

Matt was not sure he followed completely how they had gotten onto the subject of recovered memory. He wondered whether there was a message here for him about last Saturday. Was Ingrid trying to tell him that she had decided she was too drunk to have stored any memory of what they had done?

He was not left long in doubt. There was definitely something rubbing against his calf in the shadows beneath the table (he hoped there were shadows). There couldn't be a cat. Not in a bar. Ingrid must have slipped off her shoe. Gina was still talking, but he was no longer really in the room. He was a few miles west and seven nights before. *Ah*, he thought, recognition, *not* recollection. *The* then *needs a* now.

"As artists, we have a responsibility to everything we represent. Re-present," Gina was saying. "It's a kind of sacred bond."

"Matt's mother is an artist. His grandmother, too. I think you told me that?"

"Your grandmother is still alive?" Gina made it sound as if Matt himself was Methuselah, but, of course, the math was a challenge. Even if Matt were ten years younger than he was — which would make him only about ten years older than the two women — his grandmother would have to be his mother's age, which was itself already implausibly ancient.

"Was an artist, the grandmother," said Ingrid. Matt liked the tint of defensiveness and the silent deflection of the age issue.

"What does your mother do? Would I know her work?"

Matt decided not to talk about his grandmother's and mother's business. It was not that he wasn't proud of it, that he didn't think it deserved all the praise it had received, particularly in his grandmother's hands in the twenties. Some had seen in the embroidered bags and felted land- and seascapes the promise of a new and truly Canadian art. This had, of course, amused — but also pleased — his Norwegian grandmother. But the originality with which Thora and then Penelope had married principles of design with reflection of everyday surroundings and homespun media was not likely to interest Gina. And so he told them a little about his mother's experiments in the seventies.

He started with Robert Morris. There was no point in hiding the influence. Gina and Ingrid said they were familiar with

Morris's exploration of what he called "process art." They knew Morris mainly because of his interest in experimental dance in the fifties, but both had seen his felt pieces at MoMA and the Guggenheim.

"My mother was fascinated with the analogies Morris drew between felt and human skin. She loved his ideas about letting chance and the nature of the material direct the form. And gravity. My mother was a big fan of gravity. When she wasn't trying to defy it." Matt regretted the crack; he didn't want the women to think he was a disloyal son. In expiation, he decided to tell them more. "Morris worked with industrial felt, mainly. Strips of thick, machine-cut material, dropped at random to find a new form. My family has made its own felt for more than a hundred years." That was neither a boast nor a lie. Even in her nineties, Penelope still produced her own sheets from time to time. "It started as a craft business for my grandmother. She used local wool. She even engaged women to make felt for her. They would embroider scenes on the finished felt mats. Or cut the felt to make a kind of soft mosaic picture, a collage that represented a familiar scene or object from everyday life in the same way a primitive painting might. Their work was quite famous for a while, in the late fifties. A lot of Americans bought it."

He was embarrassed by the cultural-colonialist implications of this last statement, so before Gina could comment, he rushed on. "Anyway, by the seventies, the market for that kind of work was drying up, although it never entirely went away. My mother saw some of Morris's work in New York, and she read some of what he had to say about it, and she started to experiment on her own. At first, she used pieces she had around the shop, the primitive felt paintings that she and Gran had made, and the decorated bags. (She had a shop where she sold sweaters and scarves and bags. Pottery too, sometimes.) The pieces she used were what you would call 'seconds.' She put them together, or let them fall, with results that bore some resemblance to Morris's. The felt, with its skin-like qualities, reminded people of bodies. The lines were often graceful, even formal, despite how they had been achieved. Definitely abstract. But because the pictures were figurative and the felt was handmade, there was an invitation to the viewer to try to see the colour variations and the embroidered or collaged scenes that had been obscured by the sculptural process. As she pursued the work, she began creating new pieces of figurative or scenic representation and then immediately recycled them into collages and piles that hid the original work in folds and shadows, keeping it forever just beyond the viewer's grasp. Your appreciation of the sculptural form was pitted against your curiosity about the narratives of the scenes that had been hidden. Sorry. I am starting to sound like a catalogue."

He realized that Ingrid's foot had stopped rubbing his calf. "Gina, aren't you supposed to be meeting Maria?" she said, looking at Matt the whole time.

"We need to think about using some fabric, for the performance," Gina said. "Not necessarily felt, but something that can forget its old form. Or return to it, remember it. Either way. We need to think about that." Then she said, yes, she was late, kissed Ingrid, nodded at Matt, and was gone, leaving them to pay for her wine. Neither of them minded.

Jul

MATT HADN'T BEEN in a church for at least ten years, and that was for a funeral for a colleague, conducted less according to the Book of Common Prayer and more in line with Hollywood stereotypes and principles of inclusiveness. His grandmother had taken him to service every Sunday for the first ten years of his life. *Religiously*, she used to say. It was her other joke. He doesn't remember whether Penelope was with them or not, except for Christmas. On Christmas Eve they were always there together. After Thora's death, Christmas was the only time he and his mother darkened the door. He had no idea what she did all those Christmases after he left town.

The rector was just the third since the old goat with whom Thora had butted heads after the service, over sherry at Birch Hall. It was the kind of parish you didn't leave willingly. The new man — he had been there ten years — had, according to Bernie, tried to introduce the Alternative Service, which was hardly alternative in most places by then. Matt was relieved the man had eventually relented. He found it oddly comforting that his lips could automatically form the hundreds-of-years-old phrases of

Cranmer's prayers even after decades of not even thinking about them. When he dared to peek sideways, he was pleased to see his mother intoning the words of the general confession without a glance at the maroon book that she nevertheless held open in her left hand. The carols were less of a wonder. Everyone always remembered those, but negotiating the syntax of Cranmer was another matter. He thought he should write a note about it for the gerontologist.

PENELOPE IS REMINDED of how her mother used to try to get the rector to shift the midnight service to early evening, thinks how pleased Thora would be that the times have finally caught up with her, even if she can't be here to enjoy it. This way, they will be able to enjoy the big meal after church and still get to bed at a reasonable hour. Matt needs his sleep. While her lips form the familiar *there is no health in us*, her mind races ahead to the feast that is to follow. But she cannot be sure now that she has prepared any of it. Thora will have looked after it. It won't be turkey or goose. That stopped, she was told, the year her father left them, the year they were *freed of George Arnold*, Thora would say as she mixed the dough for the *pepperkaker*, evidently meaning freed of all the Arnold family traditions. They no longer celebrated Christmas. It was *Jul*. Father Christmas became a mischievous garden elf, one of dozens who had apparently been living around them all along, but you couldn't see them. Penelope marvelled at how easily her mother recalled the recipes for *pepperkaker* (*we don't call it gingerbread anymore*) and the sugary sand cakes whose Norwegian name even Penelope easily came to recognize as *sandkaker*. It was only years later, after her mother's death, when she was talking to a Norwegian tourist about customs, that Penelope learned that cod (*lutefisk*) was a traditional Christmas Eve dish. Thora would have nothing to do with regular fish; Penelope can't think why now. She always picked out the lamb for the *pinnekjøtt* in late October. Her Handworks connections meant she usually had loads to choose from. The ribs would arrive a day later and be buried instantly in the mountain of sea salt Thora had prepared. After three days, the ribs were resurrected — Penelope used to wonder whether her mother had Christmas and Easter confused — and would hang in the summer kitchen for nearly two months. This same Norwegian tourist told Penelope that some people smoked the meat at this stage. Thora disliked anything smoked almost as much as she hated fish though. A couple of days before Christmas, they would soak the lamb to get most of the salt out. Penelope's favourite part was cutting the birch sticks they arranged in the bottom of the pot to steam the lamb on Christmas Eve. Her mother let her handle the brush axe and the knives all by herself. The birch didn't add any flavour to the meat. That was part of the beauty of it, though, Thora used to say. *There is no reason; it is just how it is done.*

Matt is tugging at her elbow. "Mamma, do you want to go up for communion?" She lets him guide her up the aisle and help her kneel at the rail. It is easier than debating what any of it means to her anymore.

THEY HAD WALKED to the church. His mother had insisted. When the service ended, Bernadette joined them outside. He had invited her to join them for dinner. "Where's the car, boss?"

Penelope looked up and down King Street and then at Matt.

"We walked," Matt said, wishing his response had been quicker, to save his mother that moment of confusion. "Mamma likes to walk on Christmas Eve. Gran liked to walk on Christmas Eve. Shall we?" He crooked both his elbows and the two women latched on and tottered home along the street.

PENELOPE WONDERS WHO decorated the living room, is about to tell Matt and that old woman he has brought home with them about the *nisse*, the hobgoblins who live all around them. But then she recognizes a needle-felted sheep in the manger scene on the mantelpiece and remembers putting it there herself. It was one of the first things she made with her own hands. That's the story that goes with it, but she can't remember when that would have been, or who would have helped her. Not her mother, though her mother must have allowed it to join the *Jul* repertoire. She lifts it from the mantel and knocks a rough clay donkey onto the floor. It doesn't so much shatter as dismember itself. Another of her early works.

"Tough night in the stable," chirps the old woman as she stoops to pick up the bits. "I never liked that old ass anyway, boss."

Bernadette. *But who is minding the shop*?

"It's okay, Matt, just a minor crèche casualty," Bernadette calls out toward the kitchen.

Good. Matt is here. It is always nice to have children around at Christmas. When he comes into the living room, though, he is limping and slightly round about the middle. Taller than he should be. And balder. Perhaps he has children he has brought along with him. She can't think who his children are. Or where. "It smells delicious," she says. It is a tick. She has always done this: commented on the food when at a loss for anything else to say in a social situation. Now it is a vital survival tactic to help her navigate away from the black holes.

"It's just one of those boneless stuffed things. Sorry. I couldn't cope with the full-on turkey."

Not lamb, then. She wonders what Thora will say, wishes she could spare Matt his grandmother's inevitable rant about his Arnold ancestors.

"A man who can cook at all is a good man," says Bernadette.

Penelope is afraid she will go on to say something about how that what's-her-name is a lucky woman. It would be the wrong thing to say at this moment. Penelope knows that, although she doesn't know why.

"Mamma taught me well."

Did she? She never cared that much about the kitchen.

Bernadette is fluttering around the Christmas tree — how did that get there? — taking roll call for the ornaments. It is alarming how many of them she claims to recognize. "Do you remember the tree your mother made, boss, that one time, out of new sweaters? The war must still have been on. I was not very old. Matt, your grandmother was the most creative woman. She made a beautiful Christmas tree — although she called it something else, something like jewel without the *J* — entirely out of sweaters. Spruce green. It was the most amazing thing. Sculpture, I guess you would call it now."

MATT COULD SEE his mother's mouth tighten when Bernadette started on about the sweater tree but couldn't figure out how to head the story off, or why it mattered. Let them reminisce, he thought, as he retreated to the kitchen for another slurp of gin and to think about carving the roll of white meat and sodden breadcrumbs.

He knew he probably shouldn't be having anything to drink after the debacle of the night before. He had drunk-dialled Jennifer at midnight. Was it drunk-dialling if you could recall every detail of the call the next day? She sounded sleepy, blamed the marking, then asked if he had been drinking.

"Do I need to have been drinking to call my wife?"

"You tell me."

"I just wanted to hear your voice. With Christmas coming and everything."

"We don't care about Christmas. Remember?"

"I don't remember when we've ever been apart for Christmas."

"Before we knew each other. How's your mother?"

"She needs me." He waited for Jennifer to say that she needed him.

"And the research? The model villages?"

"I bought a turkey. Well, a turkey roll."

"Didn't you tell me your mother does some kind of a Norwegian Christmas or something random like that?"

"Fuck. Right. I'd forgotten. Not random, by the way. My grandmother was —"

"Listen, Matt, it's late here."

He didn't remind her it was actually an hour earlier.

"Maybe let's talk in a couple of days. You know, Christmas Day."

He put the phone down. "Frigid bitch." Then he remembered you had to push the red button to cut the connection.

THE POTATOES ARE lumpy. Penelope supposes Matt forgot to peel them until Bernadette congratulates him on leaving the skins on. Apparently, most of the goodness is in the skins, and people do this all the time. *Where was Bernadette during the war when potatoes were nearly all there was to eat, and they were always meticulously peeled?* She knows the answer. Bernadette was only a girl. And science was not so advanced. Advanced enough to develop that bomb that Jonathan had gone to observe, but not advanced enough to convince people to get the best out of every potato. There was a book, though, something about potato peel pie. She thinks she read that — or at least the title.

The *pinnekjøtt* is not as salty as she likes. Thora must have gotten distracted, left it to soak too long. She looks for the pickled cabbage to perk things up, finds only a cylinder of what has to be cranberry jelly, its rippled sides remembering the shape of the tin from which it has plopped.

"How did you make gravy from a turkey roll?" the old lady beside her asks.

"It's from a package," Matt stage-whispers.

"Still, you're going to make someone an excellent husband someday." Bernadette — that's who it is — laughs as she says it. Matt laughs too. Penelope chokes. There are lumps in the potatoes. Somebody — she thinks it's Matt, can't tell who through her tears — gets her a glass of water. It's good to have children around at Christmas.

AFTER THE FRUITCAKE, they said good night to Bernadette. Matt offered to walk her home (he didn't dare drive the Volvo with the gin he had drunk) and Penelope said she would start cleaning up the kitchen. When he got back, she had gone up to bed. He found the leftover turkey in the dishwasher and the cutlery in the fridge. A mountain of sea salt was dumped out on the counter.

The Moirae

MATT HAD ASKED several times in the course of his phone conversation whether the home visit was really necessary. As he explained to the crisp voice at the other end of the line, there was really no question of his mother's being able to stay in her house. They must have the gerontologist's report by now. He had to return to Toronto — he did not add *eventually* — and hiring round-the-clock, live-in help would be well beyond his mother's means, even if it were available. Finally, desperate to make a connection, he tried to work on the woman's compassion.

"My mother is quite confused. Distraught. She won't want someone walking through her house making pronouncements about it. It will upset her. And I'm afraid, frankly, that it might give her some false hopes." He never used the word *frankly*, thought it implied that a person wasn't being frank the rest of the time, but in this case he had some hopes for it.

"I understand, Mr. Reade. And we don't want to cause distress. We really don't." *Had he actually gotten through?* "But there are steps we have to go through. The protocols were developed to protect all parties. In designing a care plan, we have to have all of the data, and that includes an assessment of the home situation."

By the time the visit that had, in the end, been arranged came around, he had decided that it might after all be worth taking seriously. He had not seen the gerontologist's report, which might not have been as dire as he had imagined. Perhaps they would find that the physical space itself was not after all too badly adapted to Penelope's needs. Maybe he could delay his return to Toronto a little more, stay in the house with her a bit longer, if the presence of another person was all that was needed. At the very least, there was bound to be some waiting for a bed in the Lodge.

He was surprised when, at the appointed time, he answered the door to not one but a trio of young women. He decided at once they must be Mormons. He had put two of them off last week by telling them he had really enjoyed their hit musical, but then again, he always liked anything those *South Park* guys did. That these three should arrive at the exact time of his appointment with Social Development might be a compelling sign of their connectedness to a divine plan, but it was quite inconvenient.

"Mr. Reade? I'm Carolyn White. From Social Development? We spoke on the phone? This is Francie Nashe. She's an occupational therapist. And this is Emily Smit. She's a physio." She looked about eighteen, Matt thought. The others appeared only months older. They all had faces like pans of milk. That's what his grandmother would have said. He always remembered that phrase, though he could no longer recall whether she had meant it as a compliment or condemnation. He thought they were pretty enough, if a little bland. Carolyn wore large glasses. In a fifties movie she would have been the librarian who took them off at all the right moments. In her professional life, he supposed the glasses helped restore some of the gravitas that her youthful appearance threatened to undermine. As he helped her off with her coat, wondering halfway through whether that was an appropriate thing to do, he saw that she was pregnant.

"Don't worry about your boots," he said as all three stooped in unison. "It's not that kind of house." Was that a poor beginning? "I mean, these painted floors are tough. We keep them clean, of course. We keep the whole place clean." He looked around frantically for evidence that this was true. Carolyn was wearing white tennis socks under her boots, a trend Matt couldn't understand. He could see her painted toenails beneath the thin cotton, ten red cherries in a sack. Emily, the physio, had hiking socks that might have been from the mill in Harvey. Only the occupational therapist had brought shoes to slip on. Of course.

"I'm going to let Francie walk us around. This is really her area," said Carolyn. Matt hoped she had not caught him staring at her toes.

"Should I ... do we need my mother for this?"

"It's probably just as well. There will be some questions."

"I think she's in the back." He was afraid this sounded like he had no idea, which might be misinterpreted, so he corrected himself. "She's in the kitchen."

The house had been built as a simple three-bay Cape Cod but expanded just before the first war by a summer resident from Maryland. The addition of a mansard roof (very popular among the summer people) had allowed for larger rooms upstairs, and a large ell built onto the back of the house had afforded more bedrooms upstairs, allowing the kitchen, which had occupied one of the original two backrooms, to move into roomier quarters. Matt wondered why he was telling the women all of this, realizing, too late, this was not that kind of a tour.

He was relieved that his mother was where he had predicted. She smiled at them as they filed into the kitchen but then went on shuffling Tupperware containers from the fridge to the counter and back.

"Mamma, this is Carolyn and Francie and ... sorry, what is it again?"

"Emily."

"They've come to talk to us and take a look at the house."

"I don't want to sell."

"No. It's not about selling, Mamma." He was glad she had not heard him giving the five-cent tour a minute before.

"Everybody just wants to make sure you are comfortable, Mrs. Reade. And safe."

"Everybody?"

"Well, the three of us. And your family. And your friends."

"I'd offer you something to eat, but I can't seem to sort out what I have."

"That's okay, Mrs. Reade. We've eaten. What a lovely big kitchen," said Carolyn as Francie began ticking boxes on a form she had latched to a clipboard.

"It's freezing in the winter. You should be here in January."

Matt bit his tongue, was impressed that none of the three tried to tell his mother it was January.

"Electric stove. That's good. But not smooth-top. Also good. They can burn themselves more easily on the smooth-tops," Francie muttered to Matt. "Do you use the oven much, Mrs. Reade?"

"It's not the kind you can stick your head in. Well, you can stick your head in, it just doesn't have any effect." Penelope tilted her head as if she was about to demonstrate.

Matt was about to say something to laugh this off, but Carolyn beat him to it. "You could dry your hair." Penelope laughed way too hard at this, Matt thought. She was performing.

Francie hid any annoyance she might be feeling. "Do you bake things?"

"She was never much of a baker, were you, Mamma?"

"Mrs. Reade?"

"God no. I made a roast beef dinner last night for Matt."

Matt let this lie go. He would feel too disloyal contradicting her.

Francie had the freezer door open. "I see quite a lot of microwaveable dinners here."

"That's right, dear, that's all I eat these days. Pretty much." Penelope never called anyone *dear* unless she was annoyed with them. "They go in the little oven, on the counter." She turned to Carolyn. "Do you know whether it's a boy or a girl?" Matt hoped that it wasn't as obvious to Carolyn as it was to him how his mother had gotten from microwave oven to bun in one.

Francie had taken a measuring tape out and was recording the height of the counters. Then she opened each of the upper cabinets to the left of the sink. Matt was pleased that he had only just yesterday reorganized them so that there was one of everything his mother could possibly need within easy reach on the lowest shelf. Penelope had been furious, and then hadn't cared a bit. He had explained three times why he was doing it.

He had managed on the phone to talk Carolyn out of putting his mother through her paces in the kitchen. The gerontologist had done all of that; he couldn't see any reason to put Penelope through the ordeal a second time, he had said. He knew, of course, that Penelope might very well not remember her trials in the doctor's fake kitchen, but he did.

Francie and Emily were gently kicking the raised threshold between the dining room and the kitchen and conversing earnestly in tones too low for Matt to hear. Then it was Emily's turn with the measuring tape. She got down on her knees to get a reading on the height of the threshold. Matt wished he had washed the floor. He tried not to look at the naked crescent of her back smiling at him between waistband and shirt.

"Different floor treatments over the years, I suppose," he said, knowing at the same time the reason for the bump was irrelevant. "And maybe the ell addition never quite matched up in the first place. I suppose there might be some kind of wedge thing we could get, a very tiny ramp on either side?"

"I don't think your mother drags her feet. She knows the house. This is probably not an immediate problem, Mr. Reade."

The formal way she said his name made him worry she had caught him looking at her bared back. "Call me Matt, please." *How did that make it better?* But she was already nudging the dining room rug with her hiking-socked toe. "Should I tape that?" Somehow, he had started to behave as if the point of the exercise was actually to make the house safer for Penelope to stay when he knew it was simply to tick a box in a bureaucratic procedure for getting her out of it and into a nursing home.

"It seems to lie pretty flat."

The front living room, he found himself telling them, had, of course, originally been two rooms with a hallway and the stairs between them. The lady from Baltimore who had done the remodelling a hundred years ago had removed some walls to give her one large room with the staircase in its middle. Nice for a summer cottage, but hard to heat in the winters. Carolyn said she loved old houses and trying to figure out what had been done to them over the years. She told Penelope that she loved the house, said she and her husband hoped to have one like it one day.

"I'm not selling," Penelope said, and they all laughed.

The stairs were going to be the biggest challenge, Matt knew. Uncarpeted and worn on their treads by so many feet for so many years, they must appear as old-lady murderers, he thought.

"Do you go up the stairs when nobody is around?"

"Unless I can persuade a man to carry me up them," Penelope quipped. To demonstrate how easy she found them, she grabbed the banister and began the ascent, calling to the girls to follow if they dared.

Matt brought up the rear. Trying not to look at the rear directly in front of him, he nearly lost his footing. *They'll have me in the Lodge*, he thought. At the top of the stairs, Carolyn shot him a look he could not interpret. It was either a flirty did-you-enjoy-the-view look or an are-you-having-trouble-negotiating-stairs professional one. Her librarian glasses made it hard to tell.

The master bathroom was an instant hit. Penelope had had a tiled walk-in shower installed five years before — a ninety-first birthday present to herself — but she had retained the old claw-footed tub. Francie and Emily clucked approvingly about the shower and its built-in bench. Carolyn admired the tub, having first made sure that Penelope didn't try to use it anymore herself. Matt was ambushed by an image of the pregnant social worker soaking in the old claw foot, her rounded belly floating above the soap bubbles. Jennifer had never been pregnant. It was mostly an opportunity thing: when one of them was ready, the other wasn't, career-wise. There was also the spectre of raising a child in the city — not to mention the overall state of the world. He tried to replace Carolyn's face with Jennifer's but ended up with Ingrid's. *Jesus, what a mess.*

"What's through here, Mrs. Reade?" Francie was standing in front of the door to the workroom, which took up the entire second story of the addition. Matt hadn't been able to muster the courage for more than a brief look in it since he had been home.

"It's just storage. I don't think you've been in there for years, have you Mamma?"

But Penelope was swinging the door wide and inviting them to follow her. "Welcome to my studio, ladies!"

There was just enough empty floor space for the five of them to form a line down the centre of the room. The windows on the sides were clear, as were those at the end — the north windows his mother used to boast about — but the rest of the walls were completely obscured by stacks of sweaters and handbags and mittens, rolls of carded wool, and hanging skeins of yarn in every colour of the Charlotte County rainbow.

"Of course," whispered Carolyn. "All this wool. *Handworks*. My mother loved all your beautiful woolen things. She still has a lot."

"I remember seeing you in the shop." Penelope was beaming. Matt did not want to tell her that the woman could not have been more than two years old when the business closed. "Don't be shy. Have a good look around. Let me know if there's anything that interests you."

He couldn't be sure whether they were simply being careful not to challenge her version of reality, but the three women began to examine the stacks and rolls and skeins quite closely. Carolyn held up a heather-pink Fair Isle pullover, lining the shoulders up with hers.

"I think perhaps a cardigan for now, dear," said Penelope, patting the young woman's belly as if it were a plump lapdog.

Francie had knocked a skein of spruce green onto the dusty floor. When Emily bent to pick it up (again that crescent of flesh), a loop snagged on a rough board and the wool snapped.

Matt thought of a memory-picture from his exhibition, a mnemonic for mortality. The three Moirae, the Greek Fates: Clotho who spins the yarn of a person's life, Lachesis who draws it out, and Atropos who cuts it off. *If only it were that simple*, he thought.

Vikings

MATT TAKES HER for a drive around the point. She thinks about how they used to do this loop when he had his learner's permit. Round and round they would go, with her adding a word of encouragement here and a gentle suggestion there. They drove mainly at dusk. That was at his request. So nobody would see. He was clearly embarrassed that it was his mother giving him the lessons, though normally he was pretty good about their special relationship, never mentioned missing having a man around the place.

The grand summer places up by the hotel look very much as they have all of Penelope's life. Perhaps a little more prissy, more cared for, their gardens tamer. She names each one and identifies its owners for Matt as they pass. When they end up on the cul de sac where the Lodge glowers down at the bay, he claims he has made a mistake, taken the turn one road too soon. She nods, says she has made that same mistake herself, but — for good measure — she loudly thanks God that she will never have to stay in *that place*. Down the second left turning, the one he said he wanted all along, they admire the new houses that have sprung up above the salt marsh. Matt parks the Volvo — she has to remind him about the handbrake — and suggests a walk along the asphalt that has been laid where the railway used to run. They'll go just past the nature preserve to the big park, he says, when she doesn't respond.

"Big park?"

"At Pagan Point."

"The dump." *But no*, she thinks, *it is not the dump anymore*. It has been sanitized, bulldozed, and planted.

"I still can't believe they would have put the garbage dump right on the bay."

"People thought differently in those days." Let that be enough. She walks a little faster, wanting him to see how well she is, how fit. At least to make him regret that wrong turn he said he took.

LOOKING ACROSS THE salt marsh from the railway tracks she sees the lone figure on the beach. So he has come. His English is reasonably good, but she was not sure her directions were. She supposes that he couldn't have gone too far wrong; there are not more than two or three places that could be described as *the point*. She is still surprised by the conversation when she plays it over in her mind as she has done a dozen times in the twenty-four hours since it took place.

He had come into the shop, looking, he said, for a jumper. She laughed at this side effect of his RAF tutelage. "Sweaters," she said. "We mostly call them sweaters here. It's Mr. Nielsen, isn't it?"

"I did not know whether you would remember."

She knew from his voice that he was looking for neither jumper nor sweater. It could not have been very hard for him to track her down. A few questions in the right places would do it, but she was still impressed by his initiative. Flattered.

"The men's sizes are down this way." The aisles suddenly felt narrower, the tiny shop even tighter. "What kind of neck do you prefer?" When he looked confused, her hands went out to show him, but she pulled them back halfway to his neck and demonstrated instead on her own. "Like a turtle?" she asked, choking herself, "or a crew?" She made a throat-cutting motion.

"Like the turtle."

She did not dare ask cable or plain, couldn't imagine the mime for that being anything other than running her hands over her torso, which would never do. Not in the shop.

He tried on three before he found one he seemed to like. Spruce green. There was a full-length mirror in the north wall and they both admired him in it for a full minute.

"Is it warm, this ... sweater?"

"We think so. The sheep certainly weren't shivering." She had forgotten for a moment that his English would probably not run to jokes like this. "You can try it, if you like." This was something her mother would have absolutely forbidden. "Wear it in the wind for an hour or two to see." And then she had given him directions to Pagan Point. "But not now. Tomorrow, if you can." It would not be any cooler or any windier then, but it would be Thora's day in the shop and her own day off.

Nielsen turns away from the glittering water and sees her, waves a long familiar-coloured arm. She imagines his eyes. The blues are such a perfect match. She gestures that he should stay where he is, motions to the right to indicate that she will take the path through the woods to get to the beach. The marsh is too tricky.

"MAMMA, ARE YOU all right? Do you want to sit down?"

Where has Matt come from? There is a bench, too, that should not be there. And tarmac under her feet instead of rails and ties. She wants to climb the path through the woods, but Matt will insist on going with her, so she sits.

"I love to think about the days when there were trains running here," he says. "Summer people with their private coaches and all their servants. Trains and steamers. The place was really connected to the world. In a solid tangible way, I mean. Not just electronics."

"I like to think about the Vikings," she says. The remark will mean nothing to him but will maintain her connection to the beach a few moments longer. "Can you imagine the courage? To set out on the limitless seas?"

"There's an archaeologist, a woman from I forget where, who believes they summered in the Miramichi. The Vikings. It was their summer camp from Newfoundland."

"Oh, they came much closer than that."

"She can't really prove it. There are some passages from the sagas that she quotes to support her theory. And some wood she found at the settlement at L'Anse aux Meadows from trees that don't actually grow north of New Brunswick. But nothing remains at Miramichi. She says it would all have been temporary, the encampment, so the absence of any trace actually supports her theory."

Penelope marvels at the trivia her son can pack away, especially the historical kind. He has always been this way. She thought he would grow out of it. Instead, he turned it into a career. And used it to attract that wife of his, the professor. *Shit, what is her name*?

"You're freezing. We should walk. Sorry. Without snow and ice underfoot, you can almost forget how cold it gets here in January."

"Is it January? Oh my. The spring goes so fast." She realizes her mistake immediately but does not correct it. Neither does Matt.

The Talk

FOR HER SECOND visit, Carolyn announced she would be unattended. Matt couldn't repress the comparison with the judge who, having dismissed the jury and thanked it for its service, places the black cap upon his head. When she appeared on the doorstep, though, she might as easily have been selling Girl Guide cookies. Apart from the baby bump.

"Hi, Mr. Reade."

"Matt."

"Matt. How are you?"

Her eyes were wet. Empathy or the frigid wind? He decided on empathy, forbidding himself to debate whether it was genuine or performed. Either way, he would take it. "Um. Fine. Okay, really. Thanks. You look …" Jesus. What was he doing?

"Still pregnant."

"I guess I was going to say, um, radiant." That seemed safe enough.

"Wow. Thank you."

"I've made coffee and tea. I didn't know which you like. Oh. Maybe you're off caffeine."

"Oh, I'm off the crack and the heroin for the baby's sake, but I'd never give up my coffee." She laughed. He wondered whether she would make that joke with just anyone. Probably not: it was a little out there, definitely questionable for a social worker. Obviously, she trusted him then, liked him. Unless it was only a ploy to gain his trust. He thought of the game he and Ingrid had devised: *I'll tell you mine if you'll tell me yours.* "Is it okay if I keep my boots on this time? I think you said the last time ..."

"Of course." He supposed she had caught him admiring her toenails the other day, was disgusted with himself as he realized he had been looking forward to them again today. "Come on through and we'll find that coffee."

The coffee was really a lure to get her into the kitchen. He had spread out the pages and pages of forms and stubs and returns he was having to assemble and fill out. He thought she might have some insight. Jennifer usually dealt with stuff like this.

"Oh dear. Look at this. It's really quite daunting, isn't it?" Carolyn appeared to take the bait even more easily than he had dared to hope.

"My mother has never been a terrific record keeper. Bernadette used to look after so much of that. She was the one with the head for details and numbers, Mamma used to say."

"Your sister?"

"Someone who used to help my mother with her business."

"Oh, Miss Rigg." It hadn't occurred to him that Carolyn might have grown up in St. Andrews. "Anyway, it's not as bad as it seems. You really just have to know what her net annual income is. Her tax return is the most useful thing for that."

"It's really just the Canada Pension and the Old Age. And some small investments." He wanted to confess to her how he had been shuttling wildly back and forth between two opposite positions. On the one hand, he felt outrage that the government would want to take an old widow's mite. On the other, he could see that if she could afford to pay for her care, then that was only fair. It left more money to subsidize someone not as fortunate. "Forms just make me crazy."

"Not so many years ago, they would take your house. The proceeds."

"If they'd get rid of the contents for me, that might be attractive! I'm sorry. I don't know why I said that. I don't really mean ..."

"I know. This is all very hard. There is a whole lifetime in this house. More. It's not your lifetime. But it sort of is."

"One minute I just want to pitch it all, and the next I can't bear to let go of a broken teacup. It must be hard to do this job pregnant. Depressing, dealing with old lives, when you want to be looking forward to a new one."

"My mother said you were a thoughtful one."

"Your mother?"

"She says you knew one another when you were growing up. Amanda Williams."

Of course. Amanda of the cherry toenails. The motel in Robbinston. That would account for his attraction to this woman who was half his age. A trick of memory. Recognition. Matt was relieved. Sort of. "My goodness. That was a long time ago." He hoped Amanda had held some details back from her daughter. "I should go and fetch Mamma. You want both of us here for the talk, right?"

"The talk. You make it sound like the facts of life."

One minute ago, Matt would have wanted to find her comment flirtatious, would have bantered back perhaps. It was amazing, the instant cold-shower effect of suddenly realizing you have made love with a woman's mother. "Well, it is the facts of her life, isn't it?" To avoid any wounded look he might see on Carolyn's face, he fled upstairs to find Penelope.

Carolyn was sorting the papers on the table when he returned with his mother in tow. Bless her heart.

"Mamma, you remember Carolyn White."

"Do I?"

"Hello, Mrs. Reade. Nice to see you."

"Lovely to see you, dear. White, did you say?"

"That's my married name. I was a Gray before."

"Marriage has bleached you. Not the usual effect."

"Carolyn is Amanda Williams's daughter. You remember Amanda?" It was a risk. Penelope had never approved of his local girlfriends. But she had not approved of Jennifer either.

"Oh yes, Amanda. You were quite sweet on her, Matt." Penelope looked again at Carolyn. Matt could see her taking in the belly. "Oh my."

As Penelope looks from the aging man to the young woman who has just appeared in her kitchen, she hopes they have not come for advice. She would be the last person to be any use. Maybe Thora is around. The young woman is showing much more than Penelope ever did, either time. They wear things so tight now, an extra skin stretched over the drum. She thinks about the tents she wore. Not so much with the first, she was barely showing when that ended. But with Matt. It wasn't that she was trying to hide the fact. It was just how everyone dealt with pregnancy then. The same way some people had little petticoated dolls that hunkered down over the spare roll of toilet paper. She knows attitudes are much healthier these days, but she is still shocked to see the outline of this young woman's belly button, a bulging eyeball on the ... tumulus. A nice word, that. Better than barrow; sounds more like what it is. She learned both words reading about the Vikings years ago. A rounded mound. A tomb.

She wishes the couple had not covered her kitchen table with papers. She would offer them tea, but there is nowhere to put it.

And she hates papers, forms, applications. Maybe they are applying for a marriage licence. Better late than never. Does she believe that? Thora could help them with the forms. Or Bernadette.

"Let's go through to the sitting room," said Matt. "It's a better place to talk. Warmer. Mamma, Carolyn and I are having coffee. Would you like some? Or tea?"

"Did you warm the pot?"

"Even up the spout." He looked nervously at Carolyn, afraid she might misconstrue, but the expression was probably not familiar to someone her age.

"Milk, no sugar, please."

Matt had never known his mother to take her tea anything but clear, but he slopped some milk in the bottom of a mug that he then filled with tea.

"I'm sorry there are no biscuits," she said as she took the cup. "One day, when the war is all over, there will be biscuits again."

Matt didn't know then whether to carry the plate of cookies he had prepared into the sitting room or not. Carolyn came to the rescue. "Actually, Mrs. Reade, I was lucky enough to come by some biscuits and I brought them along."

"I hope you didn't have to do anything too awful for them."

Penelope is looking at the girl, wondering whether the wedding ring she wears is a fraud. She has seen plenty of girls put on a ring to stop the tongues wagging. War changes everything, all the things you thought you knew, thought you believed. It makes you act in ways, do things, you'd never have dreamt possible. Even for something as small as a packet of biscuits perhaps. Jonathan sometimes brings her food he smuggles off the base. But that's not why she cuddles with him.

Matt carried the tray through the dining room and around the corner to the sitting room, hoping the women would follow, too proud to look back to make sure they were.

The room had been the original kitchen, so it boasted a large fireplace that his mother had left as an open hearth until a few years ago. Then he had persuaded her to install an airtight insert, though why he had thought it would be safer for a ninety-year-old to stoke that than to toss logs onto a grate he could no longer recall.

"This is a lovely room. I didn't see it before. So cosy."

"You've been here before?" Penelope can't keep herself from being suspicious of the pregnant girl.

"Carolyn was here last week, with Francie and Emily, Mamma." Matt knew it would make no difference, was even arguably the wrong response. Better just to play along. "We weren't in here, though." In fact, he had deliberately omitted the room from the tour. It was easy enough to get away with. With all the twists and turns in the house people got confused. He had been afraid of what they would say about the woodstove.

"Do you have a favourite chair?"

Matt could not tell whether she was asking him or his mother.

"Why don't you sit in that one," says Penelope, motioning to the wingback that came from Birch Hall. She notices the stuffing is peeking out, pushing its way through the brocade, but thinks the girl with the huge belly won't mind.

"This is a lovely home."

Now Penelope remembers the girl. She wanted to buy her house. There were two others with her, with measuring tapes.

Matt wondered whether Carolyn had chosen the wisest opening for the conversation. He supposed she had done this hundreds of times before.

"But it must be quite a lot to look after."

Penelope wants to tell the girl that she should have seen Birch Hall if she wants to talk about a lot to look after. They never had any help, which had scandalized Thora's in-laws while they were still alive; possibly after they died too, rolling in their graves in the cemetery just past Katy's Cove. How could the Arnolds possibly have understood, Thora used to say. The family had come to New Brunswick with slaves. Penelope doesn't think this girl wants to talk about that. "I'm just one person. I don't make a lot of dirt."

"It's a lot of rooms, a lot of stairs, a lot to keep track of."

Cicero would applaud the number of distinctive *loci* in his mother's house, thought Matt. How useless they proved to be, though, in assisting her memory.

"Your son worries about you."

Matt shot Carolyn a look that said thank you for throwing me under the bus.

"We all worry about you."

"Do I know you?"

"We are concerned. We want you to be safe. And comfortable."

Matt braced himself for his mother's response to those words.

"Safe and comfortable. I have lived my life in the belief that nobody ever got anywhere by being either of those things." Penelope is sorry that she has also lived her life believing that you can't throw a guest out of your sitting room — even a rude one, especially not a pregnant one.

His mother's sharpness made Matt wonder whether any of this was actually necessary. He knew it was only a temporary rally, a spell of lucidity that would pass, but he wished the timing were different.

"Of course. Do you ever get lonely?"

Matt had begun to feel sorry for Carolyn as she gunned her engine in the snowbank, desperate for traction in this conversation with a wily older woman. If she thought Penelope could ever be lonely, she had even less insight into people's characters than he had given her credit for.

"I have my mother."

And there it was, Matt thought, the lost grip. He wondered what Carolyn could make of it.

"Is she living here with you?"

"No. She is at the other house." Penelope knows the young woman is angling toward something but she is too tired to figure out what. "Can I go back to the other house?"

"We have a new house we'd like you to try. It's very nice, and they do everything for you."

Matt thought she should have omitted that last bit.

"Like a hotel?"

"Yes."

Matt supposed Carolyn had to varnish the truth several times daily in her work. It didn't make her unique, of course, but he was hating this. *She must hate it too,* he thought.

"I used to go away quite a lot. My husband, he travelled. We'd meet up in all kinds of places."

"I think you'll like this place. Do you think you could give it a try?"

"If Matt thinks it's a good idea." Penelope said it without inflection, making it impossible to know whether it was mere reflex or whether she actually had some inkling of what was going on. It didn't matter to Carolyn. She was prepared to take that as the consent she was looking for.

"Good then," she said, nodding at Matt and picking up her cold coffee.

"When would I go?"

"We'll put you on the list. I don't think it will be long."

"I should get back to work. I'll take my tea upstairs." But after she said goodbye to Carolyn and wished her an easy birth, she left the room without the cup, and they heard her footsteps not mounting the stairs but fading into the kitchen.

"You have to think about her whole day. You can't let a few minutes of focus fool you. It's awful, I know, but she really can't be alone."

Matt hoped that the baby in Carolyn's belly was hearing all of this, that it would make it easier for her or him to put Carolyn away when her time came. For him, it did little to help.

"You should look up my mother," Carolyn said as she shrugged on her coat at the door. "She was in Florida for a long time, but she's back now, has a new boyfriend, a lobsterman. I don't think it's going to last." She stooped to put on her boots, realized her mistake, and laughed. For a moment, Matt saw Amanda's face in hers, and then it was gone.

At Sea

THE EMPTY HOUSE takes some getting used to. Penelope has never lived alone. First there was Thora. Then Thora and Matt. Then just Matt, the two of them somehow managing to fill the large house. The plan was always to send him away to school once he was in his teens. She and her mother had agreed on that, as they had on most things in his upbringing. He needed to experience life beyond the tiny town and, it had to be admitted, to cut the apron strings. Penelope wore an apron only in her studio so she had objected to the cliché, but accepted the premise. But doing without Matt in the house has been harder than she expected. That he is horribly homesick doesn't help. His letters home (weekly) are not so bad. She suspects that the masters read them through before mailing, if they don't actually stand over him with a stick while he writes. It's the phone calls that tell the story. These can come at any time, though never after nine p.m. They have a system. He is to let it ring twice and then hang up. She will then call him back at the pay phone in the dorm basement. That way, he is saved long-distance charges, and he gets his dime back. Penelope has had to screech at visitors not to pick up the phone before three rings. Well, to screech at Bernadette, who now finally seems to have the system down.

He always answers the phone with the same flat *hullo.* As though he doesn't know that it can only be his mother calling back on the pay phone. She supposes that the hollow sound is partly a function of the booth, tries to picture him sitting on the scratched bench, the bi-fold door pulled across to shut out eavesdroppers and the smell of teenaged boys. Her *how are you* always gets the same response: an intake of breath and *okay*. Sometimes there are such long silences that she fears the connection has been lost, but then she'll hear someone knocking on the phone booth door. Or a tiny sob. She has learned to avoid telling him about things at home. Instead, she quizzes him about his classes — he is underprepared in math but doing well in English and history and will admit to loving Latin — and sports. Not a stellar soccer player, he has been assigned to the under-fifteen football team, but so far they haven't played him much. She does not ask about discipline. She refused to sign the form giving the school permission to administer corporal punishment, though she knows that will not have spared Matt the terror of it or having to witness it. She knows something of the horror of boys' schools from her early days with Jonathan. He talked quite freely about strappings and canings, as if they were the natural rites of boyhood and not the twisted pleasures of older men whose fathers and grandfathers had done it to them. The calls always end with her assuring him that it will get better, that everything takes some getting used to. She thinks he still believes her.

She has been making more and more pictures in felt. These are a departure from the framed scenes she and her mother used to make to sell in the shop. For those, they selected, cut, and glued scraps of woolen fabric onto Masonite, sometimes sanding the edges lightly to blend them. The results mimicked watercolour paintings when seen from a distance. And a surprising degree of lifelikeness could be achieved. Thora argued that felt collage was the perfect apprenticeship for anyone who wanted to be an artist. It obliged you to reduce your composition to its elements, to think in actual physical blocks of colour and texture. Penelope can hear Thora lecturing the women to look at the scenes around them as if they were designs to capture in their rugs or bags. Line, form, colour, texture, ornament — Penelope has been able to recite the mantra in her sleep practically since she left the cradle. She looks at the dozens of unsold collages that have been neatly stacked against the walls of her workroom for four years now. She didn't have the heart to remove them from the shop until after her mother died. *One day*, she thinks, *buyers may want them again.*

In the meantime, she is trying a different approach, one that engages those old familiar principles of design at an even earlier stage of the process, she thinks. The inspiration came from the felt bags her mother used to make, though the idea itself is not a new or original one. She remembers her hands in the warm water patting out felt for the bags. And she remembers her mother's extraordinary needlework, applying colourful and intricate designs to the felt surface. What she is doing now merges the two. The design, which her mother used to apply to the finished fabric, is now being built right into the felt. It is created in the fibres even before they form a mat. The picture is fully developed by the time the fulling of the fabric is completed.

There is no stone sink here as there was at Birch Hall, and the process requires a little more control and a little less water than the basic felting they did for the bags. She has her worktable lined with a sheet of plastic and plenty of towels folded at her feet. She cuts a square from an old lace tablecloth (she does not think it is Loyalist vintage) and stretches it on the table. Then she begins tearing tufts of white roving, careful that the first layer of fibres all point in one direction. The second layer goes on at a ninety-degree angle, and the third with the same orientation as the first. She finishes smoothing what will be the backing of the picture in place and stands back to contemplate it. Her blank canvas.

She wonders, for the hundredth time, as she looks at the white expanse, whether she has done the right thing for Matt. *The responsibility of raising a child*, she thinks, *is a bet you wouldn't take if you knew anything about the stakes*. Writing on that slate, even when you didn't mean to, especially when you didn't mean to, could change the course of a life so easily. She and Thora had worried about what growing up in the constraints of Charlotte County would do to him. But what might come from the privileged brutality of an Ontario boarding school?

Today's picture will involve water. This is as much to calm her as from any aesthetic impulse. Maybe she will send it to Matt if it turns out well. Are they allowed to hang pictures in the tiny cubicles of putative privacy behind their dormitory beds?

She decides the point of view will be from *at sea*, smiles at the appropriateness of the idea. Blue rovings at the bottom of the picture, then greys and browns for the beach stones, ochre for the cliff and green for the spruce growing stubbornly out of it. She pulls the tufts and lays them carefully, patting all over before she moves to the next layer.

Bernadette walks into the workroom. Penelope thinks how old she looks. When did that happen? She is not happy about the interruption, but it is better now than when she is wetting the wool and working it.

"I was looking for Matt."

"Matt is at ..." But of course he isn't at school. He is home. Visiting. He made tea for her when that pregnant woman was here. "I am just starting a new piece. For him." When she looks down, she is patting a child's Fair Isle cardigan.

"A bit small for him, perhaps, but I like the colour."

Thank God, Bernie finds it funny. She hasn't always been so sympathetic. There were times when she was living with her, after Matt went away to school, and then when they were closing down the shop, when she thought Bernadette was about the meanest person there was.

"You never came in here when you lived here."

"You never invited me."

"Ah." She knows it was not that simple, could not have been that simple. But there is no point in challenging Bernadette's version. After all these years, it will have set hard. It no longer matters what was actually the case, only how it is remembered in the repetition. "But we had some good years."

"The best, boss."

Penelope wishes Bernadette would drop the *boss* business. She knows it is no longer anything but a shtick, but it makes her uncomfortable. Not as uncomfortable as when they were living together, but, still, it casts her in a role she'd rather forget.

"It was very good of you, you know, to keep me company." When she sees the wounded look on Bernadette's wizened face, she regrets having said it. They both know it was both good of Bernadette and also, maybe, something else. Penelope had been oblivious to it at the time. That is what she has told herself since the moment, years later, when it dawned on her that Bernadette had perhaps hoped for something more than companionship. "You could have come in."

"I'm here now."

"I came in to look for something. Damned if I can think what. It's frightening, you know. I'll find myself in a room and I don't know why I am there. You'd think something in the room would remind me. I'll look at the walls, the mouldings, the pictures, but nothing comes. And then I'll be in another room that turns out to be equally unhelpful."

Bernadette has picked up one of Thora's embroidered bags. Wherever has she found it? "I loved these things as a little girl," she says. "I couldn't wait until I grew into a lady and could wear one of your mother's bags. One day, she said to me: 'Why wait? You never know what's around the corner.' And she gave me one. Just like that."

"I don't remember her ever giving any of her work away."

"She didn't. But she gave me a bag. When I was still a child, and so I never had to grow up, never had to become a lady."

Penelope knows she should say something, but what?

"I don't know what became of the bag. Isn't that awful? It was my most prized possession for years, and then who knows what became of it?"

"Would you like that one? As a replacement? I really must clear some of this stuff out. Some days, I think I should be going through everything, so I don't leave a mess for Matt. And some days I think: *fuck it, let him deal with it*. That's what children are for: to clean up after their parents."

They look at Thora's bag in silence. The embroidered scene is of the sardine wharf in Chamcook.

Games

WEEK FOUR OF the *I remember …* workshops started off a little roughly. Gina was late. Ingrid said she didn't know what the holdup was, but Matt sensed there was more going on than she was telling him. When Gina finally blew in the door, she was already half out of her coat and uncoiling the deadly python of a scarf that he had never seen off her neck. She made no apology for keeping the group waiting. Matt wondered whether she was even aware that she had. He saw Ingrid trying and failing to catch her eye.

"Today's warm-up concerns what we call procedural memory," Gina announced, kicking off her boots. "Or has Ingrid already said that?"

Ingrid muttered that she had not wanted to start without Gina, which elicited only a snort.

"I'd like each of us to think about a repeated action, something you do each day and have done for years, if possible. It needs to have at least four distinct stages to it, sub-actions, if you will. Oh, and chiefly physical. Take a couple of minutes to select something." Gina gestured to Ingrid and the two went out into the hallway. Matt could not hear every word of what they were saying but he did catch enough to sense that the conversation was about control. Gina was suggesting that if Ingrid was going to make all the decisions herself, then perhaps she should just run the whole project and Gina would step aside. Ingrid denied that she was making decisions on her own, and then promised to do better, which Matt thought amounted to an admission of guilt.

When they returned, it was like the press conference at the end of an international summit: faces and bodies carefully aligned to say *we are in complete accord and the best of friends*. Matt could not help reflecting that both of them had backgrounds in theatre as well as dance.

Each participant was asked to describe her or his repeated action to the group, clearly identifying each stage. As they spoke, the person to their left was to attempt to mime what they were hearing. The describer was allowed to adjust the mime's gestures and poses if they thought their words were being misunderstood. The person miming was allowed to ask for clearer directions if they were having trouble visualizing what was being said. Matt thought there were some surprisingly convincing representations of making coffee and changing the diaper on a baby. There was a definite erotic charge in the room during one of the two renditions of taking a shower, while the other — was it the redundancy or the participants? — did nothing for him.

They went on to other exercises, ultimately breaking into groups to work on the recitations and movement for which each participant was becoming responsible in the developing script. Only after lunch did Gina return to the procedural memory exercise.

"Let's see those mimes from this morning again," she said, clapping her hands to get the group into the customary circle. Fewer of the participants needed prompting than Matt would have guessed. In most cases, they were able to reproduce the discrete stages of the repeated action with what he thought was a pretty high degree of fidelity.

"Now, to get a taste of what it feels like when procedural memory fails, remove a stage. Your choice, but take out one of the sub-actions."

The results were funny in the way that anything that doesn't quite add up is funny. Coffee was drunk without first having been poured, the baby's bum stayed bare, the shower became only more obviously sexy without the step of grabbing for the soap. The group's laughter spurred some of the mimes to ham it up. Even Gina's disapproving looks did little to curb them.

"May I make a suggestion?" asked Ingrid. "To take us a little deeper?"

Matt looked quickly at Gina to gauge her response. "Of course," she murmured, her shoulders screaming *fuck off*.

"Let's all try one repeated task, a common one, shared. Let's try brushing our teeth. I'm going to give you the stages and I want each of you to devise your own mime. Try not to look too much at the person next to you. Just do what makes sense to you. Ready? First stage: opening medicine cabinet. Second: picking up toothbrush. Third: putting toothbrush back down. Fourth: picking up toothpaste tube. Fifth: unscrewing cap. Sixth: picking up toothbrush. Seventh: squeezing toothpaste onto brush. Eighth: putting down toothpaste tube. Ninth: turning on water. Tenth: putting toothbrush under water. Eleventh: putting toothbrush in mouth."

Ingrid walked them through this four times, having first apologized for not returning the cap to the toothpaste tube. On the fifth pass, she omitted step seven. On the sixth, steps six and eight. Everyone was given an index card on which to write how the omissions made them feel. Then Ingrid began to change up the objects in the stages. The toothbrush became a hairbrush while everything else stayed the same. The toothpaste became liquid hand soap while nothing else changed. She ended the exercise with a statement delivered deadpan, without any trace of affect. "Some people say that memory provides the continuity necessary for us to establish an identity — even a soul, if you like. Losing your memory means losing those things. Not to mention how hard it becomes to keep your teeth clean."

There was no suggestion of a post-mortem drink. In fact, Gina rushed away before half of the participants had left the room, though she did retake the reins long enough to thank everyone for the work.

"Is everything okay?" Matt asked Ingrid. She had accompanied him when he went to his office upstairs in the museum to retrieve a file he needed to work on over the weekend.

"What do you mean?"

"You and Gina. Things seemed a little, more than a little, tense today."

"Gina is an artist. She gets worked up."

"You are an artist." If there were artistic differences, he needed to know about them, he thought, for the museum's sake. And his own. "What happened?"

"We were talking the other day. I had an idea and I told her about it. I was very excited, said I really thought it could make a huge difference to the performance."

"She didn't like the idea?"

"No, she loved it. But she said it was hers, that I had stolen it from her, that she had come up with it when we were all having a drink, the three of us. It was about using fabric in the performance — how it forgets its form, or remembers an earlier form, that kind of thing. Anyway, she got very upset. Of course, I told her I was sorry, that I must have forgotten her talking about it. That's a thing, as you know, and she knows. An actual thing with a name: *cryptomnesia*."

Matt was not sure what to say. "Right. Cryptomnesia. Definitely a thing." *When you think something is brand new, but you are really only remembering it. Where would plagiarism be without it?* "It's easy to make the mistake. That didn't appease her?"

"She said some hurtful things. About why didn't I remember her saying it? And then about you and me."

They were passing by *The Art of Memory* exhibition by then, on their way out of the building. Security was turning out the lights.

"Good night, Mr. Reade."

"Good night." Matt couldn't think whether the man was named Joe or Jim. He watched him disappear down the corridor.

Ingrid slipped her hand in his and guided him into the darkened exhibit hall. "I want you to test me," she said. "See how much I can recall. You steer me around with my eyes closed. Each time we stop, I have to tell you what we are standing in front of."

It had been years since Matt had felt excitement at being in the museum after hours. He and Jennifer had spent a whole night with the mummies once. Whether it was the flattering suggestion that Ingrid might remember his exhibit, or her hand warm in his, or the prospect of a game, he could feel the old frisson rushing back.

"How about each time you're wrong, you forfeit some clothes?"

"I won't be wrong."

And, alarmingly, she wasn't. Marvel quickly displaced any disappointment. Witnessing this fabulous parlour trick — it had to be that — was as thrilling as seeing her naked. Maybe more. "How do you ...?"

"It's a combination of things. I love the exhibit, of course." She gave his hand a squeeze. "And I did a little training when I was younger."

"Training?"

"Memory Olympics. I used to compete. Back home. It's a bit embarrassing. A bit nerdy. Not very sexy."

Matt had done a little reading on these peculiar gatherings. One event was about matching names to faces. *That*, he thought, *might be useful.* But then there were timed competitions to memorize insanely long sequences of numbers. And poems. Ted Hughes, no less, used to write new poems specially for them, so that everyone was starting fresh with a poem they couldn't possibly know. The oddballs who competed claimed to be the heirs of Simonides, devising and stocking their memory palaces with memorable (often off-colour) images that they derived through a variety of complicated systems where numbers and letters were combined in ways Matt stopped trying to understand. It was hard to picture Ingrid in such company. "But recalling it all while being led around with your eyes shut?"

"Oh that. That's an evolutionary adaptation. Women have much more developed spatial sense than men, didn't you know? It proved helpful during all those years as foragers, being able to place yourself in space, recalling where all the good mushrooms were. Spatial memory, you see?"

They were standing in front of a section of the exhibition devoted to Giordano Bruno's memory wheels. There were reproductions of woodcuts, and one replica of a nine-section Bruno wheel that had turned out so beautifully that Matt had decided it needed a plexiglass case to protect it from curious hands. To help visitors understand the general principle, he had had a second, much cruder, version made out of plywood. A placard invited patrons to try it out. Ingrid had reeled off the caption's information about the two concentric circles, each inscribed with thirty letters, and its digression about the influence of Lull's combinatory wheels on Bruno's system. She was able to name the

Hebrew and Greek symbols that augmented the Roman symbols, something Matt doubted most visitors could do. The letters on the outer wheel corresponded to a list of things and those on the inner wheel to a list of attributes. There was a key to the correspondences posted on the panel behind the wheels.

Ingrid gave the outer wheel a spin. "I have another game."

Matt looked up at the interpretive panel as the wheel came to a stop.

"No, don't look there. The answers for this game are in here." She kissed his forehead. "And here." She ran her palm over his left nipple. "The letters are the first letters of two words that conjure a memory. So an *A* and a *P* could be apple picking. You see?"

He did.

"Come on. It will be fun. Interesting. Tell me yours and I'll tell you mine."

The first two rounds yielded nothing very revealing. They might have been nodding acquaintances politely playing a game at a very dull house party. For *C* and *V*, they exchanged stories of Childhood Vacations. This was easiest for Matt, who could honestly report he had never had one. *F* and *T* elicited Favourite Teachers, more satisfying for Matt than for Ingrid, who had hated school.

When the Hebrew *Gimel* came up with *S*, Matt suggested spinning again, but Ingrid insisted they play by dreidel rules.

"What?"

"The *Gimel* on a dreidel stands for *Gadol*. That's miracle. You know the four sides: *nun, gimel, hei, shin*, standing for *Nes Gadól Hayáh Sham*, meaning *a great miracle happened there*."

He didn't know, but he didn't let on. He wondered how the hell she knew.

"So *S* and *gimel* could be Secret Miracle."

Hers, she said, was discovering she could dance.

"How is that secret?"

"I had to hide it for years from my parents. They were very strict. Not very fun."

"Mine is you." He wasn't sure it was the right thing to say, but in the dim light from the exit signs he was confident he would not be able to see her wince if she did.

"Cheating! I am not a memory. Am I? Let's make this interesting. We'll limit the kind of memory. Go ahead and spin. It's not just any kind of memory anymore but best sexual memory. So *F* and *U* could be Fellatio Underground or *M* and *B* Masturbating in Bathtub. You understand?"

It was actually less fun than either of them had imagined and they quit after two rounds, agreeing — as they returned to his office to make love on the couch — that memories and ghosts take up too much room in bed.

Bags

IT WAS NOT as though Matt absolutely needed to start in on the workroom that day. God knew, he wouldn't be able to finish up before he absolutely had to be back in Toronto; he would have to come back again in any case. And Penelope was still very much in the house, spending hours in the workroom herself. Bernadette had suggested he make a start, said she would take Penelope for a drive. They would join the motorcade of ancient townspeople who crept around and around the point at ten miles an hour, their shrunken heads peering up over the edges of car doors that had been built in the previous century. That was Bernadette's description. When he looked shocked, she reminded him she was entitled. For him to make such a comment would be cruel; for her, it was simply wry and philosophic. He told her he felt a little bit ghoulish going at his mother's things before she was ... before she was ... *dead*, Bernadette had prompted. Then she had told him that the clearing would be much less sad now than leaving it until Penelope was gone. Without her to interpret, the contents of the workroom would be a random collection of husks, mute witnesses to an irretrievable past. Besides, she said, Penelope might derive some joy from things he unearthed.

He had never spent much time in the workroom, he realized, as he opened the pitted pine door. Whether that was Penelope's doing or his own he was no longer sure. Perhaps it was both: his lack of interest as a child and her need for a sanctuary, though she had never uttered that word that he could remember. The smell of sheep and dust had been less noticeable, he thought, on the day when the Three Fates had made their assessment visit. Or perhaps his mind had been on other things. He wondered whether he should give himself an extra puff of Symbicort before getting down to work, decided that was merely a procrastinating tactic, rolled up his sleeves, and pointed himself at a pile in the farthest corner of the room.

The pile was made up of handbags, the kind his grandmother had fought over with some outfit in Québec that claimed to have introduced them. Penelope used to try to placate her mother when she became especially agitated on the subject. Matt could clearly remember her reasoning. She would propose that the notion of any kind of exclusive ownership of design in the field of traditional crafts was at the very best a grey area. This only served to inflame Thora more. He wondered why, then, Penelope never tried anything more than to repeat the exact same argument every time the matter arose.

All of the work in the pile was his grandmother's. His mother had made some of this kind of bag in her time, he knew, but Thora's hand — Thora's eye — was evident in every one of these. The top three were familiar scenes: one farmland and two seaside. He paused to admire how she had captured in felt and floss so much of the essence of the place. You knew you had been there, even if you could not immediately identify exactly where *there* was. She never completely repeated herself with her needle. But there were generic elements that ran though the designs, signature flora and strata, architectural quotations that marked the piece as hers. Matt understood why his mother had never been able to part with the bags, regardless of how unsaleable they had become with time. He tried to imagine them in a bin at Value Village, couldn't, and set them aside.

The fourth bag bore a scene unlike any he could remember. The approach was clearly his grandmother's, the way she managed at one and the same time both to reduce and to elevate her subject to its essentials of line, form, colour, texture, and ornament. But in this case, the subject was industrial. You were looking at the sardine factory from across Chamcook Harbour — *from Ministers Island, it had to be*, Matt thought. The hard vertical lines of the factory tower were cut by the diagonal of the conveyer belt. In the distance, and very muted, the model town rose in concentric circles up the hill. The design might have been made in the thirties, Soviet-inspired, if Matt didn't know the scene had to date from before the first war because of the way the factory looked. He crossed the room and leaned the bag against the door frame. He would ask his mother about it later.

Farther down the stack, after another scene of Market Wharf with a Cape Islander in the offing, and a rendition of a country dance — unusual for his grandmother, who seldom included human figures — was a bag whose entire surface was taken up by a highly distorted and impossibly compressed version of a sailboat. *The only word for the thing was grotesque*, Matt thought. It could never have been intended for sale; it would give its carrier nightmares and frighten off dogs and children. It looked almost medieval, a glimpse of a way of seeing that predated single-vanishing-point perspective. It was more in the style of brooches unearthed from Viking barrows than of the Bergen art school Thora had reportedly attended. She had managed to suggest at once the kind of yacht that dotted Passamaquoddy Bay in the early twentieth century, and a war craft worthy of Leif Erikson. Across the stern, which was visible in the same plane as the gunwale, she had stitched "Ship of Fool." Matt looked in vain for the final *s*, thought at first it must have disappeared around an impossible corner, but finally concluded that the use of the singular was deliberate.

Inside the bag was a sheaf of foxed papers crusted in dust. He set them aside. As he began to wheeze, he heard the Volvo in the driveway. Suddenly once again a guilty schoolboy, he gathered up the bag, hooked the other over his wrist as he passed through the doorway, and headed down to ask his mother how she had enjoyed her drive.

"She needs the bathroom," Bernadette announced, helping Penelope out of her coat.

"I know, I know, you told me to go before we left the house."

Matt could not tell whether this was a joke or time slippage. He watched his mother scurry through the dining room to the bathroom.

"How was she?"

"Oh, you know. She seemed to like being out anyway."

"Thank you."

"Not a problem. Not every day I get to drive. I really should have renewed my licence."

Matt laughed, then wondered if it wasn't a joke. Bernadette was pulling on her gloves. He gave her a hug, moved to help her down the front steps.

"Go to the boss. I can manage a few steps."

He watched her shuffle down the walkway. As she passed the Volvo parked in the driveway, Matt noticed that the driver's door was wide open and there was a stream of exhaust still pouring from the back end. Neither appeared to attract Bernadette's attention as she set off along the street. He waited until she disappeared around the corner before going out to turn off the car and shut the door.

"Nice drive?" Matt asked his mother as he filled the kettle. "Bernadette didn't go too fast?"

"Bernadette is a competent driver. A little timid. But she likes to get behind the wheel, so why not let her?"

"Lots of traffic?" He knew the answer. It had been a standing joke between them as long as he could remember.

"I suppose. I wasn't paying that much attention to the other cars."

"Just enjoying the scenery. That's good."

"We went up by the hotel and Lazy Croft."

Matt pretended to inspect the kettle. Lazy Croft had burned to the ground years ago, before his mother was born. There was a family story about how his grandmother had supplied some of the felt for the dining room walls. Wallcoverings made with felt had been used to decorate cottages back before the first war, his mother used to tell him. They didn't plaster and paper. They fitted planks and then covered them in felt. So it had been a kind of family tragedy when the place burned.

"Then we kept along Prince of Wales all the way to the dump."

Matt wondered whether the flock of gulls that wheeled endlessly just offshore from the park cherished an inherited memory of the old days. "It's cleaned up pretty nicely, hasn't it?"

"Has it? Don't let mine steep too long, Matt."

"Since when?"

"What?"

"Nothing." He poured the barely amber tea into both their cups.

"I think the Vaughans will rebuild."

"The Vaughans?"

"The shipyard. What an awful thing, that fire."

The shipyard fire was sometime near the end of the war. "They were making minesweepers, weren't they?"

"Fishing boats, really. They called them minesweepers. Big wooden trawlers with a few extra bits of equipment. When the war ends, they can go back to fishing."

"That's a sensible plan." Matt wondered whether any of the Vaughan trawlers were still afloat. It wasn't unlikely. A few of the old Casarco boats could still be found in the bay and they'd have been thirty years older. He pulled one of Thora's bags from beneath the pine table. "This was Gran's work, wasn't it?"

"Good heavens. That's the old sardine factory."

"Not her usual style."

"You could smell it from there, you know, from Ministers Island. That was one consolation. All those CPR folks, who owned the business, had that smell in their noses every time they visited the grand house. For as long as it lasted."

"And then they had the smell of failure after that. I wonder which they minded most." Everything Sir William Van Horne handled turned to gold, Matt knew, everything but the sardine factory.

"I could never get the smell out of my clothes. My hair. The smell of the herring and the smell of the mustard and vinegar, the tomato sauce."

Matt was about to correct her: you mean your mother couldn't. Then he thought better. "It must have been hard work. Packing."

"We were to use the French method. That just means quality over quantity. It wasn't a race. There weren't that many fish, which was just as well for me. I'd never packed a damned sardine before I washed up there."

"But didn't they bring in Norwegian girls on purpose, because of their experience?"

"Nobody ever asked point blank. They advertised for girls to work in a modern sardine-packing factory in Canada. It was printed in *Morgenbladet* every day for a week. There was free passage, and free lodging and medical care, your passage home covered if you stayed a year. And anywhere from three to five dollars a week. That was good money for sixty hours of work. Who could resist? Never mind that I'd never touched a brisling. If they chose to imagine that every Norwegian girl knew how to pack sardines, that was their lookout, wasn't it? And how hard could it be?"

"And the men who came out?"

"I don't want to talk about Nils."

"Your brother?" He nearly said *your uncle*.

Penelope laughed. "So clever. Such an original ruse, we thought. Who was fooled, I wonder? They set the men to work helping with the construction. Nils had never swung a hammer. He wasn't that kind of man."

"What kind of man was he?"

"The kind a girl's parents don't like. The kind your girlfriends warn you away from but you go with anyway. He quickly got bored with the work. Not being able to do something is one of the surest ways to boredom. He started making trouble."

"Was he deported?"

"Maybe."

"Maybe?"

"One day he wasn't here anymore." Penelope's voice broke and Matt knew not to pursue it. "Is this our usual tea?"

"It's a little weaker, Mamma. But yes, the usual. Gran loved her tea, didn't she?" He supposed this was as good a way as any to undo whatever was left of the folding over, to remind her that she and her mother were two separate entities.

"It was a way of fitting in."

He showed her the bag with the Ship of Fool then, asked her what she could tell him about it.

"She made some things like that in the 1950s, before you were born. Never really wanted to talk about them. They're grotesque, aren't they? She did tell me this one had something to do with a yacht that was owned by one of the bigwigs at the factory, the head man, but that was all she'd say. You haven't been rooting around in my workroom, have you?"

"I was just clearing some space so I could see about patching the wall." It seemed a harmless enough lie amidst all the others he was learning to tell.

Falling

THE PATH THROUGH the woods at Pagan Point is more beaten down than Penelope remembers, which means the roots of the spruce are more exposed. Twice she catches her toe and is nearly sent sprawling. The third root wins. She lands hard on her knees and palms, suddenly reborn a woodland creature on all fours. *If it weren't for the war*, she thinks, *I would have ruined a pair of stockings*. As it is, she has only scraped her bare knees and maybe smeared the line she has drawn up the backs of her legs. Everyone is doing that these days, to simulate a seam. You use eyebrow pencil. Stockings are impossible to get. If it weren't for the war, of course, it is unlikely she would be on the path at all. Her fingers stir the blanket of needles, pushing aside a chocolate bar wrapper — Ganong's Pal-o-Mine, a brand she detests, though she knows that's disloyal. Maybe even treasonous at this point.

She had better get up. It wouldn't do for Mr. Nielsen to find her in this position. How ridiculous is it that she doesn't even know his first name? A wave of something goes through her, not quite shame, can't be lust. It must be from the fall. Something is knocked out of whack. She gets to her feet, rummages in her bag for a handkerchief to blot at her torn skin. The knees matter less.

Her skirt will cover them. It is her palms she is worried about. Whatever way he chooses to greet her will involve her hands. She spits on them to help the handkerchief wipe away the dirt that has mixed with blood. Thora made the handkerchief. It will be ruined. There will be others.

He is waiting for her on the beach.

"I didn't know what your signals meant."

"Just as well. I wanted you to stay put actually. It's quite rough in the woods, and it's harder to find the path from this end." She looks back at the obvious opening in the trees, wonders if he will notice.

"I think it is very warm, very satisfactory, the jumper ... the *sweater*," he says, taking both her hands in his. "I did not know whether you would come."

Penelope wants to say the same thing. Instead, she bubbles, "Anything to satisfy a customer," and then instantly regrets the way that might sound.

"You are very kind to a man so far away from home."

"It must be awful. Knowing your country is occupied, being so far from family." It is a gamble, she knows. He may have a wife and children that she doesn't want to know about.

"I am an only child. My parents are both dead."

Not necessarily a full answer, but she decides it will have to do.

"You said your mother is from Bergen, I think. I can see that in your hair. Your eyes."

Penelope is used to people in town remarking on her resemblance to Thora. This is different. Her cheeks burn. No resemblance to Thora there; she has never known her mother to blush. "Let's walk, shall we?" It is as good a way as any to ensure her face is turned away for a bit.

The stones on the beach make progress difficult. You have to concentrate on every step, calculate which way the rounded masses will shift under your foot. Thora has always said it is good for the calf muscles. Penelope wonders again whether the seam drawn down hers has smudged, tries to sneak a peek. The beach betrays her, and she has to reach out for Nielsen's elbow to prevent a second fall for the day. Maybe it is the familiar feel of the wool that makes her hook her arm through his as they continue to walk.

"It has a very interesting history, this beach."

She wonders what he can possibly know about it.

"The geology, I mean. Such a mixture of events."

They pause and he points out the effects of wave action and wind, and the evidence of the earth's molten core. A "granitic intrusion" is what he pronounces one rock. "Forced in where it was not wanted or expected. Like the Nazis," he says, reaching down for a flat stone he can skip across the surface of the bay. Penelope doesn't know what to do with her suddenly disengaged arm, is ashamed of how much she was liking being linked.

"There are shell middens all along here," she says, anxious to show she too can interpret their surroundings, that her entire existence has not become focused on his sleeve — although it has. "From the Passamaquoddy. The native people. They loved their clams apparently. For about ten thousand years. They have been here that long." She does not add that only a handful remain on the Canadian side of the border, another illustration of his comment about intrusions.

"It makes a person feel quite small, quite ... insignificant, this beach."

She wants to tell him he is the opposite of insignificant to her. "Nature is a tapestry, I think. We weave ourselves into it for a time." She has taken his arm again, not even looking around to see whether anyone else might be on the beach. "Then out again, I suppose."

They sit on a washed-up tree, bleached like a bone by years of sun, with her arm still through his crooked elbow, both looking across the water to Deer Island. *He is as afraid as I am to look sideways*, she thinks. After three or four minutes, he wedges his toe under a stone, lifts it carefully, still balanced, until his left leg is extended straight out. His boot is scuffed, the laces frayed. Unbidden, she extends her right leg, adjusting her skirt to keep her barked knee covered. Their feet touch. They breathe in, in unison, and then, at a rate that seems one degree slower than glacial, he gently begins to shift the stone to her. The electricity threatens to upset the transfer. She wonders whether it is an actual game, perhaps a traditional Norwegian exercise for focusing the attention. Whatever it is, it is working. There is, for several minutes, nothing in the world outside the stone and their two feet. Then it falls.

"Another?" he asks. "That was very good. We almost —"

"No." She pulls them to their feet. "You haven't seen the woods."

It is not hard to find a private place. The spruce is very thick, but as long as you don't mind crawling a little you can find some bare space between. He takes off the sweater and spreads it on the forest floor. Penelope thinks how disappointed Thora would be at all this. Then he is kneeling in front of her and she is not thinking at all.

He clucks sympathetically when he finds her scraped knees, leans to kiss them, first the right, then the left, then the right again before he reaches up to hook his thumbs in the waistband of her underpants and tug them down. Penelope is not sure how she is supposed to place herself on the sweater. It is not very large. Is it to protect her bum or her head? Before she can decide, he has unbuttoned and is lying back on the sweater. The wool scratches her raw knees as she climbs aboard.

"There is less discomfort for you this way, I think," he says. "The forest floor is quite rough."

She is not surprised to find him such a gentleman. And she is relieved that he has, without knowing it, chosen a way that Jonathan would never dream of.

"More slowly perhaps," he whispers.

"Of course." *As slowly as he likes.* She should have removed her blouse. His hands are wasted on clothes.

"My name is Lars," he murmurs, just before his breath catches. For a minute, she thinks he might be about to shake her hand. She closes her eyes as the waves begin to roll through her body. When she opens them again, she spies something through the spruce boughs. Not close. She would think it was a deer, only the coat is wrong. If it is a person, she doesn't think she and Lars can be seen. Hearing them may have been a different matter. That shouldn't bother her. These woods have become a favourite since the war began, famous for furtive fucks. She catches a glimpse of RAF blue.

A PLANE FLIES over, very low.

"Must be doing photography," Bernadette says. "For tourism or something. Another brochure, or the website. People like to see a place from an angle they'd never get in real life. I wonder why. Or maybe it's just somebody out for a joyride. I thought they used those drone things now for taking pictures. Do you remember how those idiots from the air station at Pennfield Ridge used to buzz the town, boss?"

"I remember," says Penelope. "Perhaps we should go back to the car. I'm feeling a little … we should go back."

Attachment

THE EMAIL MESSAGE from Ingrid came in as Matt was getting ready to shut down his laptop. It was a reflex to check for messages just before closing everything down. He supposed it was a hedge against the darkness — in case his computer never again hummed back to life, he would at least have missed the fewest messages possible. Statistically, he supposed, there was no greater likelihood that you should receive messages in the seconds just before you shut down than at any other time, and yet he had found that was exactly when things tended to come in. Often, they were messages he would rather not have read just before going to bed, questions or crises or requests that kept him awake at night. He paused for a minute when he saw Ingrid's name in the sender line, considered leaving it till morning. And then he clicked.

She was back in Norway. He had known that. There was a new memory project, this one funded by Arts and Culture Norway, with a performance soon. She didn't suppose he'd be able to make it, wouldn't expect him to, but wanted him to know the dates. She was attaching a photo she hoped he might like. There was no salutation. Matt lamented how email had gradually degenerated to the style of text messaging. He remembered fondly the days when the speed had been in the delivery, but not in the composition. The only signature was her initial. *I*. Or was it the first-person singular?

The photo she attached might be of almost any subject. He did not think it would be anything too intimate. People were too smart these days for that. Most likely a headshot, smiling across the months and miles, perhaps to show off a new haircut or eyeglass frames. If not that, then some object, either odd in itself or shot in an unusual way, another of her homages to the Surrealists as she understood them. He was surprised, then, when it was neither. Rather, she had sent him a photo — it could have been a postcard — of a streetscape in Bergen. The very spot where he and Jennifer had the conversation that was the genesis for the Model Villages exhibition. How had Ingrid known? He remembered telling her he had been to Bergen once. And he had told her a little about St. Andrews, of course. Maybe even mused about the similarities. It could have been one of those times they had exchanged memories, between her Ikea sheets, when they were too tired to make love again quite yet.

The Tell-Me-Yours-and-I'll-Tell-You-Mine game that Ingrid had improvised at the museum had evolved, over time, into a much looser exchange of remembered experiences and impressions. As it shifted from foreplay to post-coital pastime, the revelations became less and less guarded. Too intimate, he thought now.

One night, they had been trading stories of their respective adolescences. "Did you masturbate when you were a teenager?" Ingrid asked.

Matt hadn't wanted to answer, but he knew he had to; it was the game. "Yes, I suppose. Did you?" He hoped that might cut the thread.

"Of course. Everyone does."

Matthew doubted that.

"Can you remember a specific time?"

"A specific time?"

"Yes. Can you isolate one instance? Recall what you thought. What you did."

"The doing part didn't change that much from time to time."

"Tell me."

"You know. Touching myself. Then the clenched hand. And so forth."

"The memory doesn't sound very vivid."

"I guess it's not. Just routine, you know."

"And your thoughts? Were they always the same?"

"No. Now that you mention it, they weren't. Different things went through my mind."

"Different images? Ideas? What?"

"Sometimes one, sometimes the other."

"So, you would think of a naked lady, for example, of sex with a soft warm body."

"I guess."

"Or about a sexy situation, something naughty or forbidden."

"Sometimes."

"Had you ever been in such a situation yourself, or been with a naked woman?"

"I was ... what was I ... I was thirteen, fourteen."

"When you began."

"Yes."

"So you had no experience to base the fantasy on."

"None."

"And yet you called up breasts and bushes and thighs. Maybe spankings?"

"Not spankings."

"With no experience of any of them! Interesting, isn't it?"

"Is it? It feels a little sordid. We could talk about something else."

"Interesting for what it tells us about memory. What was going through your mind when you jerked off. Is that what you call it? That does make it sound sordid. What was going through your mind was essentially an act of memory, wasn't it? You called up in your mind's eye bodies and situations that were not present. That's obvious. But they had never been present for you. Never. It's like false memory. Paramnesia."

"And I thought you were going to beat me up for not being able to recall a specific incident, for mixing them all up together. I thought you were going to use my pathetic adolescent onanism as some spectacular illustration of the difference between semantic and episodic memory."

"Oh, well, that too. Obviously." She laughed then and pinched his nipple.

"And you? Can you remember specific times?"

"It's odd. I can remember the doing in detail on several different occasions. The thinking is all a blur."

And then she treated him to accounts of several discrete occasions. Was *discrete* the right word? Yes, he assured her. She had also been the other kind of discreet, no doubt.

When she was finished, he said, "But they still fall into categories that repeat themselves, don't they? How can you be sure now that you haven't substituted one for another? Every episode involves your nipples. Two of the five include your bum. In three, your fingers are doing one thing and in two they're ... well ... mainly rubbing. Spread that over a whole career of masturbation —"

"A career?"

"You were the one who started this conversation, the one who said everyone does it. Spread that over a career of pleasuring yourself and how could you possibly isolate a single instance? How could you tell them apart?"

She thought for a minute. "I have an excellent memory. Have I told you that before?" She laughed.

"An excellent memory for body parts and what they do. A Rabelaisian memory."

"The two go hand in hand. Or something in hand. Your classical memory heroes knew that. Lewd images were their favourites for stocking their memory palaces. The dirtier the better. People try to tell you the invention of writing put an end to the art of memory. I think I even read that on a panel in your exhibition. It's nonsense. The Greeks knew how to write, for heaven's sake. It was the Puritans who put a stop to the ancient art of memory. Too rude for them. They thought they'd go blind or something. Speaking of masturbating and memory, would you like to try sex with an actual woman, in the present, again? It will be nothing short of memorable, I promise." She rolled over on top of him before he could answer.

It might have been later that same night — or was it another? — that she asked him why he seemed so gloomy. Was what they were doing bothering him, making him feel guilty? She had never raised it before, never once alluded to his marriage.

"I've never been ... unfaithful ... before. I don't think Jennifer has. It will hurt her."

"If she finds out."

"Is that supposed to make it better?"

"Think about it. If I remember that I have a bunch of boxes stored in my basement, that memory remains valid even after my neighbour comes in and steals them. Isn't that so? The thing is that until I see an empty basement, or am told of the theft, my memory of those boxes in that basement is absolutely true, right?"

"I guess." Matt had never liked these epistemological plums.

"Why should it be any different with infidelity? Her memory of your being faithful is what matters. Until that is challenged, there is no problem." With that, she had rolled over and fallen asleep. Matt had lain awake for an hour, then dressed and gone home.

He reread Ingrid's message, tried to compose a response, although he knew he shouldn't. He thought opening the attachment again might help him. It was still Bryggen. He didn't know what had led him to hope it might somehow have become an indecent photo to remember her by.

Canned

THEY ARE LISTENING to *Information Morning* out of Saint John. The transistor radio in the kitchen sometimes struggles with the signal — the CBC usually surrenders to that station just over the border in Calais — but today it is strong and clear. Matt has offered a few times to do something about it with his phone. Apparently, you can get the radio over your phone if you know what to do. It doesn't make any sense, she has told him, stopping short, though, of admitting it's confusing. When he tried to demonstrate it to her, with her trusty transistor still blaring, they had discovered that the phone or the internet, or whatever it is, lags a little behind the radio. She was able to use that as her trump card: her news is fresher than his.

Matt has an irritating tendency to try to correct everything he hears on the show. The host sometimes muddles his words (who wouldn't, getting up at three for a six a.m. start?). The newscaster has a number of habitual mispronunciations (who cares how the *u* is supposed to sound in *municipal* or that the *l* is not silent in *vulnerable*?). And some of the weekly featured guests consistently offer opinions that Matt pronounces ill-informed, illogical, or ill-expressed. Some mornings it is hard to hear any of the program.

When she suggests he turn it off, though, he always insists he is loving it.

This morning, a piece from one of the stringers Matt has been known to mock quite mercilessly has captured his attention enough to shut him up. During a recent nor'easter, a herring-brining shed in Maine was blown off its pilings into Lubec Narrows. It floated south, neatly navigating the trestles of the international bridge before washing up on a beach on Campobello Island. The building is on the National Register of Historic Places as the last traditional smoked-herring facility to have operated in the United States. A heritage group has been trying for years to restore it as a museum. The reporter tells them that the shed crossed the border remarkably unscathed — even with its chimney intact — but it was met by scavengers on the beach, many of them wielding chainsaws and claiming salvage rights. It all has the makings of an international incident if you believe the CBC. The piece ends with a clip from a Lubec councilwoman: "The last sardine house has met its grave."

"RIP," says Penelope.

SHE IS IN the sparkling, white-tiled packing room when she hears the first of the rumours. The fact that there is actually any idle time for gossip adds credibility to the story. The herring just are not running. Most of the little that is being caught is going to Maine or to Connors' plant up in Blacks Harbour. The girls, even she, could easily pack three times what is coming to them in a day. Most of the clams and the beans they have canned in the off-season are still sitting in the warehouse, so those alternatives have already been exhausted.

Hilde, a girl with unpleasant breath whom Thora suspects of having slept with Nils before he disappeared, has heard from one of the men who run the boilers. It is not hard to picture her sweating in the bowels of the factory with her skirt up around her waist in exchange for the information. "They plan to shut the steam off at the end of the month. They'll be letting us all go. All except the office people, of course." She licks the olive oil off her fingers before reaching for another handful of herring without cleaning her hands.

"Hilde!" shouts one of the really religious girls. It is either Nora or Hedvig. Thora can't tell them apart.

"What? What would they do? Fire me? Nobody is ever going to eat these sardines, that's what I am trying to tell you. We could pee in the cans for all the difference it would make."

Hedvig (or Nora) mumbles what may be a prayer against the Evil One, but most of the other girls laugh.

By the evening meal, the stories have multiplied. The manager is running from the sheriff; his yacht has been seized in Eastport. The stockholders are selling in panic. Sir William Van Horne will turn the model town into guest houses for his overflow on Ministers Island. The Norwegian consul is coming the next day, and the day after that they will all be on a boat back to Bergen. Nobody is complaining about the food, for once. Every last mealy potato disappears. Some of the girls stuff their blouses with the bread they usually sneer at. You never know where the next meal is coming from.

Only one of the stories, the one she heard in the packing shed, is true, though several will become true in the months that follow. They are all told at breakfast the next day that they are to report to the concert hall rather than to their usual stations. Mr. McCann has an announcement he wishes to make.

Morris McCann is an object lesson in the mysterious operations of fate. He lived into his surname at the age of thirty when he registered patents on no fewer than five types of tin cans with key openers. Van Horne poached him away from Eastport to run Casarco, giving him carte blanche in the construction of the plant and town. McCann arranged a contract that set his salary at a percentage of the costs of building and equipping, which meant that he had spared no expense. The workers didn't like him, said that he didn't need the factory to be a success. Between his special contract with the company and the steady income from his patents, it didn't matter to him whether the herring ever ran or not.

Her dealings with him had been different. It was unlikely they should ever have met in the first place. The lines were clear. While on special occasions — well, Christmas and New Year's as it turned out — the bosses and the workers were all to gather together for an evening of eating and drinking and dancing, the rest of the time there was to be no fraternizing. Even around the Christmas tree, the groups remained separate, eyes cast upward to the star as they sang, with only the bravest souls venturing a sideways glance. And at midnight a week later, following speeches about what a great year 1913 would be and the singing of some song none of the Norwegians knew, they parted, oil and water — the workers back to their dormitories and shared cottages, the bosses to the larger cottages or their mansions in the town a few miles away.

It was before all that, in the fall, after the sardine girls had moved out of the makeshift living quarters in the clam factory in town and had started using it for practice runs, that her path first crossed McCann's. Fate. Her ears were bruised from the yelling of the supervisor who threatened to let her go if she didn't improve. Daily, the woman asked her where the hell she had learned to pack sardines. She didn't dare tell her she was learning on the job. She wished she had never listened to Nils. There must have been a simpler way to foil her parents' orders that she stop seeing him. People didn't go halfway around the world just to be with their boyfriends. Especially when the boyfriend turned out to be not the person you had thought. She had gone for a walk along the shore, arriving finally at the rocky bar that connected Ministers Island to the mainland when the tide was low. The bar appealed because it was a path that also wasn't a path, being wiped clean, eradicated, twice a day. She had no certain idea of what the tide was doing at that moment. From the look of the beach it was still going out, so she decided to venture. She knew Van Horne, the millionaire railwayman who owned the island, was in Montréal. Everyone knew the comings and goings of the rich and famous. She wouldn't care about being warned off by one of the barn workers or a gardener.

Once you were on the bar, there was no cover, of course. You were out there for anyone to see. And your purpose could hardly be in doubt. She wondered, later, how long the man had watched her. *Long enough to develop a plan and rehearse a speech.*

She was just starting up the cedar-lined lane that branched off to the right once you were on the island when he called out, "A nice afternoon for a stroll." The man held a cigarette in his right hand — one of those black ones from France — and was leaning against a stone gatepost. She thought instantly of portraits of the devil.

"Very," she muttered, uncertain whether she should be addressing him at all, thinking that she now must turn around and make her way off the island.

"Have you seen the house?" He spoke to her as though she were an equal, another casual visitor to the island.

She could only shake her head.

"Well, you mustn't go back without at least a glimpse. There's nobody at home. But then I suppose you knew that."

She didn't like the suggestion that she was there for some nefarious purpose. It was as if he were accusing her of planning to rob the empty house. "I came to walk, sir. Just to walk. I have no interest in the house or any of the buildings. I needed to think. I think perhaps I should return —"

"Nonsense. Please continue your walk. I will accompany you. They know me here. We don't even need to talk." After a few hundred yards of silence, though, he had begun to pry. She supposed a man who knew so many ways of opening a can couldn't leave things alone. "You are from Norway?"

It was a diplomatic way of saying he knew she was one of the cheap labourers at the company that he ran. She nodded.

"And you have a lot to think about." When she just continued walking, he went on, guessing, "You are a long way from home, from family."

"I came with my brother, Nils." She thought it important to let him know she was not without male protection. If that is what Nils was or had ever been.

"Ah." McCann had evidently heard enough "brother" stories that he had cracked the code long ago. "I come here to walk quite often. To think. I have quite a lot to think about." When she didn't respond, he said, "I am the manager of the plant, the one across the harbour there." He gestured vaguely back in the direction from which they had both now walked for five minutes.

"I know who you are."

"Then you have the advantage of me. Morris McCann." He held out a hand she could not refuse.

"Thora Halvstad." It would do.

"I wonder, Miss Halvstad, whether we might be able to help

each other: two people who like to walk and think, who have lots to think about."

"What could I —?"

"I think you might be a good listener."

"Oh." Men often said that when your ear was the last hole they were interested in.

"No, not listen to me. *For* me. I wonder whether you might listen to others, for me. I need a pair of ears on the ground. Sorry. That's not the image I want to portray. I need someone to listen to the workers, to tell me things I need to know."

"You want me to spy for you."

"To provide me with intelligence. Yes."

She knew there had been trouble with the Italian crews they had brought in for construction. Everybody knew that. Their foreman had not been shy about making his crew's demands known. But there were others who supported the Italians, shared their grievances. McCann might not know so much about them. Most of the Norwegian men were fed up. With the plant still not operating, they were being ordered to do jobs they would never have contemplated. There had been some vandalism — nothing major, some broken glass and smashed walls, and one small fire. She had known about all of that before it happened. Nils still confided in her, even if he had transferred his affections elsewhere. She thought about how the supervisor had threatened her. It might not hurt to have a friend in high places. The highest place. "Perhaps we can come to an … arrangement."

That arrangement had weathered nearly a year — ten months of setbacks in the business and assaults on her position as a packer. Her information had been crucial in fending off two potentially violent incidents and once resulted in a visit from the Norwegian consul to sort matters out. McCann, she thought, was getting good value for his protection of her. Had they known, her coworkers would view what she was doing as betrayal. She knew it was simply a matter of survival.

But now, as he addressed the assembled workers, outlining how they would be paid off and the plant closed down, she knew the old arrangement no longer served either of them anymore. Intelligence about what the workers were thinking when they were no longer the workers was no use to the boss when he was no longer a boss. And it wasn't her ability to keep her job that was at stake. It was whether or not she would be able to stay in the country, because staying is what she had decided she must do.

THE RADIO HAS moved on to the eight thirty news. Matt is making faces, pushing on his cheeks with thumb and middle finger to make his lips form the *ew* sound in *municipal*. The newscast ends with a brief clip from the piece on the brining shed. Penelope hears again the councilwoman from Lubec: "The last sardine house has met its grave." She thinks of her mother and what things must have been like for her.

The Smoked Mackerel

MATT'S LUNCH WITH Amanda Williams had been inevitable, he supposed, since the moment Carolyn mentioned her. Having not thought of Amanda at all for at least twenty years, he suddenly could barely think of anyone else.

She was not difficult to find once he decided to look for her. He didn't ask Carolyn. That would have been mixing the professional with the personal. And might have sent the wrong message. He was curious, not mating. Bernadette gave him a funny look when he raised the name but told him where to look anyway.

In what appeared to be the completion of a circle, Amanda could be found at one of the restaurants along Water Street. It was not the same one she had worked at in the summers when they had dated. That had changed hands — and names — at least twice since. This one was newer: a conversion of an old three-story sea captain's house that was previously a boutique. A patio had been added on the water side, for dining in the warmer months, and the interior had been completely redone. The menu, however, seemed from an earlier era.

"What can I get you, m'dear?" Her face was more lined, of course, but she was perfectly recognizable. The voice was rougher too, and he didn't approve of the folksy affectation. "Oh my God. Matt! Carolyn said you were in town."

"Carolyn? Oh, yes, right." He didn't know why he was pretending indifference. "What's good?"

If she was surprised by his coolness, she didn't show it. "Not much," she whispered. "I'd go with the halibut cheeks."

"The halibut cheeks then. Oh, and a Moosehead. Please." He hardly drank beer anymore. Ordering it was to make up for treating her like a stranger: Moosehead was what they had drunk together in those summers. He wondered whether she remembered.

"I'll put the order in and bring that beer right along." She smiled. *Recollection or rote?* "It's good to see you, Matt."

As he watched her retreat to the counter in the back, he thought he could still see traces of the elegant creature she had been. She was still slim, still moved like a dancer. He felt ashamed of the roll that was daily increasing its doughboy creep over his belt, and was glad that she had not seen him arrive, favouring his left hip as he did now most days when it was damp. It was stupid to have just shown up here like this.

She poured the Moosehead for him, making a little sommelier joke of it all, twisting the can with a flourish at the end. He didn't remember her being funny, supposed she must have been. Was he?

The halibut cheeks were actually terrific: not too much batter, but not pretending to be dietetic. He burned his tongue on the fries. When she came to ask how everything was tasting — the script hadn't changed — he was swishing beer around to soothe the pain. He only had time to nod before she turned away.

They didn't have portable terminals so she took his card to the cash desk to process it. He thought she might pause to chat when she delivered the slip for him to sign, but an American was gesticulating in a way she couldn't ignore. He added twenty per cent — wondering, too late, whether that was insulting somehow

— and signed the merchant copy. As he went to fold up his copy, he noticed there was writing on the back: "Let's have lunch. ANYWHERE BUT HERE. Call me" and seven digits. She had managed to keep her parents' phone number over the years.

AND SO, HE found himself two days later waiting at a table for two in the library bar of the hotel. It was the only other place that was open for lunch, she had explained when she suggested it over the phone. Did she think he was worried she planned to take him upstairs afterward?

He hadn't been inside the hotel since the major renovations a few years back. Some people said the place had been sterilized, homogenized, all traces of character removed. Others argued that the new owners had respected the bones of the old hotel but had to make changes. Single glazing, dry-rotted mouldings, and faded chintzes didn't cut it anymore — as if they ever had. Matt thought the lobby and the huge salon were very well done but instantly hated the wallpaper in the bar.

Amanda was late. He couldn't remember whether that had always been a thing with her; he probably hadn't cared so much about time in those days. When she appeared in the archway that separated the bar from the salon, he thought — uncharitably — that she might have planned to be late in order to make an entrance. You almost wouldn't recognize the beleaguered server from the Smoked Mackerel. The lines on her face had been erased and her hair was down. Black leggings and an electric blue tunic suited her better than the T-shirt and carpenter jeans she worked in, he thought.

"Sorry. There was a thing with my mum. It held me up."

So, her mother was still alive too. "How is she?" Matt had never liked Amanda's mother, was certain she had never liked him. No doubt she was suspicious of his intentions. Rightly.

"You know how it is. She's still in there in that body somewhere, but most days it is hard to tell. They're wonderful at the Lodge, but Jesus I hate going up there. That's awful, I know."

Instinctively, he put his hand on her forearm. He hoped it said sympathy and not something more. Her perfume was the same as forty years ago. *L'Air du Temps* — the name came back unbidden. He used to watch her dab it behind her ears, her knees, then put a drop on one wrist and rub the other on it. "Not awful. Just honest."

"You look great, by the way. I didn't say so at the Mackerel, well ... you know."

"I should have called first. It was weird just showing up."

"It's a restaurant. People come in. Mostly I don't care. I work in a restaurant just like I did forty years ago. Only now I do it in the winter as well as the summer."

"I work in a museum. Same as I did those summers forty years ago."

"I feel like a glass of wine. Can we do that?" She moved her arm. He hadn't realized his hand was still resting on it.

Their server brought her a glass of Pinot Noir instead of Pinot Grigio, but when Matt said she must send it back she waved him off. "They'll take it out of her pay for the day. I don't care. Actually, I prefer red. I was mainly afraid you'd think I was a lush if I ordered red at lunch."

He instantly regretted ordering a Guinness and whatever frumpy message it had sent her about his attitude to daytime drinking.

"Do you remember ..." they both started at once.

It was a picnic on a Sunday — the only day they both had off. They had driven to Oven Head, nearly tearing the muffler off his Cortina as he eased it in and out of the craters in the dirt road. The menu was modelled on one in some book they had both read that summer. Neither could recall anymore what it had been, though they agreed that it had seemed life altering at the time. There had been a mix-up about who was to bring the wine. Fortunately, it wasn't the kind of mix-up where they were left with none. He had brought a Chardonnay and she something with bubbles. No, his was a Sauterne, she corrected him. He cringed, knowing she was right.

"There was a fog bank just offshore in the bay," she said.

"I remember it as full sun."

"Well, where we were on the beach, yes, but not on the water."

He thought she might be confusing it with some other occasion. God knows, fog banks were common enough. Just not that day.

"We got quite tiddly."

"Squiffy." They were words they had enjoyed that summer, probably also from that same book.

"Are you ready to order?" The server saved them from revisiting the consequences of their two-bottle lunch: the hungry lovemaking, the nap in the sun (with or without the fog bank lowering), and then the weaving drive back to St. Andrews. *It's what we did in those days*, they would have agreed, *you just didn't think about it.*

They ordered the lobster chowder — bowls, not cups. She had heard the servings were very generous but suggested they not risk it. "There's nothing worse than wanting more, is there?"

He decided to let it go as an innocent remark, though he knew it wasn't.

"They used to experiment with how much potato they could get away with in the chowder. If nobody complained on a given day, they added a little more the next. And sea legs, remember that? Pollock coloured up to look like lobster or crab? They'd slip that in. As long as you had a sandwich board outside announcing 'The Best Lobster Chowder,' you could sell almost anything. The town was booming."

"Was it? Maybe in the restaurant business. I seem to recall a lot of pretty quiet days at the museums." Matt had worked in each of the town's three museums over successive summers. If there were three tour groups in a day, they counted it a bumper.

"And retail. Your mother's shop did very well."

People always thought that about Handworks: that it raked in profits. The illusion was helped by the houses they lived in, and the school Matt was sent away to. In fact, the business was usually just a step ahead of the bank. It was the family money — Grandfather Arnold's money — that allowed them to live as they did. And that drove a wedge between Matt and just about every other young person in town. Even Amanda, he remembered now. "My mother worked very hard."

"I know. She was the hardest-working boss I ever had."

"You?"

"I worked there in the fall and winter of '75 to '76. You would have been in second year at Mount A. She never mentioned it?"

Matt thought back to August 1975. He could feel the fist in his gut, taste the snot of their tearful last kisses. Amanda had said they should see other people, admitted she already was.

"I think she felt sorry for me. That you dumped me." She smiled.

"Oh. I may have changed the story a little for her." At twenty, he wasn't about to admit to being the jilted one.

"That's all right. It got me a job. She was very sweet to me. Although she did find me something else in the spring before you got home again in April. And she said maybe it was better if I didn't come around."

So Penelope had seen through his lie all along, Matt thought.

The chowder came in bowls with rims broad enough to drive a small car around. Matt nearly tipped his over trying to extract the spoon from under the overhang. Amanda was already eating and cooing by the time he got sorted out. He watched her lift her spoon to her lips, smiled at how fast the thin white moustache had formed.

"Jesus, this is good. I should probably be sick of lobster, but it never happens."

Of course. Carolyn mentioned a new lobster fisherman boyfriend. Matt wondered whether this was an invitation to ask about him, decided not to.

"I was in Florida for a while. Working. I think I missed the lobster most of all."

"So you came back for it?"

"I couldn't live in the States anymore. I mean, I could. They weren't throwing me out or anything. I just couldn't be a part of ... of all that."

"Chump."

"Exactly. Do you go? To the States? I suppose for your work you must have to. Conferences and so forth."

"Mostly to Europe." He hated himself for saying it, thought she probably would too. There was that old wedge again.

"Lucky you! Of course, I pop across the border to Calais, sometimes go as far as Eastport or Lubec. As long as I know I can get back home within an hour or two."

Was she thinking then, as he was, of their adventure to Robbinston? At eighteen they had both felt old to be virgins, but they had wanted to do the thing properly — not in the back seat of the Cortina or in the bushes at Pagan Point. They had climbed Chamcook Mountain one evening with a bottle of Baby Duck, but it had started to rain and they had come back down still intact. The plan for the motel in Robbinston ticked all the boxes: comfort, anonymity, and the sense of occasion that goes with international travel. In the end, it delivered two of the three. The bed had squeaked so loudly they had ended up doing it on the floor, which was no more comfortable than his car or the spruce roots at the point. Matt had recounted all of this to Ingrid during one of their games. He wasn't sure how much of it was true and to what degree he was relying on what usually happens rather than on what actually did. When he tried to recall details — the exact hue of her nipples, who had been on top, even whether she had come — he couldn't be sure they were not mixed with memories of other women, other times. He suddenly felt ashamed, sitting there with this woman who was his first lover, unsure that he could reliably remember details of the experience.

"It's a funny thing, memory, isn't it?"

Had she been reading his mind? They were always pretty much on a wavelength, he recalled.

"What it does as we get older, how it lets us down little by little. I see what's happened to my mother and I'm scared about my turn coming."

"Your mother is an old woman. My mother is a very old woman."

"Carolyn has told me about your mum's situation. I'm sorry, but I guess it comes to us all. Don't you sometimes forget things already? I don't just mean details. But those too. I can't remember the name of that motel in Robbinston, for instance. It had a red roof, do you remember?"

"What motel would that be, now?"

"Oh, very good." She smiled and then, "Sorry, does it make you uncomfortable? We can forget it ever happened." She took a spoonful of soup.

"No. I don't want to forget it." He owed her that much, owed himself. "It's just funny talking about it. The Redclyffe. That was the name." He silently begged her not to reminisce about the noisy bed.

"Of course. Shit. How hard could that be to remember? Anyway, it's not just the details I'm worried about forgetting. It's more the big things, like why you know something, or forgetting why you don't believe something."

"The problem of forgotten evidence and the problem of forgotten defeat," he said reflexively.

"I knew you'd have names for it."

"Philosophers love that stuff."

"You've probably started reading up on everything about Alzheimer's too."

"How did you know?"

"Carolyn said she thought you were taking it all very seriously. I can't bear to read anything about it."

"It doesn't help, as it turns out."

"Can I interest you two in some dessert today? Or another beverage?" Their server couldn't have been older than Amanda was in 1975. Matt wondered briefly about her love life.

"You?" they asked one another at once, then shook their heads. It might have been rehearsed. Or they were slipping back into old ways.

"I have to pick up Jim's truck for him. He was having the brakes done or something."

So the lobsterman boyfriend's name was Jim. "I should get back to Mamma."

And the spell — whatever it had been — was broken, and they were just two old acquaintances with new lives.

Matt insisted on paying the bill. Amanda wanted to look after the tip. "She's no twenty per cent," she laughed.

He couldn't tell whether it was a rebuke for the other day or a joke. He couldn't remember whether she had always been funny.

Arrangements

PENELOPE WISHES MATT would leave her house alone. He wouldn't like it if she went to his house, wherever it is, and started tossing things about. That woman he married certainly wouldn't. He says he is helping her organize, which shows how little he knows about organization. Everyone has their own system. Just as everyone is entitled to their own space. The two things go together. You organize your space your own way. Nobody else can do it properly for you. What he has done in the kitchen, she will admit, is quite helpful in terms of putting things where she needs them. She knows she had spent a lot of time searching through the cabinets for a juice glass or the right bowl for her oatmeal. Having all the breakfast things on the one shelf saves time — although, she wonders, saves it for what?

Matt was never a tidy boy. And now there is this mess he has gotten into with the Williams girl who was here the other day with her burgeoning belly. It's a wonder he doesn't see the irony of his trying to put order into her life when his own is in such disarray. Maybe when the baby comes he will be distracted, leave her alone. She doesn't know whether she can wait that long.

His invasion of the workroom is the worst. She should have put a lock on that door, wonders who you would call to get something like that done. Matt would know. But she doesn't want him involved for some reason. What was it?

She sits with one of her mother's bags flattened across her lap. It is one of the grotesque ones: the Ship of Fool that she hasn't seen for years. Ugly as it is, it demands your attention. There is a kind of magic about it. She follows the blocks of colour around the design as they evoke an impossible boat, a kind of Cubist boat, she thinks. Its real name suddenly comes to her, although she would swear she has never heard it before. *The Molly McCann.*

MOST OF THE girls are happy about going home, though they worry about what they will find there. Nothing has improved in Norway since they took up the offer to come to Canada to pack sardines. But at least they will be with family and in a place where everyone speaks their language. For her, neither is a draw. Her family will not have her back, and her English is very good; she has never had a problem making herself understood in St. Andrews.

She must go to see Morris McCann.

They have nearly always met either on Ministers Island or halfway up Chamcook Mountain. Once, they used the woods at Pagan Point. It is important that no one see them together at the factory or in the sardine town. Neither of them has thought to worry that someone might suspect they were having an affair. They know they are not, and so, she thinks now, they have been blind to the possibility of any such interpretation. But her value to him as a source of information has relied on people speaking freely around her, and they wouldn't do that if they suspected any connection to him. With the end of their arrangement, the need for discretion has also vanished, she decides. So she goes to find him in his office at the plant.

She times her visit for a few minutes past noon when she calculates, apparently correctly, that his secretary will be absent. He hurries her in, shutting the door sharply behind her. The office is smaller than she has pictured, much less ostentatious. Although the walls are painted and hung with paintings, they are still cinder block, and the furniture is plain oak, not the mahogany she imagined. The window is the nicest feature, with a sweeping view across Chamcook Harbour to Ministers Island.

"Miss ... ah ..." He pretends they are strangers, though she can't imagine why. There is no one else near them. She waits for him to offer her a chair, and when he doesn't, she sits down anyway, realizing too late that this gives him an advantage over her. He chooses not to exercise it, though, and retreats behind his desk, sinking into his half-turned swivel chair. "Well? Do you have something for me?"

It hasn't occurred to her that she might eke the arrangement out a little longer by pretending to have valuable intelligence, making up plots and counterplots. She thought the market for all that had vanished with the closure of the factory, wishes she were quick enough to manufacture something on the spot. Instead, she settles for the plain truth. "I want to stay on. Here. I don't want to go back to Norway."

"You could go up to Connors'. Or down to Maine. A good packer can always find —"

"We both know I am not a good packer."

"How is your arithmetic?"

"What?"

"Can you operate a typewriting machine?"

"Of course." *How hard could it be?*

"Be here at eight tomorrow. Do you have something appropriate to wear in an office?"

The typewriter proves to be harder to master than she thought, though the volume of his correspondence is not vast. She is able quite quickly to memorize the keys and find them reliably with a few fingers, which seems good enough. Her knowledge of arithmetic turns out not to matter. He teaches her a whole new kind. She doesn't ask where his previous secretary has gone. No doubt, she objected to some of what she was being asked to type and had reservations about the novel uses of arithmetic. She had the luxury of quitting. She was not facing deportation.

Although she is now one of the office staff, Thora is allowed to stay on in the dormitory. A month ago, this would not have done, but any potential issues of mixed echelons have been eliminated with the eviction of the factory workers. There are no meals, of course; she would be the sole diner. Sometimes she walks into St. Andrews to buy dinner. The rest of the time, she helps herself to cans from the warehouse. McCann has said he doesn't mind. She keeps the large kitchen stove kindled so she can have hot water to bathe and heat the occasional can of beans and bread. As the fall wears on, she moves her bed to the kitchen so she doesn't freeze to death at night.

In late November, McCann announces he is making a trip to Norway. He has developed a new process for soldering cans and there is a factory there that is interested. He offers to take her with him. As his special assistant, he says.

"I have told you I don't want to go back there."

"It is unlikely I will come back here."

"What does that mean?"

"It is time to move on. I have done what I can here."

She knows this means he has squeezed what he can from the company.

"Will there be a new manager?"

"Yes. They are still trying to get the bank to invest more. People say the herring will run well in the spring."

They both know that neither will happen. "But the new person won't want me, will he?"

"He will be looking for a more ... conventional arrangement. More standard skills."

"I'll need somewhere to live." She doesn't ask him for money. That has been well looked after over the last few months. She insisted that if she was going to sell her soul it must fetch a very good price.

"You can rent in town."

"A single woman without work? Besides, I will need to disappear for a while. I want to reappear in a few months as somebody else, a complete newcomer, somebody who doesn't stink of herring and desperation."

"Then come —"

"Not Norway. No. I've said."

And that is when he suggests the *Molly McCann*.

PENELOPE LETS THE bag slip from her lap. Thora will be home soon with Matt. Her mother likes the walk to pick him up at school. She would not be happy that Penelope has been going through her things, these things. There is stock for selling in the store, and there is what Thora makes for herself. Penelope needs to understand the difference between the two. That is what Thora will say if she arrives home and finds this bag out on the floor. It has happened before. Though Penelope can't think of when. Then there is the creak of the front door and she knows it is too late to do anything.

But there is no sign of Thora. Only Matt. Something is bothering him, she can tell. She thinks he is about to tell her that Thora has died. But she knows that already. It is something else.

"Mamma, do you remember when Carolyn White was here the other day?"

She may. She needs more to go on. But she nods tentatively, hoping it will encourage him to provide more context.

"And we were talking about other houses, other places."

Still nothing.

"And Carolyn talked about the place where they could do everything for you."

He means his little knocked-up paramour. They are after her house. "No."

"Well, the thing is, Mamma, that you really can't be alone here anymore, in this house."

"I've been alone in this house for more than twenty years."

"Nearly fifty. And that's amazing. Truly remarkable. Something to be proud of."

"Nobody should live this long."

"It's an achievement."

"See if you think that in thirty years."

"A room has come up, a space. And they'll take you. It's just a short walk away."

"Will I be walking back?"

"Well, no. We think you'll like this new place, and you won't ... you won't feel the need to walk back. You can take your own things. Many of them. Pictures. A chair. The long-case clock, as long as we disable the chimes."

"It's not a nursing home, is it?"

That stops him for a moment. He was never good with a direct question he didn't want to answer. Like her mother. "Well, yes, I guess it could be called a nursing home. It's really more of a —"

"What do the people who run it call it?"

"A nursing home."

"I'd rather die." Except, of course, she knows she can't. If only wishing could make it so. If only we could choose our own time. Her mother seemed to manage it, to the doctor's amazement. But Thora was much younger: three score and ten. And more determined. Penelope has never forgiven her. "There was something I wanted to tell you about her."

"Who?"

"My mother."

"Your mother?"

"Yes. Something. I don't know. It's gone now. I'll think of it in the middle of the night and call you."

"Okay. I bought some scallops for supper. I'll sear them in butter. Does that sound good?"

"Have I shown you my collection of scallop pearls?"

"We can look at them again after supper."

"You know where they are?"

"No."

She is afraid that he is going to ask her whether she knows where they are, but he doesn't, which is both a relief and not. "It's nice to have you here, Matt." Here in this house. He has said something about the house. Something important, she thinks, but it's gone.

Program

AS THE *I remember* ... performance drew closer, Matt became more and more convinced that it was going to make a truly important statement. The impact he had hoped to make with his *The Art of Memory* exhibition paled in comparison to the new insights he was sure Gina and Ingrid's project would provide. When he mentioned this to Ingrid, she kindly said it was only because *The Art of Memory* had closed while *I remember* ... was still going on.

The weekly workshops gave way to nightly rehearsals. Ingrid and Gina argued endlessly about the inevitable effects of this kind of repetition on the freshness of the original memories, and about how to account for those effects in a responsible way, but they all agreed that rehearsal was a necessary evil. Since it was impossible to rehearse the oral elements and the movement elements all in the same room at the same time, Matt arranged for an additional space in the museum. Gina asked him to attend the sessions where the performers — for that is what they were becoming — honed their monologues and recitations, while Ingrid worked with the dancers and Gina would float back and forth. He thought it was a clumsy attempt to keep him apart from Ingrid but quickly became obsessed with his new responsibility. He would make suggestions here and there, and came to see himself as something approaching an associate director, though he would never have admitted it to either Gina or Ingrid.

The monologues and recitations had been carefully curated with an eye to the variety they could add to the presentation. He found something new and interesting in each of them every night.

There were readings from Proust and Márquez: the madeleines of *Swann's Way* and the almonds of *Love in the Time of Cholera*. Matt had suggested those, said he couldn't see how they could be left out. Gina resisted at first — he suspected it was the gender of the writers — but eventually relented. Matt supposed Ingrid had had to concede on some other point in order to buy Gina's assent.

The highlight on the oral side of the performance, Matt thought, was the segment in which three people recounted their personal memories of the destruction of the Twin Towers. The accounts were very detailed. And identical. After the third had been delivered, the witnesses were asked to state where they were on September 11. One was in Yellowknife, one in Toronto, and one in Fredericton. They would then project on a screen the widely broadcasted video footage that was responsible for creating this stunningly homogenized "memory."

Ingrid's enthusiastic nightly updates on the development of the dance performances were often long and significantly reduced the time available for lovemaking before he had to return home. Although he always felt the dance portion must lose something being translated into words, he could tell from her enthusiasm that something impressive was being created. When the two groups finally reunited in the week before the performance was to take place, his faith was vindicated.

The show would open in very dim light with Ingrid and Gina performing a pas de deux. The idea was very simple: Ingrid repeated Gina's movements on a five-second delay. Originally, they had planned to be nude. Matt was relieved when they decided to wear body stockings after all. He knew the decision had nothing to do with modesty, but the outcome was the same so he didn't care. As the finale of the dance, four yards of Kraft paper were to be unrolled and Ingrid and Gina were going to leapfrog over one another, printing a row of fading images of their bodies in blue pigment. Neither, it turned out, had wanted to roll naked in the paint.

Beginning at a point three minutes into the opening pas de deux, a delayed video feed of the entire evening's performance would play on a large screen, interrupted only for the showing of the Twin Towers footage. This had been Gina's idea — a nod to Sontag, she said, and what she called *living by proxy*. Ingrid found it a distraction and cautioned against trying to say too much and splitting the focus too widely, but in the end she agreed, in the interests of peace. Also running throughout the evening — although at intervals, and live — was a demonstration of the endurance of procedural memory. The oldest woman in the group (Matt thought that was just by chance) repeated a mime version of her nighttime ablutions while groups of other performers bombarded her with distractions that ranged from shouted instructions about doing things differently to recited lists of medical products and litanies of recipes for complicated lemon desserts.

Matt was most nervous about what he and Ingrid had come to call "The Fuckin' Foucault." He didn't doubt the performers' ability to pull it off. It was the voice-over that he had provided that he was afraid might fall flat, pulling the rest down with it.

The idea had come from a passage Gina had read, second-hand somewhere, from Foucault. It went, she said, something like this: in our time, history is that which transforms documents into monuments. They had already been developing, in the workshop, a piece about how acts of memory become reliant on the preservation of physical objects. Modern memory and the archive, they wanted to say, have become one and the same. We save even our garbage on the off chance that it might become significant later, creating a new class of objects and events: *the potentially memorable.* The Foucault passage supplied the organizing image they needed, and Ingrid went to work. The entire group would be involved. One after another, they would pile cardboard banker's boxes onto a pyramid that would finally tumble, with the contents of the boxes spilling at the audience's feet. The papers and receipts and candy wrappers, condoms, and champagne corks that littered the floor would then be slowly and reverentially gathered and re-boxed and the pyramid rebuilt. The piece would end with the performers inviting the audience to join them in venerating the monument. Matt's voice-over, which developed the idea of the potentially memorable, seemed to him overly obvious, but Ingrid and Gina assured him it was only because he was so familiar with the work. An audience would need the guidance, they insisted. He was more than a little afraid that some of what he had to say might be misinterpreted by his museum colleagues, who, after all, might be seen to earn their livings on the backs of items and events that were deemed merely potentially memorable.

"I don't think the fabric is working."

Ingrid made this announcement as he was unhooking her bra and it took him a moment to understand that she was referring to the performance.

"If we could have got the felt pieces to cooperate, that would have been great." She and Gina had experimented with the Robert Morris / Penelope Reade idea for weeks. They had auditioned different weights and cuts of felt in hopes of getting them to morph before the audience's eyes, remembering and returning to their former form. Or forgetting their current one (it didn't matter which). When they could get no result that was really telling, they had decided to try a different fabric-based approach. Ingrid had demonstrated it to him with one of her Skogsnarv sheets, first clarifying that in the performance she would probably not be naked.

"Gina will drape me with a length of cloth so that I am completely covered. I'll be standing like Jesus on the cross so the fabric will take on a pretty recognizable form," she had said. "Then she'll turn her back and when she looks again my arms will have drooped. Then again, and I'll be squatting. She'll set me up again and I'll sag again. It's as close as we think we can get to your mother's experiments."

But the fabric was not cooperating, she said. They couldn't make the idea work. Unless it was tightly wrapped around individual body parts, making a mummy of Ingrid, the cloth tended to slip off and reveal the body beneath. They had tried Velcro but there were distracting sounds of tearing when it got stressed, and the soundtrack for the piece (slow breathing) wasn't enough to cover them up.

"I'm sorry, Matt. I really wanted to make something work."

Matt didn't tell her he was relieved. Ingrid and Gina had worked so hard, but he had really never wanted his mother involved in the first place. "Do you have an idea to fill the gap?" he said.

"There's something I've thought about, but I need your help."

Migration

PENELOPE HAS OFTEN wondered whether she would have liked to have led an itinerant life, trying one city and then another, maybe even new countries. Perhaps a life similar to the one she and her mother invented for Jonathan after he deserted. In those early years after the wedding, it was true, she had made some small journeys, purportedly to meet up with Jonathan, but there was never any question where home was. She supposes she inherited this from her mother, at least learned it from her. Once Thora had settled in St. Andrews, she apparently lost any wanderlust she had ever had. Thora was what they might these days call a *thriving invasive species*, with her roots deeper in Charlotte County soil than most of the native sons and daughters. It wasn't the shopfronts that enraptured Thora, Penelope thinks. Those had changed with the winds of the economy and their family situation. And it wasn't the houses. Her mother never really liked Birch Hall, complained it exhaled soul-numbing Loyalist spores every time you opened the front door even long after George Arnold had left.

SHE DOESN'T CLEAN up the dining room until George has been gone almost a week. It isn't that she is afraid he is coming back to add to the mess, not for a while anyway. There are just so many other claims on her time. Penelope, now three, needs her for the hundreds of attentions, tiny and big, that children demand. And there is the business to run. So, she decided the day George left that the mess in the dining room could wait. She and the child never eat in there by themselves, and George's family has made it clear they expect no more invitations.

The Arnolds were against the marriage from the moment George proposed, and their position has not changed in the five years since, though they have perfectly honed their performance of accepting her, and even showing love for the child when she finally came along — all for the benefit of the community. People like them don't make bad marriages, so once it was clear that George was not to be dissuaded, they had undertaken the charade, if not enthusiastically then at least credibly. Thora knows it is too much to expect them to recognize that, in the end, it was she who had made the bad bargain in the marriage.

George was frail, vulnerable, when he returned to St. Andrews at the end of the war. That was part of his attraction, she thinks. He was a project, someone she could make better. Who wouldn't have been damaged by what he had seen — what he had no doubt done too — in the war? The army itself recognized that. They had stopped calling it "shell shock" partway through the conflict but it did not go away. *Neurasthenia* was the new word, and the proliferation of proposed cures confirmed it was a genuine affliction. There were those who championed the use of electric-shock treatments, in a kind of cruel variation on the old hair-of-the-dog remedy. George had thankfully avoided this. Others saw the condition as a kind of nostalgia, which they carefully defined as a dreadful homesickness for one's native soil, for happier times, even for one's own body and mind. George was lucky enough to be sent to that place in Scotland where they espoused talking as the way out. But that same talking cure also ended up as a way back into the war. Apparently relieved of their burdens, many of the officers treated at Craiglockhart had been sent right back into action, with what Thora thinks was the inevitable, and surely foreseeable, result.

She begins picking up the shards of Limoges, shrapnel scattered around the dining room at Birch Hall thousands of miles and half a dozen years from the trenches. He might as well have smashed the whole ridiculous, impractical china service and done her a favour. But his outbursts were never that prolonged, which was a mercy for the sake of the child. She holds a half of a broken saucer against her cheek to cool the patch where she still feels the warmth of a blow a whole week later. She hasn't tried to hide the bruises from his last outburst any more than she ever did when George was still around. Then, she thought they were useful reminders to him of the devastation he had wrought. Now, they are a defence against the Arnold family — irrefutable evidence to be called up if and when they decide to come after her for helping George make the decision to go away. At no time has she felt ashamed of the marks his violence left. They are not her fault. In this, as in dozens of ways, she is very different from her Loyalist in laws.

There is a scar across the mahogany top of the dining table where he dragged the smashed wine bottle. Thora thinks she will be able to treat it with some of the dye she has developed for infusing her wool with the local sandstone colouring. She can rub that in and then French polish over it. The table is the only piece of furniture in the room she has ever cared about. She supposes it is a sentimental weakness, something to do with the way a table, with the memories of shared meals around it, builds a sense of family.

Family was a large part of what she was looking for in marrying George. That had surprised her at the time. It ambushed her one evening not long into what was for him becoming a courtship, and for her, she thought, was still a dalliance. Her experience with men up until then was hardly domestic — not that that experience was very broad. There was Nils (had they ever made love lying down?) and then that corporal during the war. Oddly, she thinks, Morris McCann might be the closest she came to a domestic partnership before George Arnold, but she wisely stopped that one short of sex.

The stopper of the whisky decanter is nowhere to be found. She wonders whether George left for Montréal with it in his trousers pocket. She has seen him dozens of times palm the thing and stuff it in his pocket when he became frustrated by its willful rolling after he'd set it down too quickly on the drinks cart. Surprisingly, there is still an amber inch in the bottom of the decanter. Perhaps he wasn't as drunk as usual for the final episode then. She doesn't like to think about what that might mean.

Persuading him to seek help was a slow, months-long campaign, with no end clearly visible. She had to choose her moments carefully, capitalizing on the short-lived bouts of genuine remorse that usually followed his outbursts by about a day. Even then, she felt she had to come at the matter obliquely. George Arnold had learned well the game of nothing-is-happening-here pioneered by his forebears. But, even more importantly, he was acutely sensitive to any suggestion of mental weakness or native cowardice that might cling to a diagnosis of neurasthenia. Her usual beginning, then, was to ask whether he had heard anything from Dr. Rivers. Early in their acquaintance, George talked fondly of Rivers, though only occasionally did he allow himself to mention Craiglockhart. The person was within limits as a subject; the place was not. Craiglockhart was closed down at the end of the war, its work officially done, but Rivers continued to correspond for a while with some of his patients, and George felt special to be one of those. That feeling of specialness was crucial to Thora's campaign. It was as close as she could hope to bring George to an acknowledgement that there was something not quite right with him. Gradually, she would then bring up a story of someone she had heard of who was getting a similar kind of talk therapy at a facility in Québec. Her hope was that George might feel that being one province away, and in a culture where English was not the only language, would provide the anonymity he seemed to require.

There is a wine stain on the woven runner. Wine or blood — after a week it is difficult to tell. He had cut himself on the broken bottle and refused her help binding it. He might have wiped his hand across the runner in a moment of self-possession, she supposes. Thora doubts the stain will ever come out. The blot looks like a map of Norway though, which makes her smile, not out of nostalgia (she was glad to wipe her feet of the place) but at the way fabric can reveal an insight that words might shy away from. The runner, loosely woven of the bright colours of New Brunswick summer, did not belong in the sober polished-mahogany-and-old-silver dining room of the Arnold family for more reasons than the obvious aesthetic ones. It was a reminder of the differences in background between her and George, of course, though he only knew the parts of her story that she chose to tell. But, more importantly, as a reminder of Thora's handcraft business, it shouted out a reality that George never truly came to terms with, even though he tried to make all the right noises.

When they met, right after the war, Handworks (she still regrets the loss of the old name) was already well established. The Arnolds always held that against her. The only thing worse, apparently, than being a gold digger (an expression Thora resented) was being a single woman of independent means, particularly if those means had been piled up through commerce. She smiles when she thinks of how the word *commerce* could ever pretend to describe what she is doing. Her refusal to abandon the business after the wedding, and then again after Penelope was born, promoted her from stubborn eccentric to outright subversive. The unassuming but by no means innocent woven runner was her revolutionary banner staked in the staid Loyalist dining room. She wonders now whether keeping it there was a petty provocation.

It is never clear what sets George off, except, of course, the liquor; he turns from a pale, shivering, often quite kind soul into a raging stag. When she looks for a deeper cause, she doesn't think it is her independence, or her undeniable peculiarities, or the differences in their backgrounds that drive him to drink. It is something deeply, darkly his own, stoked by the memories from the war. Only with help from professionals can there be any hope of a change. His parents have denied all of this, but she has known it for years, since before the baby. And finally she has persuaded George.

That is not fair. In the end, she persuaded him of nothing. It was an accident that made up his mind. The wave of rage had crested by the time a sleepy Penelope appeared at the dining room door, but the evidence of the storm was everywhere. George was winding the runner around his bleeding hand (so it was blood and not wine); Thora had started to pick up bits of china but then cast them aside. The child stood and stared. Nobody spoke. The next morning, George packed a bag and set off for a small private clinic in the Laurentians.

UNLIKE HER MOTHER, Penelope knows she can love houses as homes. She felt a wrench that Thora would never have experienced when she had to sell Birch Hall. This house, this house where she has been for fifty years — where have they gone? — she sometimes knows is too big for her, impractical. Now they are claiming it is dangerous. That sneaky girl who has Matt wrapped around her ... well, it's not really her finger, is it? What business is it of hers? Even if she is carrying Matt's baby (how can anyone be sure?) that doesn't entitle her to boss around his mother.

She has thought about taking a trip. Packing her things and getting Bernadette to drive her to the train. Is there still a train? She would leave Matt a note suggesting they wait until after she returns to talk over her living arrangements. No, she won't open that door at all, simply say she is going on the Grand Tour and will be in touch when she gets back. But the thought of packing is exhausting, and she'd have to change money, which would mean dealing with the bank — and she can't lay her hands on her passport although she is sure she must have one somewhere. People do.

Things have begun disappearing from the house. Whoever is taking them probably thinks she won't notice. She is prepared to accept that occasionally she cannot immediately recall exactly what day it is (or year), but she is quite sure she knows the location of every item in her own house. Besides, when the pictures go they leave behind a darker-coloured rectangle on the bare wall. Anyone would notice.

It is the same in the shop. She knows every piece of inventory, and which shelf it sits on. She can also give a provenance for the core stock, right back to the sheep's great-grandmother in some cases. Thora was the same. Bernadette is bright but she has not been able to master it, says it must be genetic, which Penelope thinks is a lame excuse. Once, years ago, Bernadette made a comment about how it would be impossible ever to pilfer from the shop since Penelope knew every piece of stock so well. It was supposed to be a joke, but she wondered why Bernadette had felt compelled to make it. For weeks afterward, she had gone through the entire inventory every evening before she closed up. Not that she suspected Bernadette of anything, but the idea had been put in her head.

Knowing the stock on the shelves is a good skill for a business owner, but it would be better to know who has bought what. And that is a problem right now because nobody is buying anything. Thora told her there would be times like this. She herself can remember the dirty thirties and how things were then. Her mother had to move to a system of consignment. The decision was not popular with the craftswomen, of course. They preferred getting their money up front. But, as her mother reasoned, those women were at least growing their own food and catching their own fish. That put them in a better position for survival than a shopkeeper in town. When the bank had refused help — nobody was getting loans — Thora had arranged to barter with O'Neill's: sweaters for groceries. Penelope knew that Mr. O'Neill had no need of the sweaters; he was doing it out of charity and to spare Thora's pride. She didn't know whether he knew that more than half the sweaters were on consignment and therefore not Thora's to dispose of in this way. When the war began and everyone got back on their feet again, O'Neill sold everything back to Thora and she, in turn, bought up all of the consigned goods. So the women got their money in the end.

Penelope doesn't think a barter arrangement would work now. There is no worldwide financial crisis. Just a market slump for handcrafted clothing and knitting supplies. Is it a slump when you can't envision an upward slope again? Having had her sixty-fifth birthday, she supposes she could declare herself retired, maybe try to sell the business, though she doubts there would be a buyer. It is not as though the shop has ever been her main source of support. She thinks about Thora's money, the Arnold money. It has kept her until now. And Matt is completely independent. Bernadette would easily find another job in another shop.

But there is her mother's memory to consider. Selling the business, or simply closing it down, would mark an end to what Thora created and built. Handworks is her monument, even more than twenty years after her death. The business has lasted nearly three-quarters of a century. That may be more than Thora would have said she ever planned for, but Penelope knows she would be disappointed nevertheless if the doors closed now.

There is a kind of symmetry about the timing, though, that is inescapable, even aesthetically appealing. When that land developer got the army in last week to blow up what was left of the sardine plant, Penelope was reminded of her mother's beginnings in St. Andrews. That early chapter in her life was something Thora seldom spoke about and only to Penelope and only just before the end. She was evasive when others brought it up. As the plant was reduced to a pile of concrete and reinforcing bars, Penelope could almost imagine Thora's ghost breathing a sigh of relief. Like her work there was finished.

The bank will be happy if she decides to close. Her accountant less so. Something about the losses at the shop helping offset her income from the family investments. Bernadette has explained it to her every April. She wonders now whether that is because Bernadette has not wanted her to abandon the failing business and leave her jobless. In the end, she must do what is best for herself.

Someone seems to have anticipated her decision and made a start on her workroom. The stock has been shuffled around.

It can't be Bernadette. She never comes into the workroom. Penelope doesn't remember moving things herself, although she has been known to sleep-organize. Once, she rearranged all of the living room furniture without waking up. But this is the opposite of organizing. This is chaos, an assault on her system. Who would want to buy a business in such disarray? Perhaps it is a message to her from the universe to just let the bank take it all.

"Mamma, are you ready?" Matt has his parka on, but where are they going?

"I was just looking for ... I was just looking for ..." But it is no good. It has gone out of her head what she was looking for. She wishes people wouldn't just barge in and interrupt her.

"Maybe we can look later," Matt says in that voice people use. He really means *maybe we can look never* because he thinks she will forget. Or they won't be back here. That's it, actually. Something about moving.

He has warmed up the car, an extravagance she has never allowed herself. Even her seat should be nice and warm, he assures her.

"You said this place was in walking distance."

"Yes, but the ice."

"Ice? What month is it?"

"January."

"Oh God." She lets him fasten her seat belt. Anyone who doesn't know what month it is maybe deserves to be infantilized, she thinks.

They drive past the hotel and the gardens and turn left. Penelope feels a knife in her bowels. It should be in her back. *The Lodge or the Bay, and I choose the Bay*. It is too late, though, now.

She waits for him to come around to open her door, hopes he will think it a quirky nod to the manners of a bygone era and not a bid for ten extra seconds of freedom. The wind can take the blame for the tear she can feel forming. For a second the car won't let her go. *Loyal servant, bless it.* Then Matt leans over and releases the seat belt. *Oh.*

There is a uniformed block at the door, as wide as she is tall, black pants and a polyester top in swirls of colour that should never be seen together. The pants say she can mourn with them that mourn, and the shirt that she can rejoice with them that rejoice. *Which will it be with you*, she seems to be asking. With her mouth, though, she is saying "Welcome, Mrs. Reade." *Abandon all hope.*

Matt and the block — she has said her name but Penelope has not taken it in — steer her through the gauntlet of wheelchairs just inside the door (one crone tries to pat Matt's bum) and down a corridor where the tang of bleach has struggled with and lost to the much more potent reek of pee and despair. They pause at a closed door. Matt points to the glass case outside it: *the two Hummel figures that have been missing from the mantel for a week.*

"We'll have your nameplate next week," chirps the block as if she is offering an OBE. "There was a problem with the spelling." Penelope remembers Jonathan's joke about those who can't read omitting the final *e*. Something like that. It is alarming how many of Jonathan's jokes she can recall. She doesn't remember him as funny. Most of the jokes support that.

Matt is clearly very excited about opening the door. She nods.

"We encourage the families to get everything ready," the block is saying. "We want you to feel at home right away."

Penelope is glad to see the missing mahogany lady's chair and the walnut library table and the set of Bartlett prints, but these things do not make this cell seem like home.

"We don't often have a single room for our new residents, but your son was very persuasive, and considering your place in this community and all that you and your mother did for the women of the county, well, we were able to make an exception."

She wonders how much Matt has had to pay. Or was it sleeping with that pregnant girl? Almost certainly, somebody died at the right moment for Penelope. She supposes she should be grateful for small mercies. Very small mercies.

Matt takes her coat, afraid perhaps that she might bolt. "It's a lot to take in, Mamma, I know." She cannot tell whether he is inviting her to congratulate him on the decorating details or acknowledging the enormity of what he has done to her. Then she realizes it doesn't have to be one without the other. Guilt works in interesting ways.

The block mutters something and leaves them alone but she does not shut the door. Penelope hopes that is not a rule. She can sense two old biddies with walkers just around the door jamb.

Matt continues to look at her expectantly. "It's a nice room, isn't it, Mamma? Lots of light."

She wonders how he can tell that in March. "We'll see what your grandmother thinks. You're staying for supper, aren't you? I'm not sure what I have, but there's always something in the fridge."

Conversable

MATT PARKED THE Volvo on Water Street. He wasn't ready to go back to the house, couldn't quite imagine it without his mother in it. Even harder to imagine her in the Lodge. She would be sitting in the dining room now in front of a white-bread bologna sandwich and a bowl of tomato soup. If she was lucky, the wizened face across the table from her would be conversable. He couldn't remember hearing many of them speak. Maybe they were shy in front of visitors, suspicious lest their words be used against them.

The sandwich board outside the Smoked Mackerel promised a lunch special easily confused with the fare at the Lodge, but he went in anyway. It wasn't the food that he was interested in.

He thought Amanda blushed when she saw him. She definitely smiled. He had forgotten about the dimples, more pronounced on the left than the right cheek. She was taking an order and had to ask the customer to repeat it. Matt liked that he was having an effect. Unless she was just not very good at her job. She bobbed her head in the direction of a booth in the back of the restaurant. When she came over a few minutes later, she announced she was on a break and could join him, if he didn't mind.

"Is it okay? They don't mind?"

"Who? Candace? We're not that busy. She'll gladly scoop up the extra tips."

"The management." He remembered tales of Amanda being reamed out as a teenager for even saying two words to her friends when they came in to eat where she was working.

"Carolyn didn't tell you."

"What?"

"I'm the management. This is my place."

He flipped frantically through his memories of his last visit to the Smoked Mackerel, and of their lunch at the hotel. Had he said anything really stupid or offensive? Why hadn't Bernadette told him? "Oh." It was the best he could do.

"You didn't think I was really still just doing my old summer job, only year-round? How sad would that be?"

There was no right answer to that. "It must be a lot of work."

"The summers are. The winters are a lot of fretting about whether anyone will come in. And here you are. Twice in a week. Don't have the halibut cheeks again. Or the special. Mushroom soup and ham and cheese, like school lunch or something, but lots of people actually like it. The lobster roll is pretty good."

Matt couldn't let the invitation to probe about the lobsterman go again. "So, the restaurant must take up all your time. Do you have ... do you have ...?"

"What? A home life? Is that what you're afraid to ask? My domestic arrangements?"

"I guess. Yes."

"I live by myself. Upstairs here, in fact. I've been seeing a lobsterman. But Carolyn will have told you that. Jim. She doesn't like him."

"She doesn't have to." It seemed like the right thing to say, the gallant thing.

"She's got pretty good instincts about people actually."

"Can we have a drink? Is that okay? Can you have a drink?"

"I can have a whole bottle if I want. And I can go and get it from behind the bar. What did you have in mind?"

"Bourbon?"

"Ah. This must have been the day. Your mother?"

"Yup."

"I'll be right back." She brushed her hand lightly on his shoulder as she passed.

He felt a jolt of electricity, willed it away, unsure whether the infidelity would technically be to Jennifer or to Ingrid. A lobsterman was probably quite strong, too, possessive, able to swing his fists. *L'Air du Temps* hung in the air just below the guilt and the fear. He made a show of scrutinizing the menu.

"They need to come up with better names for bourbon," she said as she plunked two glasses on the table. "Almost all of them sound like they come from a hillbilly still."

"You didn't really need to bring the whole bottle." It was Knob Creek. Small batch. He decided he would have to reassess the restaurant.

"I've always wanted to do this. You know. The padrone and the customer sitting at a table in the back with a bottle between them chewing over old times. Like in the movies. Who better to do something like that with than your first real love? There should be a piano player though."

He decided to leave the first love comment alone and focus on the musical one instead. "You have live music here, don't you?"

"At night. Late. On the weekends. You should come." She blushed (it was not the exit sign). "If you like that kind of thing." She poured them each a generous inch. "I got drunk every night for three weeks when I had to put my mum in the Lodge."

"It didn't help, right?"

"Oh no, it did. It really did. Just not during the day. I really wasn't ready for the full-on descent."

Matt remembered that she had had the best head for liquor of any woman he had known. Any he had slept with at any rate. Male friends used to take him aside and ask whether he was resentful. They thought it must be annoying to share a bottle of wine or a case of beer right down the middle. Annoying and expensive. Their key criteria were their partner's tolerance for alcohol consumption and her willingness to round the bases — low tolerance and high willingness being the desired combination. Amanda was an outlier. He loved that about her.

"Your mother will be all right, you know. Some of the time she will be miserable. And some of the time she won't really know where she is. That's one of the mercies, I tell myself. And she won't remember the times she was miserable when she isn't."

"It felt like dropping her off at boarding school or something."

"You hated boarding school."

"Exactly."

"How do you think she felt when she sent you there?"

"She thought she was doing it for my own good."

"Bingo. She'll understand. Somewhere deep down."

"It's just —"

"When I left Carolyn's father, I moved to Florida. Did you know?"

"I think I heard."

"I didn't take Carolyn."

"How old —"

"Fifteen. It was better for her to finish school here. With her friends. And I wasn't ... well, I wasn't in the best shape to take care of her."

"I'm sure it was the right thing." He wanted to make it clear he got the message, so they could move on. "Sometimes you have to do what doesn't feel right because it actually is right."

"She was my daughter. Do you know what that is — ?" She stopped herself. Matt suspected she had remembered that he didn't have any children. No doubt people in town talked about things like that. "She was fifteen. A girl."

"I am sure she was very capable."

"Inexperienced."

"But she could handle herself."

"A virgin, I think."

"She seems very capable now."

"She was the grown-up of the three of us."

"But you still felt guilty. She was her own person by then. Nearly as old as we were when we started seeing one another."

"She was way more mature."

"So, there you go." He reached for the bottle, splashed an inch into her glass before adding to his own.

"You were always a good listener, Matt."

"Because I never really had anything to say."

"And a good deflector. Carolyn asked the other day how come we didn't end up together, you and I."

"And you told her what?" He thought he was strong enough to hear again her speech about seeing other people.

"I told her it was because you were a good listener. And a deflector."

"You wanted to see other people. You said —"

"That seemed kinder at the time."

Kinder than telling him he was boring, he supposed, kinder than saying she suspected she would never get to know him, the real him. If there were one.

"Who knows what I was thinking? It was a long time ago. I can remember a lot of it, of course. If I set my mind to it. Though I sometimes wonder how reliable that is. But only some of the detail comes back. Do you find that? Like that motel in Robbinston. I've forgotten its name again." She wasn't meaning to be hurtful. He didn't think she was. "The one we went to, to, you know, pop your cherry."

"*My* —?"

"Oh sweetie. You didn't seriously think that *I* ...?"

Hadn't he?

"You got so drunk on gin as soon as we checked in."

Had he?

"And then you puked half the night. I felt so bad for you. All that hard-earned money for the room and we didn't even do anything."

Matt thought he might throw up now.

"Sorry. Look at you. I didn't mean to get talking about all of this. I shouldn't drink during the day. Do you notice that? That you get drunk a lot faster before five than after? Maybe we should get some food." She added quickly, "On the house."

Matt was afraid the lobster roll would stick in his throat but he was too shaken to object. Amanda took the Knob Creek back to the bar when she went to put in the food order. He wished he'd asked for a Guinness in the first place. He wished he'd just gone back to his mother's empty house. More than either, he wished he hadn't taken that bottle of gin with them to Robbinston

Ship of Fool

PENELOPE IS GLAD to be one of the few mobile and continent inmates in her new circle of hell. The attentions of the attendants — she will not call them *caregivers* — are consumed by those in wheelchairs who must be lifted with mechanical devices into and out of bed, and by those who no longer have control over their own bladders and bowels. She is relatively at liberty to roam the halls, although the locked front door is a reminder of the illusory nature of this freedom. And she is among the last to be readied for bed in the evening. They have insisted that she not do this for herself. It is, they have said, part of their duty of care or something. She should remember exactly; they have repeated it several times this afternoon, as if she is an idiot or struggles with English.

She thinks there can be no harm in laying out her things for the night. Matt offered to help her unpack this morning, but she sent him packing. The waves of guilt coming off him were unbearable. It was as if he were the injured party. Now, confronted with the old black suitcase on the bed and the grey metal armoire in the corner of the room, she wishes she had accepted his offer. There are so many ways in which things could be arranged. She has no idea which would be the best or where to start. Colours quickly present problems as there are not enough shelves or drawers to segregate them, and all her underthings are white and take up more than one drawer. Texture proves equally to be a dead end. Halfway through an attempt to organize by function, she gives up, wondering whether the garment she holds in her hands is even hers. She can't begin to imagine its purpose.

The room looks as though it has been ransacked but there is nothing to be done. She sits on a pile of satin-feeling things and clutches the grotesque handbag she must have tucked in at the bottom of the suitcase.

IT IS REMARKABLE how little anyone seems to care about the *Molly McCann*. For the first few days on board, she refrained from lighting the stove, afraid the wisps of smoke would betray her presence. She stayed below during daylight hours, emerging on deck only at sunset to empty the bucket she had pressed into service as a toilet. Whenever the wind shifted and the boat adjusted, she was afraid someone had boarded her and was taking control. She shivered for hours below decks, dreading the moment of discovery. But by early December she has become convinced that everyone has forgotten about Morris McCann's yacht, moored in plain sight in Chamcook Harbour. She lights the stove and sits up on deck sometimes in the watery midday sun. There is no sign of life at the factory. Occasionally, she will catch a glimpse of the barn workers on Ministers Island, but if they are surprised by the presence of a lone female figure on a boat, they do not show it. They probably have become as incurious as the dairy cattle they tend.

McCann saw to it that she is well provisioned. He rowed across sack after sack of the company's cans in the dinghy under cover of night. Also, bags of onions, which he must have actually purchased. She is to eat one a day even after they begin to feel rotten, he said. Scurvy is a threat, he seemed to think. Water will soon be a problem as the barrel is nearly half down already.

She has barely touched the rum. McCann brought that out on his last trip, the night before he was to catch the train to Montréal to get on his boat to Norway. He poured them both a glass and proposed a toast: to survival, at whatever the cost.

"I'm not very used to spirits," she said as she put her glass to one side after taking the tiniest sip, hoping he would not contradict her, remind her of what he knew about the night after Nils disappeared.

"But you are a survivor. What will you do with your little nest egg?"

She didn't like the way he constantly brought up the money. She was ashamed enough on her own of how she had earned it without being reminded every time they met. People like him, she supposed, were able to cross things out and move on. Nils would have been the same. *Once a thing is done it is done*, he would say, *no amount of worrying about it can undo it*. "I will start a business."

"I know one you could get pretty cheaply." He gestured toward the shore. The man really had no remorse.

"A smokeless factory, mine will be." She was proud of the phrase, had hammered it out over the last few weeks. "Making beautiful things that are also useful."

If he had not laughed, she thinks now, she would not have weakened and reached for the glass of rum. She might easily have been drinking molasses, except for the burn in her throat, the fire behind the eyes. He took a long draught from his glass and poured some more, never once taking his eyes off her.

"To beautiful things, and their beautiful makers," he said after a minute.

She knew she should blush prettily, maybe tilt her glass toward him without drinking, look down into her lap. She knew all of the next steps too. He was a good-looking man, Morris McCann, no matter how rotten his insides. She suspected he might be a good lover. Finding that out for certain would be a natural act of gratitude for all he was doing for her: providing his boat to help her disappear, making sure she had food and water. It would also, she knew, give her another hold over him. He was a married man, with children, and one of the bosses who should never consort with the workers. The scandal of a sexual liaison with someone like her would rival the one that was sure to erupt once his financial manipulations were discovered. He would pay as dearly to cover up the sex as he had the embezzlement. But she couldn't do it. "Time for you to row back across, I think," she said.

He looked almost grateful. She felt sorry for him then, this spider who was also a moth that could not resist the flame. "Don't forget to eat the onions," he said as he slid over the side of the boat and dropped into the dinghy. She thought it was one of the oddest endings to a near seduction that anyone could have imagined. Just as he was about to cast off, she realized she would have to row him over. She would need the dinghy. It wouldn't do to be stranded, a prisoner.

She pours half an inch of rum now and looks around the yacht's saloon at her work. It has been a busy two months. Every available surface is covered with drawings. Skeins of wool hang in the companionway. A map of Charlotte County is spread out in the galley, with arrows and circles marked in India ink.

She has drawn from memory and sketched from the deck of the *Molly McCann*: scenes pared back to line, form, colour, texture, ornament, and then recreated on sheets of the twenty-pound bond paper she liberated from the office at the sardine plant. Some she has tinted with watercolours, while with others she has relied on the strokes of her pencil to suggest the light and to hint at the colours. Drawn over most of them there is a fine grid of lines that will help the embroiderer or hooker transmit the design to cloth. For the rugs, she has carefully counted the strands on four old feed bags to get an idea of a standard grid. The decorated felt handbags she has in mind will be trickier, but the principle, she knows, is sound.

The wool she has gathered is far too dull. She has festooned it around as a goad rather than an inspiration. She can hardly wait to begin trying out her ideas for dyes. The colours will be drawn from the colours of spring and summer and fall, not the dull greys of December and January. Sometimes, she sits up on the deck and squints her eyes, trying to conjure the greens of the hardwood leaves and pinks of summer sunsets. The reds of the cliffs and the mud, and the blues of the sky and the water are easy on a sunny day; they don't change much from one season to the next.

The map of the county, like the wool, is more conceptual at this stage. She has marked it up at random. Once the winter is over, when she emerges from her water-borne chrysalis as a complete newcomer to the area, she will hire a horse and driver and cover the roads recruiting craftswomen. Each one will earn a mark on the map until she has workers in every corner. Then she will rent a shopfront in the town — the real town, not the sardine town — and start her new life.

"HELLO, PENELOPE."

She cringes. Strangers don't call her that. *Mrs. Reade.*

"Or Penny, is it?"

Jesus. Never. Who is this woman?

"It's time to get you ready for bed, okay, dear?"

Not dear, either.

"Things are a bit all over the place, aren't they? Were you looking for something?"

Freedom, she wants to say.

"My, that's an interesting bag you've got there. Is that a picture of something?"

"A boat. A boat I lived on before the war."

"My grandfather was evacuated at Dunkirk. You know, like in the movie."

"No. Before the other war. The first war."

The young woman nods and smiles and sets about looking for nightgown and toothbrush.

Rabbit Holes

THE CALL FROM Jennifer woke Matt from a sound sleep. It was midnight. She always forgot about the hour's time difference.

To his mumbled account of recent events, she responded, "You did? She has? It's done?" She sounded as though she were actually concerned.

"When 'tis done, then 'twere well it were done quickly."

"What?"

He decided the Lady Macbeth reference was a little harsh. "Nothing."

"So you can come back." If the prospect afforded her any relief, she hid it well.

"Soon, I think."

"How soon?"

He wondered why she wanted to know. Was there someone who would need to move out of her bed? "There are a few things."

"Of course. The research."

"And the house. And I need to make sure she's settled, happy — as happy as she can be."

"It's not as though there is an alternative if she isn't."

"Still."

"Right. So another week? Two?"

"I'll have a better idea in a few days."

"Can't somebody help you with the house? There must be services like there are here. People who come in and help you clear out. They sell what they can and give the rest away. Or chuck it. You don't have to do anything but make a few decisions."

"It's not Toronto."

"Well, just somebody your mother knows, then. Her cleaning lady."

Matt was too tired to try to explain to Jennifer about his mother's domestic arrangements. "Sure. I'll ... ask around." He didn't mention he'd already had a surprise offer of help. "How are classes going?" He knew it was the surefire way to distract Jennifer. Bracing himself for a twenty-minute diatribe, he slid his back down the hallway wall until he was sitting on the chilly floorboards.

Amanda had phoned the house the morning after their awkward drunken lunch at the Smoked Mackerel. If there had been caller ID on the land line he probably would not have picked up. When he heard her voice he thought she was maybe calling to apologize, but she didn't mention lunch. Carolyn had apparently thought that Matt might need some help, some support, she said, going through his mother's house. She'd suggested that Amanda should call. It was either the clumsiest effort at matchmaking or genuine professional concern, but Matt decided he could, in fact, use some company as he waded through the contents of the house.

When Amanda arrived the next afternoon, straight from the restaurant, she was still in carpenter pants and T-shirt. "Sorry, I look a mess. Good for pitching in and working, though, right? Actually, I could use a coffee before we start. Is that okay?"

She followed him to the kitchen. "Wow."

"What?"

"This place."

"Oh. Right. Was your mother's house —"

"Also stuffed with things, but she had moved around a bit, so things got rearranged. And her things weren't ever as interesting."

As they took their coffee through to the living room, he prayed she would not reminisce about the late evenings when they had fumbled on the carpet in front of the fireplace, giggling and hushing one another so they wouldn't wake Penelope.

"We should make a plan," she said. "Tackle it room by room."

"I don't want you to feel —"

"The restaurant's not very busy. I can give you a few afternoons a week."

He wondered for a second whether this was a negotiation, whether he was supposed to suggest an hourly rate.

"Nobody should have to do this stuff alone, Matt. I'd like to do it for you, for ..."

He was afraid she was about to say "old times."

"For your mother." She looked into her coffee cup. "And it will be fun to have a little time. That's all."

They decided to continue what Matt had begun in the workroom.

"You say you've *started* on this?" She laughed when he opened the door.

"The problem is, you go down rabbit holes. I'll pick something up and start looking at it, thinking about it, and suddenly half an hour's gone."

"That's what you need me for. Somebody completely disinterested."

Matt decided not to take that the wrong way. He also doubted it was true, or that it would be true once they got going.

"Some of this stuff looks really old. I mean older-than-your-mother old."

"She kept everything of my grandmother's."

"Who started the business."

"Right. My mother only took it over after the war. In '46, I think. Not long after she was married, anyway."

"So, when did your grandmother start it? After she was married?"

"You'd think so, wouldn't you? After the first war. Grandfather Arnold would have been the one with all the money. That's what you'd think. But she had the business before she had him."

"He must have been pretty progressive, you know, to marry a woman who had her own business. He must have seen how good she was at it."

"Maybe he was proud of her. Or maybe he just liked having her out of the house. I've always wondered about that. But then he left anyway, so it can't have been that."

"He left her?"

"He was what they called neurasthenic, shell-shocked. His life wasn't great. He was miserable."

"PTSD before PTSD."

"I guess so."

"Oh look. She saved his ... his cap badge, it must be?" Amanda cupped in her palm a bronze-coloured maple leaf. There was a large number 4 in its middle. At the top of the leaf was a crown with the word "Canada" beneath it, and around the perimeter: "Overseas Pioneer Battalion." Behind the number 4, a rifle and a pick were crossed. He had to get quite close to read all the lettering.

"Maybe."

"Maybe?"

"I'm not sure about the number four. I thought Grandfather Arnold was with a different numbered troop."

"Take it to your mother when you visit. Trust me, you'll want things to talk about. She'll know all about it, and that will make you both feel better."

"Where was the badge exactly?"

"No wonder you get stuck down rabbit holes. Does it matter? In this bag."

She handed it across to Matt. The decoration on it was another aberration from his grandmother's standard Charlotte County scenes. The background was identifiable, with Deer Island in the distance across the bay, but the figures in the foreground were from another world altogether. It took him a minute to decode. A nearly naked female figure was chained to a rock, with a saw-toothed sea monster in the offing. Between the two, and above, a male figure was swooping in on a horse — to the rescue, Matt supposed, though there was something more than a little sinister about the severed head the deliverer swung in one hand. Perseus and Andromeda. On Passamaquoddy Bay. "Let's put it back for now."

"Matt. You'll never get through this."

"Just for now. Just while I try to work something out. Let's tackle some of these boxes."

They worked until the light faded, pausing over the odd recipe for blueberry dye or notes for mixing a particular pottery glaze, sometimes chatting but mostly not — each, Matt thought, contentedly aware of the other's animal presence in the room. He was anyway.

"Oh shit. Is that the time? I've got to get to the Mackerel. Sorry, Matt. I'll come round again tomorrow. Same time?" She gave him a peck on the cheek. Before he could think what that meant, she was gone.

Supper was a chicken breast he had found in the freezer, furry and forlorn. He braised it in white wine and made a mustard-caper sauce to drown out any lingering traces of where it had been and for who knows how long. There were roast potatoes left over from Penelope's Last Supper the night before last, and frozen peas. The peas might have been pressed into service, more than once, as a cold pack for pain in shoulder or hip, but he ate them anyway. *Everything has a history*, he told himself, *even the bottle of bourbon he had found tucked in the back of the sideboard*, though with the bourbon he couldn't imagine what that history might be.

After finishing the dishes, and armed with a fresh dose of whisky and a zip-lock freezer bag, he returned to the workroom. A faint trace of Amanda's perfume lingered. He fought the distraction and focused on finding that sheaf of papers, the ones he had liberated from the Ship of Fool bag. The bag was nowhere to be found. He remembered having it in the kitchen but it was not there now. His mother must have returned it to the workroom, he thought, but, if she had, he couldn't see where.

He closed his eyes, tried to reconstruct where he had originally found the bag. It was the northwest corner, he thought. So he stood there and called up the sensations of the dusty tickle in his nostrils and the catch in his throat when he had taken the papers out of the bag and set them aside a few days before. He located them almost right away then.

What had been, in memory, only a nondescript pile of papers quickly resolved itself into several distinct subcategories as he sat on the floor and sorted through them. There were pages from some kind of ledger, filled out in a beautiful copperplate hand. Interleaved with these were what looked like diary entries in the same careful hand, the dates entered in capital letters at the tops of pages. A quick rifle through indicated they were all from the fall and winter of 1913–14. His breath caught when he unfolded a series of delicate sketches of harbour scenes. Even with the fine grid of pencilled lines that overlaid each one, you could tell the artist had been really gifted.

On the floor beside him, he found two items that he supposed had fallen from the stack of papers when he first took them out. The first was what must be a passbook of the kind they used to use for banks. He remembered the printed ones, of course, but this was entirely in hand entries. "The Bank of Nova Scotia." "Miss Thora Halvstad." The dates matched those of the diary pages. The autumn pages showed a series of what were probably quite substantial deposits in those days. There was no activity through the winter, and then in the spring several withdrawals before a more balanced rhythm of back-and-forth was established.

Whether it was the dust or the drink, Matt suddenly felt too tired to continue. He tucked the papers carefully into the zip-lock bag and took himself to bed. When Jennifer called at midnight, he said nothing about the documents he had discovered. Neither did he mention that Amanda was already helping him sift through the contents of the house.

Cap Badge

MATT TOLD BERNADETTE he was inviting her to go to the Lodge with him to cheer Penelope up, but it was really because he couldn't face visiting alone. She likely knew that but said she had been meaning to go anyway and would be happy to join him. A ride up the hill would be very welcome. The ice was quite tricky. She didn't want to break a hip and end up in ... well, he knew what she meant.

Bernadette had always been a slightly eccentric dresser, but Matt was stunned when he pulled up in front of her apartment. She was wearing one of the Handworks hallmark tweed coats with self-scarf. A bright pink enamelled brooch of a kind Penelope had carried in the shop for only a year or two was pinned to the spruce-green coat. On her head, she had perched a Fair Isle toque (blue), and below the coat he could see the matching socks peeking out over her mukluks. Either she had lost all of her winter clothes and had to resort to discontinued stock squirrelled away before the store closed, or it was a nutty but sweet tribute to Penelope. He decided not to comment.

"I can drive, if you like," she chirped when he got out to help her into the car.

"It's a bit icy around that side of the car. Safer here," he said, helping her over a snowbank that was easily as dangerous to negotiate as the ice on the road. "Maybe on the way back." He would think of another excuse in the parking lot at the Lodge to cover the return trip.

"How are things going in the house? I hear you have a little help."

Matt supposed she had picked this information up in the coffee shop or the post office. It was a small town. People talked. "Amanda's daughter is Mamma's social worker. She suggested it. And Amanda worked in the shop one winter."

"I never understood why the boss did that. We sure didn't need the extra help."

"Well, I do now." He felt ridiculous defending himself like this.

"I could have come over."

So that was it. "Of course. I'm sorry. I didn't want to bother you. And ..."

"Spit it out."

"Actually, I thought it would be way too hard, going through it all with you. Hard for me and hard for you. You know."

"I'd just pitch the whole lot."

"You know you damn well wouldn't."

"No. I wouldn't. What's the rush to get it all cleared out? You're not thinking of selling?"

"No rush. And no, I'm not. Not now anyway. But you've seen it. It's a disaster area."

"Remind me not to invite you into my humble abode."

"I need to go through things. Not only to tidy up. I need things to pass through my hands. I need to hold them, think about them."

"You must be driving that Williams girl crazy."

"Gray is her married name."

"She left him years ago. She's been seeing a lobsterman. You know that, right?"

He was touched that she so clearly still wanted to protect him. "Jim. Right."

"He's a bigger ass than that Gray fellow. Don't they ever clear this parking lot?"

The usual honour guard greeted them at the door. Bernadette no doubt knew most of them but she ploughed straight by. He had to hurry to keep up. "Those ones would have you talking there all day," she puffed once they were around the corner. He doubted that but nodded. "Keep moving, that's what you have to do in a place like this. Otherwise they'll nail you down."

He wasn't sure who *they* were, assumed she meant the people who ran the Lodge. "It's not like anybody's held here against their will." They both laughed.

Penelope was sitting in front of the window in her room, looking out at the parking lot. She must have seen them arrive, Matt thought.

"Matt! Am I ever glad to see you. And Bernadette. Oh dear. Is something wrong? The shop?"

"Everything's fine, boss. We just wanted a visit." Bernadette sat on the remaining chair, leaving Matt the bed.

"How long have I been here?"

"Just a few days, Mamma."

"It feels like longer."

"I know." He hoped it sounded sympathetic and not presumptuous. Of course, he couldn't know how long it must have seemed to her.

"Aren't you boiling in that coat?" she asked Bernadette. "It came out quite well, though, didn't it?"

"It's January, boss. Nearly February. I need my woollies."

"It's a remarkable coat," Matt said. Not a lie.

"Didn't I come here in the summer?"

"No, really, just a few days ago."

"They try to do everything for me. I suppose that's very nice. It's just not ..."

"No, it's not home. I know." He still really couldn't know. He wondered then about the wisdom of bringing things from her house to show her. Amanda had said it would help conversation but now he thought it might only upset Penelope. He should try to find Amanda's mother, he supposed, one day when he came to visit, knowing, however, that he probably wouldn't.

"Your things look good here, boss. And I like the pictures."

"Yes. I can't think who that portrait is of. It must have been here when I came."

He was about to tell her that the things were all here when she arrived, that he had arranged the furniture and hung the pictures before moving her in, didn't she remember? Instead, he said, "The young woman in the portrait is very beautiful." And Bernadette clucked her agreement. Matt got up off the bed to straighten the picture. As soon as he stood, the cap badge fell out of his pocket.

"What's that?"

"Oh, just something I found." It was too late to put it back in his pocket. "Do you recognize it?" He handed it to his mother.

"Hmmm."

Bernadette got up and perched on the arm of Penelope's chair. "It's a cap badge, isn't it? Old."

"Would it have been Grandfather Arnold's?" he asked his mother.

"He was Twenty-Sixth Battalion. Infantry. This is the Fourth Pioneers." She said it right away as if she were telling him something as obvious as the colour of the sky, or the time of year. "Pioneers were engineering units. Don't you see the pick there, crossed with the rifle? They dug holes and built bridges and that kind of thing. Your grandfather would never have wanted to do any of that."

"It was with some of Gran's things."

"Was it? I suppose it was. The Fourth Pioneers were stationed here, briefly, during the war. The first war, about halfway through. One summer. Your gran told me about it. A little."

"Before she was married to Grandfather Arnold then."

"Oh yes. They didn't marry until 1919."

"But she already had the business by halfway through the war, right?"

"Who told you that?" Penelope's voice was like a knife.

"You did. She did. It's part of the story, isn't it? Gran's heroic story of self-determination that you'd always tell me?"

"She started the business after the sardine plant went tits ... after it closed."

"Right. That would make sense of this, then." He produced the plastic bag of papers from the inside pocket of his parka and extracted the bank passbook.

"Don't let her know you've got that, Matt. She's very private about money." Penelope seemed genuinely afraid.

"She's okay with it, Mamma." He leafed through the pages, though he already knew them by heart. "She put quite a lot of money into the bank during the fall of 1913. I wonder where she got that kind of money."

"I wouldn't know anything about that. It was all a long time before I was born."

"Your mother was a great lady, boss. A real pioneer herself."

"You'll stay for dinner, won't you? I don't know what there is."

Matt stuffed the bag of papers back into his coat. He could try again another day. Or leave it alone.

Bernadette suggested a walk around the halls. "Good to keep moving, boss," she said. She didn't add: *so they don't nail you down.*

Matt offered to fetch tea while they walked. There was a little kitchen that family members were allowed to use. He couldn't face the promenade among the bent bodies and blank faces.

He knew there was a set of four mugs that he had bought for Penelope to use for visitors, but they were nowhere in sight in her room. They weren't the kind you would leave out on display and he couldn't find them in the metal armoire. Penelope wouldn't know where they were. They hadn't come from the house so it was unlikely she would even recognize them if she saw them. He would have to ask one of the caregivers. In the meantime, they could manage with Styrofoam. The tea provided at the Lodge was pretty bad anyway.

On his way to the kitchen, he caught a glimpse of Bernadette and his mother talking to the woman who used to run the movie theatre. Matt couldn't think of her name, which was annoying. He wondered whether she had a new roommate yet.

"You see, boss, there's lots of your old cronies here to visit with," Bernadette said as they sipped their tea from the Styrofoam five minutes later.

Matt had never thought of his mother as someone with cronies, was pretty sure she didn't see herself that way. So he was not surprised when Penelope merely snorted and pretended to be intent on her tea. There were cookies, too, that Bernadette had produced from the pocket of her outlandish coat. Penelope reached for two and stuffed them both in her mouth at once in case it was not already clear that she had no further interest in talking.

After he had kissed Penelope goodbye, Matt spotted the Ship of Fool bag and scooped it up as he left the room. He thought his mother's eyes were closed.

Forgotten Evidence

AMANDA WAS EARLY. She let herself in. Locked doors in St. Andrews were only for come from aways and, even after decades in Toronto, Matt was not that. He was in the kitchen. His plan had been to surprise her with lunch served up in the dining room, so the pleasure of seeing her was diluted a little by her premature arrival.

"Something smells good."

"You smell good." It was a joke they used to share. He was afraid he shouldn't have made it. "Sorry. Too creepy?"

"Just the right amount of creepy."

"You haven't eaten, have you?" He realized, too late, he thought, that there was another way the surprise could fail.

"I'm starving. It used to be that smelling food all day, slinging it to other people, and busing their smeared dishes, ruined my appetite. Now it makes me ravenous."

"It's just soup and bread and cheese." He hoped she would ask for details so he could elaborate on the pains he had taken to produce what sounded misleadingly like a very simple lunch. Admittedly, everything for the soup was somewhere in his mother's kitchen. The package of split peas came from the back of the pantry. The lettering had worn off the plastic but he was sure split peas couldn't go bad. The ham bone in the freezer had no date on it (he had tried in vain years ago to persuade Penelope to start labelling things) but it looked perfectly fine once the frost was knocked off. There was a jar of yeast in the refrigerator but it had expired three years earlier, so the baguettes benefitted from a fresh batch he had located with some difficulty at the back of a shelf in the grocery store. For the cheese, he had broken a long streak of fearfully avoiding what he still thought of as the Hippie Deli. The young woman behind the counter had been quite helpful in recommending a local brie. The experience had felt like a normal retail transaction in the end. He hoped Amanda would ask about the cheese so he could offer it up as a demonstration of his efforts to produce a lunch of just soup and bread and cheese.

"There's something about the smell of fresh bread. I can't believe you make your own bread, Matt."

Matt wouldn't have believed it either. Jennifer certainly wouldn't have, although she also probably would not have noticed. "It's something about being in this house." He hadn't known that was it until he said it out loud. "You want to make things." He doubted the house's influence was as simple as that. After stirring the soup, which was starting to stick to the bottom of the pot, he unwrapped the cheese and put it on a chipped plate that reminded him of his grandmother.

"You went into the Larder! Is that their goat brie? Wow."

So she did remember his phobia. "I think so."

"Very brave. I've forgotten why you never wanted to go in there."

"Me too," he admitted.

He had put wine glasses out: squat Provençal tumblers stamped with dragonflies. He hoped they said that wine with lunch didn't have to mean anything special. When she saw them, she said, "Thank God," and produced from her bag a bottle of Tempranillo that he suspected she hoped said the same thing as the glasses. She poured them both a splash, paused a moment, and then filled both glasses nearly to the rim. "Economy of movement. It saves energy, filling them right to the top," she said. "You get up twenty per cent less often to pour. Can't do it at the Mackerel, though. I'd be out of business." She raised her glass. "Here's ..." Matt thought she might complete this with *looking at you, kid*, but she surprised him. "Here's to the problem of forgotten evidence. That's a thing, right? You said the other day. Your encounter with the Hippie Deli reminded me about it. Here's to not remembering why we don't do certain things. Or is that forgotten defeat?"

Amanda made all the right noises about the soup and the bread. He thought there might be a hint of freezer to the ham but decided not to mention it. It would sound too much like fishing for compliments. The bread would have been better, he thought, if he'd been able to dust the cookie sheet with cornmeal, but he had had to throw out the cornmeal bag when he found it had been gnawed open by mice.

It was after two when they got up from the table and stacked the bowls and dishes in the sink. Without discussing it, they left the empty wineglasses in the dining room. Matt wasn't sure what it meant, but he thought it must signal something.

He had turned the heat up in the workroom. Years of trying to second-guess the inferior thermostats that controlled the baseboard heaters had left him no wiser, though, and the room felt warmer than the twenty-two degrees he was hoping for. "Sorry. I can open a window."

"And waste all that heat? Not on your life." She peeled off her sweater. The T-shirt underneath was not one from work. It fit completely differently. He hoped she didn't see the overheated room as some kind of teenaged ploy to get her out of her sweater, then wondered why she had so obviously chosen so carefully what she wore beneath it.

"The cap badge apparently has nothing to do with my grandfather," he announced, producing it from his jeans pocket. "Some earlier outfit. Engineers, essentially. Where's that bag it came from?"

"Does it matter?"

He told her then about his developing theory about Thora's filing system, how he suspected the decorations on the outsides of the bags bore some kind of relationship to their contents.

"Like a kind of ... felted archive?"

"Exactly. What a great way to put it." He showed her the Ship of Fool bag, which he had rescued from the Lodge the day before, and told her about the bank passbook and what it revealed about his grandmother's money, the money she had amassed quite quickly over one fall half a dozen years before she married George Arnold. "The boat is a yacht that was owned by the boss at the sardine plant. I think the money is connected somehow. Gran connected the two things, anyway."

While he talked, Amanda dug through the piles until she found the Perseus and Andromeda on Passamaquoddy Bay bag. "So, here it is. But there's nothing more in it. There was just the cap badge. If there's only one thing, does that really support your filing-system theory? Maybe the badge just fell in. Your mother said it had nothing to do with your family."

"She said it had nothing to do with my grandfather." He did not want to admit that Amanda might be right. "Toss it over. Please."

"We're supposed to be clearing out. If you put that cap badge back in this bag, it will be like we haven't accomplished anything. At least with it empty we've made some progress." To demonstrate, she turned the bag inside out.

"Just a minute. The lining. What is it?" He knelt beside Amanda, struggled to ignore her scent, tried not to notice the outline of her breasts beneath the T-shirt. "She always used cotton. Muslin. This is too smooth."

"Silk, it feels like. Satin, maybe even. There's a bit of border here. Lace? Oh my God. She used an old slip as lining. Very thrifty. See? It's torn here and here. Not useable anymore, at least not if you thought anyone might see it, so she sewed it into this bag."

Matt took the bag from her and turned it right side out. If it made him a prude that he felt uncomfortable examining his grandmother's torn slip — even fifty years after her death — then that was just too bad. As he returned Perseus and Andromeda and the monster to the outside, he quietly slipped the cap badge back into the bag. However grateful he was for Amanda's help, it was his family's stuff, and he needed to do what he needed to do with it.

Any chance of Amanda's noticing what he had done was obliterated by her excitement over a new find. "My God! This is even crazier than the boat bag. Sorry, Matt. I don't mean that meanly. Your grandmother did some beautiful work. Your mother did too. But this is ..." She held the bag up for him to see. "It's like one of those Flemish paintings, you know, the ones where they are harrowing hell or whatever they called it."

Matt knew she knew that was exactly what they called it. He wondered why Amanda so often insisted on playing just a little bit dumb. They held on to the bag together, their shoulders touching. "It's some kind of factory," she said. Her index finger moved from detail to detail. "Look at this little devil turning this crank. What's coming out the other end? Boxes? And then look at this one with the hot poker. Is it a hot poker? There is smoke coming off it. I wonder what he's going to do with that? And here, down in the corner in what looks like a kind of crypt, all the tormented souls. The damned. All women. All blonde. What a wild nightmare."

"The boxes are cans. Sardine cans. The poker is probably a soldering iron." Matt had read up enough on the sardine industry to recognize the context for the allegory immediately. The damned souls were dressed like the packers he had seen in old photos.

"She must have really hated that place, your grandmother."

Matt was already reaching inside the bag. He half expected to find an ancient tin of sardines or at least a label from Casarco — some artifact from the factory — but his tingling fingers found only crumbling newsprint.

He drew the clippings out slowly, setting the bag aside once he had extracted them, and unfolded them on his thigh. There were three separate articles, each with a date written by hand across the top. He recognized the writing as his grandmother's. They were much later than he had expected: from 1952. So they were not about the building of the plant. The dates were at intervals of a month. The first piece reported a fire at York House, one of the dormitories of the old sardine town in Chamcook. The dormitory had been unoccupied for years, the article said, and the cause of the fire was under investigation. There was a paragraph devoted to the failed model town and another on the current operators of the nearby plant, who were Latvians. One of them was quoted as saying it was a mercy that nobody was in the building at the time. The two subsequent articles merely established that there were no leads in the investigation, which tallied with what Matt had learned in his own recent research. On the one with the latest date, Thora, or someone, had sketched a tiny Viking ship on fire.

"I remember when they blew the factory up. In the eighties." Amanda was reading over his shoulder. Her breath tickled his neck when she spoke. "They called it Operation Seabreeze. Can you believe it? It was all very exciting. You wouldn't have been here, of course. Carolyn was very little. Her father made a video. Lots of people did, although the army wasn't crazy about it. I imagine your gran would have — if she'd still been alive and owned a camera."

Matt was about to stuff the clippings back into the bag when Amanda grabbed his wrist. "Matt, you can't. We'll be here forever."

He didn't know why he should feel hurt that she apparently saw that as a bad thing. "She put them in there for a reason."

"Her reason. Her system. Hers. What if this house had burned down? Or what if your mother had pitched everything out?"

"But it didn't. She didn't."

"Anyway, it's not like you are going to forget. The clippings about the fire went with the crazy Breughel bag. The cap badge was with the Andromeda and sea monster bag lined with ripped flimsies. The bank book was in the ship. Jesus, I am getting stiff." She stood up and stretched. "Let's go find some wine."

Joining

WHEN THE PREGNANT girl comes through the door, Penelope looks in vain for Matt. She cannot imagine that he has sent her along to see her on her own. They barely know each other. Penelope cannot remember the girl's name, for God's sake.

"Mrs. Reade?"

Why is it a question? Is the girl as muddled as she?

"I'm Carolyn White. It's nice to see you again."

She had thought the name started with *A*, but at least that is cleared up. "You too, dear."

The girl seems surprised by this response, as if she expected Penelope to have forgotten her, as if meeting the mother of her grandchild is something Penelope would not remember. "How are you today?"

Penelope cannot tell whether this is a trick question, designed to lead to an admission that she doesn't know what day it is, or whether it is an avoidance tactic, suggesting they need only address how she is right now and not overall, not generally. "Is Matt parking the car? He has trouble getting it straight between the lines."

"Your son's not with me today."

Shit.

"I wanted to have a chat, just the two of us. Is that okay?"

"Matt hates to be left out."

"I'll fill him in later. I'm going to be visiting you regularly now, once a month, just to touch base, just to check in."

She wants to say something about baseball and hotels and mixing metaphors. Or to tell the girl that once the baby comes there will be no time for idle visiting, though she would like to see the child, naturally.

"We want to be sure everything's going well, that you're … that you're … happy here."

The girl has a set of brass ones, Penelope thinks. She wonders whether that is what attracted Matt. "I suppose it's where I have to be, isn't it?" She doesn't bother to cross-examine the girl on the meaning of happy. "Is somebody in my house?"

"I think your son is there still, isn't he?"

Does she really not know? Penelope thinks she divines the purpose of the visit now. Matt and this whatever-her-name-is have had a tiff. They have broken up. She wishes she could tell the girl that the final trimester is very tough on relationships, that she and Matt need to invest in theirs a little — but of course she can't speak from any experience. "My mother had this room before me, didn't she? Some of her things are here."

"It's nice to have your own things around you, isn't it?"

Penelope is so relieved to have steered the conversation away from the girl's romantic troubles that she instantly agrees, even though the things, out of context, mean very little to her.

"Have you been doing some of the activities?"

The girl will have to give her more to go on. The question is both too generic — what activities? — and circular — doing is what you do with an activity. "Mmmmm?"

"The Lodge organizes lots of things. It's good to participate."

Good for who?

"I think they are making cookies today. You know what? You could maybe start a knitting group or something."

Socks for soldiers. She thinks about her mother's stories of the dreaded knitting machines, the threat they posed to her young business. When the Great War broke out, Thora had seen an opportunity. Trench foot was one of the greatest threats of battle (believe it or not) and extra socks the easiest antidote — armistice apparently being out of the question. Thora had organized the women and approached the army. But then the Red Cross had gotten in on it. They provided families with automatic knitting machines and wool, and set a target. If they met their quota, the families got to keep the knitting machine and could use it to make socks to sell. With a practiced hand on its crank, a machine could turn out a pair of socks in under an hour. There was no competing with that.

"Would you like some tea? I must have some biscuits somewhere." She remembers being ravenous when she was pregnant.

"Are you eating well? Sometimes it's a little hard adjusting to having your meals in a big dining room with a lot of people. But it's important to eat."

For you, thinks Penelope, *not for me.* "A full stomach and clean underwear: those are the only things that really matter."

The girl laughs. Uncomfortably, Penelope thinks.

"My mother used to say that." She doesn't know why she says this. Thora had never said any such thing. She made it up herself, on the spot, just now. But it does have a ring to it.

"I'll remember that. You haven't lost your sense of humour."

People who say that usually wouldn't know where to begin looking for their own.

"Anyway, it's good to see you are doing so well."

Penelope wonders when this happened.

"As I say, I'll be in for a chat every now and then."

She is a pretty thing, with a kind voice. Penelope hopes she and Matt can reconcile their differences. It can't be any fun bearing a child on your own. Or raising it. Thank God she had Thora. "Of course, dear."

"And think about that knitting group." The girl takes both her hands as if they are going to play London Bridge. Then she smiles — white teeth, wet eyes — and is gone.

SHE JOINS THE White Feather Girls largely as a form of insurance. It is hard, as the war wears on, to have a foreign-sounding name. She changed the name of the business in the first year of the war. It was too difficult to explain that *Håndverket* was a Norwegian word and not German. She and her business were swept up by the larger movement that renamed cities, and breeds of dog. But people still remembered they were originally *Berlin*, and *dachshunds*, and that her business had started out with a German-sounding name. Her actual origins haven't helped — when she has dared to mention them. Norway's decision to remain neutral might as well have been a vote of confidence for the Kaiser. And then there was the business with the damned sock machines, accusations that she was trying to undermine the Red Cross and therefore the war effort. It is best in times like these to join something, to belong to a larger group, the more blatantly patriotic the better.

She tries to ignore the central purpose of the organization. Shaming men into joining up and going to the front has led to so many tragedies, not to mention what happens when a mistake is made. There are dozens of stories of White Feather Girls in London handing the feather to a veteran or a soldier home on leave. In St. Andrews, the chance of such a mistake is slim. Everyone knows everyone. But she has looked on enough times with a shudder as her fellow members bully a young man into a choice that will almost certainly end in the trenches and death. The reports coming back from the Somme are worse than grim.

Not that she would have the nerve to take the side of the conchies. And she certainly wants nothing to do with the efforts she has heard are going on to help deserters cross the border at St. Stephen. There is a cobbler, an American, who is rumoured to provide this service, though he has yet to be caught in the act. She is a believer in seeing things through. If you take the King's shilling — is that still what happens? — you have made your bed and must lie in it.

Fortunately, since the arrival of the Fourth Overseas Pioneers in May, the White Feather Girls spend at least as much of their energy in good works for those who are already soldiers as they do in recruiting more for the meat grinder. They have set up a lending library where Thora volunteers twice a week and a recreation centre where she goes one other day, and there are picnics and dances practically every week.

She prefers the library to the recreation centre. The soldiers who are looking for books are, predictably, a more thoughtful group. And quieter. She has had some very good conversations with some of them about the classics and Rider Haggard, though she is embarrassed that the majority of the books that have been donated for loan are by writers like G.A. Henty — boys' adventures for grown men. At the recreation centre, some of the soldiers arrive drunk and, despite the rules, get drunker. You don't get through an evening without a row or a grope or both. She wishes she could opt out of the table tennis and cards and improvised dancing but is afraid the alternative would be standing on the street corner scouting young men who are candidates for white feathers.

There is a city of tents that went up overnight on O'Neill's farm, across Katy's Cove, when the Pioneers arrived. She supposes this feat is not so surprising given what they will be expected to do in France, building bridges and roads and fortifying trenches. Nobody seems to know exactly when that will be. In the meantime, they have given the town a kind of carnival atmosphere. The innkeeper at the Kennedy House thinks he has died and gone to heaven with all the camp followers needing rooms. Thora has had handbills printed up, trying to lure these wives and lovers into the shop. She has experimented, following the latest fashions, with boiled-wool jackets with a distinct, if fanciful, military cut and lots of brass buttons, and she has a line of caps in pastel colours that otherwise look just like what the soldiers are wearing. But either the camp followers care nothing for fashion or they have no money; traffic in the shop remains only a trickle.

She makes the young corporal's acquaintance at the lending library, which should augur well. He has been in several times before they actually speak. She has noticed what he borrows. It is mostly poetry, books the other girls laughed at when they came in, hooting that no soldier would want to read that stuff. Poetry is not her favourite, English poetry especially, but she is curious and dips into a few of the volumes when he returns them. They do little to change her opinion, but she finds a few poems to like. Henley's "Invictus" and Kipling's "If" seem not too bad.

It is late in the summer when he approaches the desk and asks her for a recommendation. This has never happened to her. When she sees it occur with other soldiers and other girls she is convinced it is just thinly disguised flirting, but she is equally sure that in this instance it is genuine literary interest. She has just this morning uncrated a new donation: the works of Ibsen, translated by William Archer. It is a beautiful set with leather spines and corners and marbled endpapers, and only a few years old. She wonders why anyone would give them up.

"Do you read plays?" It seems a safe bet that anyone who borrows volumes of poetry would. "These have just come in." She suddenly wonders whether, like her, the playwright might have fallen victim to the general hatred of all things Teutonic. "They are in translation. From the Norwegian. Actually, he wrote most of them in Italy." She thinks the corporal might like *Peer Gynt*, whistles a little of the Grieg incidental music. He signs the volume out and is back the next day for more. They talk about some of the plays when he returns the books: *The Master Builder*, *When We Dead Awaken*. Not *Ghosts*, fortunately; venereal disease is not something she wants to talk about with anyone. She wonders afterward whether *Hedda Gabler* is responsible for what happens next.

It is time to close the library and they are still talking about the play. Corporal Cooper — *call me Coop* — shows a sensitive grasp of Hedda's boredom, Thora thinks, of her *ennui*, stuck in a place where she barely feels alive. When she tells him she really must turn out the lights and lock the doors, he moans that they have only scratched the surface and asks if he can walk her home at least, to continue the conversation.

She doesn't like people to know where she lives — strangers, that is, newcomers; everyone who lives in town already knows. It is not exactly that she is ashamed to live above the shop and it is not that she hasn't made the place very comfortable and attractive once you get inside, which nobody ever does. Rather, it is a pattern she set in those months when she was camped out on the *Molly McCann* and she hasn't felt like changing it. But she decides that it is all right for Coop to walk her home. And then — thank you, Hedda — she invites him in, conscious the whole way up the uneven wooden stairs that his face is not three feet from her bottom.

He admires how she has decorated the apartment, stopping to gaze at the felted pictures she has made for the wall and gently handling the pottery animals she has been experimenting with in a makeshift kiln she had put together with bricks left over from the new bank building. Obviously, she has made the right decision. This man reads poetry and plays and has an eye for beauty. He is the opposite of Nils. It has been three years. She asks if he would like to stay for tea, puts the kettle on without waiting for an answer. He produces a hip flask and pours a dollop of rum into each of the teacups she has put on the table. *What would Hedda do?*

In what follows, there is neither poetry nor beauty, but she does not care. Cooper's lust for reading pales beside this passion. Nils was sometimes rough, but this comes from a different place. As he tears at her slip, she shuts her eyes to complete the escape, a release for a moment from the wave-battered rock to which she has felt chained. It doesn't hurt to know that he could be shipped off to France at any point.

"MAMMA?"

She is surprised to see Matt. Where has he come from?

"Were you asleep?"

Not exactly. "I was thinking about the war." She supposes that is true. "We used to entertain the troops."

"The Mercury Club. You've told me about that. It's where you and Pappa met."

She flinches when she hears him call Jonathan Reade — a man he never even met — Pappa. "The *other* war."

Matt looks at her oddly. Is her nose running, her hair a mess? Then he says, "Really? The other war? Why don't you tell me what you were thinking about that."

Memory Wheel

IT IS A fact of life for museums that you simply cannot keep everything. There was a standard process for disposing of artifacts that had been declared surplus. From time to time, the practice raised a public outcry when pieces of precious pottery were found in dumpsters, or ancient sideboards appeared at auction, but for the most part museums go about their business of sloughing off very carefully, and unnoticed. As a curator, Matt had managed dozens of these processes. He knew the forms that had to be filled out and the committees that had to be convened. He knew the criteria off by heart; he had been part of the group that authored them in the first place. The nine-sectioned Bruno memory wheel (not the plywood demonstrator, which was pretty well destroyed by the time the exhibition closed) fit the bill without ambiguity. It was large and therefore difficult to store. It was peripheral to the museum's core collections, having been part of a special exhibition that was unlikely to be remounted. And it was a reproduction, no matter how convincing. Matt had engaged an old hippie who had a woodworking shop tucked away behind St. Michael's College to craft it. There were enough compelling reasons for getting rid of the thing. What was unusual — *irregular*, the Director was eventually to pronounce — was that the deaccession protocol had been triggered neither by space concerns, nor relevance, nor provenance. Ingrid had simply asked Matt if she could have it. Even that irregularity might have been forgiven were it not for what had then been done to the object in front of an audience.

Ingrid was desperate to devise a replacement for the failed fabric choreography. She didn't have all the details worked out, but it had come to her that the wheel was to be central. Matt made her promise that the choreography would have nothing to do with the erotic game they had played with the plywood wheel that night in the museum, and then he filled out the paperwork. The committee was a rubber stamp. The museum's van delivered the wheel to the studio of a friend of Gina. Ingrid insisted that she needed privacy to develop the work, and more time than she could possibly take in the room provided by the museum for rehearsals and the performance.

In fact, she apparently needed so much time that her trysts with Matt had to be put on hold. "It will be worth waiting for," she said, unaware of the irony of the use of that particular phrase for Matt. How many times had he been put off as a young man, in the back seat of a parked car or at the doorway of a dorm room, by exactly those words?

In the end, it had been worth waiting for. When he saw the piece for the first time at the final rehearsal the night before the public performance, he was sure that Ingrid had created something that made sense of all of the work they had been doing.

Ingrid began by drawing a large circle on the polished concrete floor with a chunk of sidewalk chalk. Matt thought it should be easy to erase; he would warn maintenance. Inside the circle, she inscribed squares and triangles in a quick approximation of something you might see in Vitruvius. Watching her work, one of the participants whispered that it looked like the drawing on her vitamin-pills bottle, only without the spread-eagled figure.

Another immediately corrected her: it must be the twelve houses of the zodiac. Then Ingrid ground the chalk stub under her heel, scooped up the dust, and blew it from her palms.

At each of the twelve points where the triangles touched the circle, she placed an object. She did it slowly, ritualistically, investing the objects with more gravity than their banality might seem to merit. The objects were in pairs and they recalled aspects of the performance that had gone before. There were two toothbrushes to stand for the procedural memory segments, two file boxes for the archive fever piece, and, to represent the Twin Towers exercise and the constant time-lagged video feed, two outlandishly large VHS video cameras that she must have gotten from a yard sale. All of these, she placed with the members of the pairs facing off at twelve o'clock and six o'clock, three and nine, and two and eight. At one and seven, four and ten, and eleven and five, she installed facing pairs of paint cans, small bunny-eared television sets, and tiny cakes that were supposed to be madeleines. You could barely see their oval shape and the ribs were invisible, but Matt thought the audience would get the drift. The almonds that went with them were impossible to make out.

Once the objects were in place, Ingrid danced lines between them, drawing connections, first moving from one member of a pair to the other, and then gradually beginning to mix them up, travelling in a quick step from twelve to two or a long glissé from eleven to four. On the large projection screen, she had arranged for a series of still images of functional MRIs, linked together in a way that made them seem animated. At about four minutes into the piece, she registered awareness of the projections, stared at them for a full twenty seconds, and then began feverishly rearranging the objects, moving more and more frenetically until she finally collapsed on the floor. Matt thought that might be the end, though he knew it shouldn't be. Then she gradually rose up to her knees and began — with a cloth she must have had tucked up her skirt the whole time — to wipe away the chalk markings. Once the drawings were blurry, she tackled the objects, packing the pair of toothbrushes and one of the paint cans into a black sack, which she then slid under one of the front-row seats. The nine remaining objects were rearranged into a tighter circle. That was when Matt knew she would bring out the artifact she had asked him for. The wheel had nine divisions, not twelve. He was curious to see how she was going to make the transition, wondered how the broken pair would come into it. But immediately after she had installed the wheel at the centre of her circle, she stopped and called for lights and announced that the rest was still in development.

Matt thought Gina might have a fit, but she simply nodded and thanked everyone for an excellent dress rehearsal, reminding them about their call time for the next night and urging them to get some sleep.

"It's going to be amazing," Matt said to a sweaty Ingrid as he took his turn in the line that had formed to give her what he had come to think of as those obligatory theatre hugs.

"Here's hoping," was all she said back. "I'll work on it tonight. Sorry."

He supposed he should have expected that, although he had been hoping they might go back to her apartment, celebrate a successful rehearsal, and toast the coming performance. Both of them knew that the project's end would also almost certainly mark an end to their affair — if that was what it had been. He went to the bar on Bloor Street by himself and drank three bourbons before heading home to Jennifer.

He wished afterward that he had worked harder to get Ingrid into bed that night. The piece could have ended perfectly well with her sinking to the floor exhausted. Then the wheel would never have come into it.

Jennifer had a faculty thing she was supposed to go to on the night of the performance, which removed that potential awkwardness quite neatly. She had half-heartedly offered to skip it, but he had said she must go; it was important for her career. Matt was looking forward to sitting anonymously in an audience of strangers, he said, taking in the work just as they would.

About two minutes before the lights were due to go down, the Director spotted him and went to the unusual length of asking a woman to move one seat over so he could sit with his friend. Matt had never thought of them as friends, but he could hardly raise that objection and ask the woman to stay put.

"Quite a good crowd." The Director said it as though he were personally responsible. Matt wondered whether he would have been as quick to take credit if attendance had sucked. "Great outreach for the institution. It's so important to be in the public eye whenever we can." Matt waited for him to thank him. "I was talking with a few of the participants this afternoon. They are very excited. They say the two women have been wonderful."

Matt wondered if the Director even knew Ingrid's and Gina's names. He wanted to point them out on the program, but the improvised house lights started to fade.

Inevitably, there were a few stumbles in the performance, and a technical hiccup with the delayed video feed, but the audience, including the Director, remained rapt. Matt got one sidewise glance from his boss during his voice-over on the subject of how collection policies are driven by the potential memorability of objects, but he thought it was more quizzical than defensive.

The early parts of Ingrid's finale unfolded as they had the night before, with a few small tweaks that Matt thought were brilliant. The toothbrushes had been supplemented by other brushes of various kinds — hair, scrubbing, and toilet — to make a pair of bouquets. And to erase the chalk triangles, rather than producing a cloth, she simply removed the skirt she wore over her black leotard and rubbed that across the floor.

Rather than reducing the objects to nine, Ingrid gathered them all into a much larger black sack than she had used the night before. She disappeared with the sack for a moment, and when she stepped back into the lights, her head and face were covered in a balaclava-like sock. Combined with the leotard and tights, the impression was of an all-black Spider-Man. Matt dismissed the analogy as trivializing and disloyal. Stuck to the balaclava (presumably with Velcro) was a pair of neon-pink ears, a large nose, and an open cartoon mouth that might have been Mick Jagger's. The effect narrowly avoided Mrs. Potato Head by the addition of outsized, red-framed sunglasses. Ingrid turned around to be sure the audience could see that there were Velcroed patches on her crotch and bum as well. *The nine openings of the human body.* What had started as a summary of the collective's work had become suddenly and weirdly personal. And almost certainly sexual. Something with a message for him. *Lewd and therefore memorable*, she would have said. Matt missed the cans of paint and toothbrushes.

When she dragged the memory wheel to centre stage, Matt didn't need to look at the Director to sense his dismay. His sharp intake of breath must have been audible to everyone in the room. Matt wanted to turn to the man and ask him, hadn't he read the week's lists? He wanted to reassure him that the deaccessioning had been done strictly according to the book. Whether or not the wheel was any longer the property of the museum was unlikely to matter to him though. People would inevitably identify it as such.

Ingrid was now pulling the patches off herself and affixing them to the nine positions on the stationary outer wheel. The nose tore in half to allow each nostril a spot, and the sunglasses broke at the bridge so the eyes could be separated. Matt worried that the

Velcro that she must have affixed to the wood of the wheel would ruin the lettering. It was gold leaf and had taken days to get just right. Then he noticed that the letters on the two inner wheels were gone altogether. No wonder she had needed privacy. He might have stopped her if he knew she was altering the beautifully crafted wheel. The letters had been replaced by crudely painted images of ears and eyes and nose and mouth, and what he could only imagine were supposed to be renditions of anus and labia.

As a few people in the audience giggled and the Director went rigid in his seat, Ingrid began spinning the two inner wheels, watching intently until they ground to a stop. Her reactions each time suggested there was indeed a set of rules in place for whatever game this was, but they were not immediately apparent. Only when three ears finally lined up on the three circles and Ingrid replaced a Velcro ear on her head did Matt sense what was happening, though he still could not tell what she meant by it. The audience quickly caught on when she was able to restore half her nose, and they soon came to sound like a crowd around a roulette wheel. The Director was stonily silent. After a dozen further spins with no positive result, suddenly the stereo speakers — which had been silent since Ingrid erased the chalk triangles — came alive. Bob Dylan. Matt thought the choice was too obvious, blamed it on Gina, who he now thought must have known Ingrid's plans all along. "I'll Remember You," Dylan promised from a too-tight throat.

Then came what Matt had heard Gina and Ingrid call a Brechtian moment. Did people really talk like that? In stark contrast to the musical backdrop of slow, measured nostalgia — memory as bittersweet — Ingrid began to thrash about: memory as torment. It was as if she was moving to a different soundtrack altogether. She pushed the wheel off its stand and began to jump on it. When it did not break (the hippie's work was very good) she began to work more methodically, but still at a frenetic pace. Within a minute, she had separated the three wheels. This was not difficult, Matt reflected. There was a central hub with a bolt that could be freed with the removal of a wing nut. *Wing nut.* He smiled for an instant at the aptness of the word. A glance at the Director wiped the grin away. Ingrid had begun to spin the wheels on their edges. The largest didn't work very well — Matt supposed the bodily orifices stuck to it spoiled the balance — but the smaller two twirled like dimes. She kept them going until the Dylan song approached its end and then she let them judder to the floor, where she joined them as the lights snapped to black.

"What the fuck, Matt?"

Matt had never heard the Director swear. And he seldom called Matt by his first name. "The last part was new. Since last night. I hadn't seen it."

"That was an artifact. A museum piece."

Matt debated whether to remind him it was actually a reproduction, then decided against it. The very public act of destruction tonight rendered moot any such quibble.

"People would have seen it in the exhibition. Your exhibition."

Matt doubted any of the same people had witnessed both *The Art of Memory* and the *I remember ...* performance.

"And then to see it desecrated here tonight. I just hope none of the board was here." The house lights had come up — they had agreed there should be no curtain call — and the Director nervously scanned the audience, muttering something about the public eye, which had obviously, suddenly become much less attractive to him. As soon as their row cleared, he fled the room.

Matt shook hands with the fellow who had run the projections and then headed behind one of the sets of velour panels they had hung to create improvised wings. The Twin Tower trio had popped a bottle of champagne and were passing it around, the froth slopping on the composite flooring. Matt couldn't see either Gina or Ingrid. He crossed the performance area and parted the curtain on the other wing. The mood could not have been farther from the jubilation not thirty feet away. Here there were tears and sad hugs. Matt was reminded of scenes on wartime train platforms or at hospital bedsides. The participants had formed a community, a society, and they did not want to let it go, though they knew that was exactly what they must do after this night. Gina was comforting the old woman who had done the teeth brushing. When she saw Matt, she broke away.

"Where's —"

"She left this for you." Gina handed him a cream-coloured envelope. It smelled of lemon. When he opened it later in his office it contained a slip of paper with the words "We'll always have Toronto."

Jennifer found it crumpled in his jacket pocket two days after that. She had never gone through his things before.

Excavation

"IT ALL SOUNDED so believable, though, every embarrassing detail. Sex with a total stranger. My mother. I thought it was just going to be some story about the war. I shouldn't have asked. She talked like the guy was rescuing her somehow. Can you imagine hearing your mother talk about having sex? And Ibsen?"

"But it can't have been true, Matt. At least it can't have happened to *her*. Not in the first war. You said she was talking about the first war. She can't have had sex before she was born. Could your grandmother have told her the story?"

"My grandmother didn't tell stories of her youth. At least, I don't think so. And why would my mother tell it as if it happened to her?"

"They do that. It's called *confabulation.*" Amanda took a long sip of wine. "My mother tells me how she's just been to the Superstore, or out walking the dog this morning. She hasn't been able to walk for over a year, and she hasn't left the Lodge for months. We never had a dog. It's not lying. Not really. Just tangled wires."

"Do you think she might have been trying to tell me something, though? About herself or about Gran? Folding one war over another like that? Or was it just that she saw that cap badge?"

"Only two people can help you with this, Matt. One's dead and the other won't remember telling you the story in the first place. Sorry if that sounds cruel." She reached across the table and rested her hand on his forearm. "Delicious lunch, by the way. Again."

He was afraid Amanda was beginning to tire of their lunches. It had gotten so that he spent the whole of every morning planning and tweaking and puttering away in the kitchen. Each day, he tried something more ambitious than the last. By noon, the prospect of seeing her was so exciting he had to wash dishes to calm himself down. When she came through the door at exactly one o'clock, he always pretended to be surprised. The two carefully laid place settings in the dining room gave him away, of course.

He started to clear away the dishes. "This is probably starting to be a pain in the ass, helping me every day."

"Would you rather I didn't?"

"No. Of course not. I'm just thinking of you."

"I'll worry about me. It's my ass where the pain would be. And I'm going to keep hauling it into that workroom, starting with right now." She never offered to help with the dishes or cleaning up the kitchen.

Amanda had persuaded him to buy dozens of banker's boxes. If she couldn't convince him to part with things right away, she said, at least having them organized into batches would help when the time finally felt right. He doubted that, but it was a way of putting things off while seeming productive. He was no longer sure whether his desire to drag the process out had more to do with his reluctance to throw things out or his need to have her stay around.

Deciding how to group things had taken one whole afternoon. She had suggested approaching it chronologically but he had thought that was too cold. And some of the things were hard to pin down or to limit to one epoch. He thought about how his mother seemed so often now to occupy several periods at once, rewriting time. So then Amanda proposed colours, though he thought that was only a joke. They both thought that genre might do, handbags with handbags and scarves with scarves and papers with papers and so forth, but there would clearly need to be subgenres. There was no way even a fifth of the handbags would fit into one banker's box. Amanda suggested attractive and grotesque as subcategories, but that did little to solve the problem; there were still too many of each. In the end — over Amanda's protests that they hardly needed the banker's boxes if this was what they were going to do — Matt had settled on what he called an archaeological approach. "If we think of the room as a series of cubes and we record exactly where we found each thing and label the boxes to correspond with the cube where we found its contents, that could work. Like a dig."

"How is that different from just leaving everything in its place?"

"It'll be in actual boxes. We can move them around without losing touch with the original order. We could even empty the whole room and give it a good cleaning."

"I'm not helping you clean this place."

"No. Of course not. I just think there's maybe something significant about where everything is." He didn't mention Simonides and the collapsed banquet-hall roof in ancient Greece.

She had agreed to indulge him in the end. He hoped it was partly that she too wanted the task to go on longer.

The system divided the room into sixteen cubes with edges a metre long. Four portions at the tops of the end rows and the top ones of both of the side rows weren't perfect because of the slope to the ceiling, but there was less stuff piled that high anyway. The rows were assigned letters going one way and numbers going the other, with a Greek letter denoting height, so that A1Gamma, for instance, was at head height on the left just inside the workroom door.

They had begun to tackle B4Alpha — on the floor at the far end of the room — when Amanda let out a little squeal. She held up a coil-bound sketchbook. "I don't know whether you are ready for this."

"Mamma's or Gran's?"

"Neither. At least I don't think so." She handed it over with a grin he could not read.

The graphite had faded, rubbed with the years, but you could still tell the technique was exquisite. All of the sketches by Thora and Penelope they had found up until then were designs, meant to be transferred or executed elsewhere. Lovely, some of them, but definitely a means to another end. These were perfect little works of art all in themselves, although they too were also clearly studies for other work. The hand that produced them was classically trained. Matt flipped through heart-stopping renditions of apple-round breasts, dimpled buttocks, and S-curved hips before coming to a sketch that united them all and added a face. Penelope's face. Younger. Before he had known it. But definitely hers.

"That portrait that used to hang above the mantel in the living room. Do you think ...?"

Matt did. He struggled to remember the painter's name. Something Sparrow. Jonathan? No. The bird was the first name. So obviously not Sparrow. Robin. Robin Humphreys. How did Humphreys come so easily once he had Robin? "What's on the outside of the bag?"

Amanda held it up. "Hard to say. It's not really a scene, is it? I guess a series of symbols. No, look: it's like a coat of arms or a knight's shield or something."

Matt took the bag from her. She was right. A green lozenge-shaped escutcheon with a yellow pale running down the centre was topped — where the helm or coronet should be — with the twin masks of tragedy and comedy. On either side, the lozenge was supported by a dancing maenad. Crossed paintbrushes and facing-off treble clefs lay across the green field. The imagery was cliché, he thought, and then reminded himself that that was precisely how heraldry actually worked.

"Did your mamma belong to an arts club?" Amanda had taken the bag back and was beginning to unpack more of its contents.

"Mamma was not very clubbable."

"That's what I would have thought." She unfolded a newspaper clipping. "Oh. I remember hearing about this. The summer that Myrna Loy and Kostelanetz and Lily Pons were all here together. The old people used to go on and on about it. It was before we were born. Myrna Loy. I loved the *Thin Man* movies. They used to play them on TV late at night when I ... They used to play them late at night."

"Mamma had recordings of Lily Pons. She never let me touch them. I used to ask her what's a recording for if you don't ever listen to it. It didn't change her mind. I wonder where those are now."

The article was little more than a social notice, a registry of artists who were summering in St. Andrews. Matt recognized Miller Brittain and Robin Humphreys along with the ones who were more nearly household names. The date was 1954. The article might, then, have been clipped by either his mother or his grandmother, although, given the contents of the sketchbook, he was betting on his mother. A second carefully folded article was devoted to a notice of an opening of a show of paintings by Robin Humphreys. It was from the *Montréal Gazette* two years later.

Amanda produced an envelope from the bag. It was unmarked, had never been sealed. The adhesive had turned to powder, some of which stayed on her hands. When she shook the envelope, a small photograph slipped out. A baby in a knitted suit. Matt recognized it immediately. He held it carefully between thumb and forefinger, looking at his chubby face.

"There's a story about Shelley, isn't there?"

"Shelley Trenholme? From school?"

"The poet."

"I know. Percy Bysshe." She pronounced it with a posh British accent.

"Something about how he grabbed a baby once and held it up and demanded that it tell him what it knew, what it remembered of the life before."

"You mean all that Wordsworth stuff about 'trailing clouds of glory. Our birth is but a sleep and a forgetting.' All of that."

Matt liked it when Amanda stopped pretending she hadn't read anything.

"What do you think this little fellow is trying to tell us? Probably that he needs to be changed." She kissed Matt's cheek lightly as she took the photograph and put it back in the envelope, which she then returned to the bag. "I bought a photo album for Carolyn. I've told her I want it filled up with pictures of the baby when it comes. She says that's stupid, that I'm going to be right there, that she'll have lots of photos on her phone. Were we that cavalier? Our mothers certainly weren't. Thank God."

Matt didn't want to remind Amanda that he and Jennifer had no children. "Carolyn must have been a cute baby."

"Fairly ugly, actually, at first. But you still want pictures. You should take this bag to your mamma. Maybe not the sketches of her bits, but the rest of it. She'd love to see the baby picture." She tossed the bag toward the workroom door.

"I should tag it somehow," said Matt. "So I remember where it came from, which box it needs to go into."

"I can remind you."

"But what if you're not ..." He trailed off, not willing to finish the thought.

"I'll be around. And I have a very good memory. Extraordinary, in fact. You might be surprised."

He wished she hadn't said it. He was doing such a good job of forgetting Ingrid.

Summer People

THE COUGH IS nothing unusual at first. She has had plenty of coughs. You don't get to be however old she is without having had coughs. The nurse who looks like a chest of drawers — a highboy — makes more fuss than Penelope thinks is necessary. Matt comes to visit. Penelope hopes the nurse has not called him. He assures her he was coming anyway, that he comes every day. She doubts that, but it doesn't seem worth challenging him. He is looking happier, she thinks, though happier than what she does not know. When was the last time she saw him?

They sit in the solarium. That's the name they have given the plastic bubble at the end of the hall. She laughed at the pretentiousness the first time, but she has come to accept the name, to use it when she can remember it. The other prisoners tend to avoid the sun. She is tempted to make a vampire joke to Matt but she is not sure how he will take it. As a small child he used to come out with the most outrageous things. Thora and she would laugh and laugh. But she is not sure he is funny anymore. So she just tells him it's nice and quiet in the greenhouse, or whatever you call it.

He has brought along one of her mother's bags — or it may be hers. "Where did you find this?"

"In the workroom. I've been doing a bit of organizing."

She suspects she is supposed to apologize for something here. "Clearing out, you mean?"

"I thought some of it might be fun for you to look at."

Fun. How little he knows.

He unfolds a yellowed square of newsprint. "Would you like me to read it to you?"

"How do I know? What if it's my obituary?"

"What if it's mine?"

Good. Maybe he is still funny. "I can read just fine." She takes the paper from him. It is and it isn't an obituary. She looks through the names. Lily Pons. The singer. She died of something miserable. Pancreatic cancer. Penelope remembers that because her Mount A roommate died of the same thing a few years later. Myrna Loy. The movie star lived much longer, she thinks, into her late eighties at least, though she had two mastectomies in the seventies, not long after Penelope saw her on Broadway in that play with all the women. Then there is the painter. Is he dead? She cannot recall. He was older than she, though she didn't think much about that during that long-ago summer.

IT HAS BEEN years since she has been to an actual party. Since the war, really, and at first she tells Robin no, she can't join him, but then she relents when she sees his face fall. She knows she should be flattered that he has asked her, that he is so obviously prepared to be seen with her on his arm. What the townspeople will think is another matter. If they see them. Penelope doubts that any locals will be at the actual party itself, so it's really only the getting there that's a problem. She suggests she meet him there, pleads responsibilities at the shop that will claim her until a bit after the cocktail hour begins. She doesn't want to hold him up.

She regrets the plan as soon as she begins the walk up the long driveway all by herself. With every step she takes, the house grows larger, more imposing. Thora has always told her the summer people are only people; *somewhat foolish people*, she often says, *with more money than good sense*. She had a hand in decorating some of the summer palaces forty years ago and she pronounced several of them utter follies — though she still cashed the cheques. As the three-story shingled facade looms above her, Penelope has a hard time convincing herself that everyone inside is just a person and the house just a house. She thinks she can hear the party around the back of the building and debates whether she can simply slip around or whether she must ring the front doorbell. Mercifully, Robin appears on a side verandah just as she is about to mount the steps. She throws herself into his arms with more fervor than she had meant to, hopes nobody else sees.

"You'll spill my drink!" But he gives her a long kiss. His tongue tastes of gin. "Let's go get you one."

He sweeps her across the verandah, through an arbour, and onto the emerald expanse of the rear lawn. There is croquet set up. The slight slope in the direction of the water would pose some challenges, Penelope thinks. At a table with a linen cloth and a pyramid of cocktail glasses there is a barman who is somebody she went to school with, but he maintains his professional distance, pretends he has never seen her before. Or maybe he has forgotten or doesn't recognize her.

Penelope does not really like martinis, not that she has had a lot of occasions to test her taste for them. But before she can ask for white wine, Robin has told the man to shake her one of what he's having. "Olive or twist?" her schoolmate asks, and she thinks he is reminding her of the Dickens they read. "Olives. Two," says Robin before she has caught up. She would rather have had lemon, looks at the pair of olives floating in the glass and can't avoid thinking of testicles in formaldehyde.

Robin steers her past the croquet pitch to a terrace at the bottom of the garden. He wants her to see the view of the water, he says, but she sees that there is a knot of painters and poets that is probably the real draw. Surely, he knows she has seen the water from every possible angle, isn't much impressed by new views of it. One of the artists, a woman in her late fifties who works mainly in pastels, is apparently quite popular with collectors in the States right now. She is Scandinavian but she draws and paints under an Irish name and didn't burst onto the scene until she was a grandmother. Penelope wonders whether that isn't what's needed to make it in the art world: letting everyone know you are using an assumed name, or that you are a remarkably late bloomer. Something unique about you, unusual. Talent will only get you so far. Robin introduces her to the woman, whom he seems to know quite well. Penelope wonders whether he is trying to make the other woman jealous by showing off this thirty-two-year-old on his arm. He doesn't call her his model or his mistress but both labels sit in the air around her, she knows. Rather, he describes her as a painter.

"And what do you paint, my dear?" The *my dear* sounds like the woman is expelling a turd.

"Actually, I work in felt. I make paintings out of felt. Landscapes. Seascapes." She expects the woman to sniff and turn on her heel.

"How wonderful. How authentic. I want to know more. Come, walk with me. I need another drink."

Penelope can't tell whether the woman does actually want to know more or whether she simply wants to separate her from Robin, but she has no choice but to follow her back toward the bar. The woman seems genuinely interested to hear about Thora and the business and all of the background, but her eyes glaze over a little as Penelope begins to describe her methods. Perhaps it is the fresh martini, which she has downed in two gulps.

She is not reunited with Robin until the dinner gong sounds half an hour later, but she has by then been dumped by the Scandinavian-Irish grandmother and fallen in with a poet whose work she admires. They don't talk about poetry or pictures. Rather, the poet fills her in on the guests of honour for the evening. When Penelope confronts Robin about why he has failed to mention their names to her, he shrugs and dismisses them as just people. She thinks of her mother, wonders how she would be faring in this milieu.

If you squint, Myrna Loy looks not much older than when Penelope first saw her on the screen in *The Thin Man* and *Manhattan Melodrama*, and that must be twenty years ago. She calculates, though, that Miss Loy must be about as old as Thora. Robin says she doesn't do much film work anymore. She is busy with UNESCO. With her husband. Her fourth. Even from a distance, you can tell she is exactly the witty, bubbly person you saw on the screen. Penelope wishes she could read lips.

"She started out in the silents, you know," Robin says. "Usually as a femme fatale. Asian or Eurasian, if you can believe it."

Penelope can believe it, having just spent time with the Scandinavian who markets herself as Irish.

"All serious roles. Heavy. Louis B. Mayer didn't want her cast in *The Thin Man*. The director really had to push."

She knows that the director had in fact had to push Miss Loy into a swimming pool. He did it just to see how she'd react. That was her audition. Penelope had read all about that kind of thing when she was twelve. *Robin seems to lose forty years and become about twelve around the celebrities*, she thinks.

Lily Pons, she recognizes from her advertisements for Lockheed and Knox gelatin. She has heard recordings, of course, but she missed seeing her movies, not being a fan of the RKO operetta. Miss Pons is maybe a bit younger than Myrna Loy but it is impossible to tell. Robin is full of information about her too, but Penelope manages to tune much of it out. She'd be more curious to hear about the singer's Russian husband, the conductor, but there Robin is no help.

After dinner, they are ushered back out onto the lawn where folding chairs have been set up in rows facing the house. From the upper-story windows an enormous white cloth has been hung, anchored at the bottom by the planters that line the rear verandah. Their host — somebody from Montréal to whom Penelope has not been introduced and whose name she has forgotten — stands in front of the makeshift screen, making obsequious remarks about Miss Loy and Miss Pons. Finally, he assures them all they are in for a huge treat, gesturing behind him at his oddly draped house.

There is the whir of a projector. "I love *The Thin Man*," Penelope whispers to Robin. She has had a lot to drink and she nibbles his earlobe a little. But it is not Myrna Loy who appears on the huge screen. It is Lily Pons.

The film is in black and white and must be from the thirties. Even two decades later, Miss Pons's costume draws gasps from the after-dinner crowd assembled in the cooling summer evening. Her breasts, about a quarter of the size to be expected in an opera singer, are held high and firm in a bandeau. Her midriff appears unapologetically bare (though likely encased in a stocking, Penelope thinks). But to call it a *midriff* is too clinical, and *bare* does not do it justice. The exposed belly button and the sensual curve below her tiny waist are eclipsed by the cross-gartering at her hips. Her long skirt is held up by two crossed straps that mark a spot exactly above where her bush must be. Between the upper and lower straps at either side, the smooth bare flesh of her hips pouts a tiny bit, beckoning, daring. It may be one of the sexiest outfits Penelope has ever seen. She squeezes Robin's hand, puts it on her own thigh.

Although the sound is scratchy, the Little Nightingale's coloratura is nearly as breathtaking as her costume. Mostly, what she is singing sounds like nonsense, although Penelope can pick out the odd French word. Diction is obviously thrown to the winds in favour of the incredible, exquisite high notes, though she thinks some of the highest may not have words assigned to them anyway. Robin tries to explain that this is the famous "Bell Song" from Delibes's *Lakmé*, but she hushes him right away. It doesn't matter. She wants to listen and watch and nothing more.

The piece is being sung as part of a staged performance, with an onstage audience made up in three equal parts of officials dressed in the awkward trappings of the British Raj, heavily made up Brahmins, and a third distinct group of sailors and soldiers. Penelope watches Pons charm them all with her waving arms and warbling voice. Several times during the five minutes the scene lasts, the camera cuts away to an audience bedecked in Western evening dress listening sedately in an ornate theatre auditorium. The tight tuxedos and stiff gowns and what you can tell, even in black and white, is blue-rinsed hair all send a chill through her. More menacing, though, she thinks, are the two men watching from a private box — a pair of leering pencil-thin moustaches and bow ties.

As Miss Pons finishes the song, the onstage Indian audience congratulates her while the onscreen theatre audience — Paris? New York? — rises to its feet. Moments later, as the fifty-eight-year-old singer steps in front of the now lifeless screen to take an awkward bow, the dinner guests in St. Andrews also offer a standing ovation. Penelope tries and fails to map the delicious hips and belly button of a few minutes before onto the evening-gowned body of the aging star. She thinks about all the levels of watching, of looking, wonders whether others too are trying to reconcile the celluloid memory of Lily Pons, tricks of light projected on a billowing screen, with the flesh-and-blood woman of the present moment.

Over a nightcap, Penelope meets Myrna Loy's (fourth) husband. He says she looks very familiar and haven't they met somewhere? He never forgets a face. Robin says that Penelope has been modelling for him a little this summer. The man says that must be it. Penelope thinks about Lily as Lakmé and Lily tonight and hopes that it is indeed her face and only her face that the man has not forgotten.

She and Robin have an argument about it as he walks her home to Birch Hall. She has tried to tell him about trying to reconcile the singer with her nubile former self and how she couldn't look at Miss Pons the same after seeing the film. He claims not to understand. And then she asks him how many people have seen the paintings he has made of her.

SHE LOOKS AT the bag Matt has spread across his lap, the childish effort she had made at a coat of arms or something. And she thinks she knows what he is about to pull out next.

Chest

MATT IS SITTING in the dining room finishing the bottle of wine and staring at the two bowls of cold soup when the phone rings. He thinks about letting it go wherever calls go when there is no voice mail. *Nowhere. They just end.* He has always known the day would come when Amanda would simply not show up for lunch, when she was fed up with his pathetic efforts to please in the kitchen and his lamentable lack of decisiveness in the workroom. It would be the sign that he must go back to Toronto, to his marriage and his job and whatever he could salvage of either. But he has decided to allow himself some brief mourning anyway. Knowing she would stop coming is not the same as experiencing it. As he worked his way through the wine, he composed half a dozen versions of a goodbye letter. He will find a blank card among the stacks that are still in boxes from Handworks, write with the fountain pen he almost never uses anymore, and deliver it to the Smoked Mackerel at a time when he sees that her car is not parked outside. Finding the right tone is proving to be a challenge. He has tried everything from a bouncy limerick — to hide his feelings — to what sounds remarkably like a suicide note — which exaggerates them, if he is honest. He doesn't remember whether he ever wrote to Amanda when they were young and — he thought — in love. If only he held on to things the way Thora and Penelope did, there would be old letters and he would be able to find out, perhaps to match the tone, at least to remind himself that he survived the first time around.

The phone, when it rings, could be the Lodge, he thinks. Or Jennifer. It is still lunchtime in Toronto. It won't be Ingrid. She doesn't have his mother's number. Even if she found it somehow, he is not sure she actually knows how to operate her mobile as a telephone. Her emails have slowed since he wrote that he was not interested in the new collaboration she was proposing. He wonders now whether spending some time in Norway might be just the thing, but is pretty sure he has closed that door quite firmly.

He picks up the receiver. It is Amanda on the other end.

"Matt? It's me. Sorry I missed our lunch. Things got a little crazy."

He knows this is a lie. If the restaurant has ten people at lunch these days, it's a miracle.

"Carolyn went into labour! Mike wasn't around so I had to drive her."

Matt is happy to hear this, though the wine has dulled his reactions. He imagines the hour-long trip to the hospital in Saint John with a moaning, contracting daughter and thinks that the hell she has been through in the past two hours may actually rival his.

"He's here now. She's dilating nicely. Sorry, is it okay that I said that? Anyway, I'm headed back. They'll call me when it's born and they're all bonded and everything, and I can run up again. Maybe you can ..." She trails off. "What was the soup?"

"What?"

"Lunch. What did I miss?"

"I can warm it up. I drank the wine but there's another bottle."

"I'm sorry. I should have called. It just all got a bit hectic."

"No worries. I knew there must be something serious," he lies.

"Maybe I'll come by on the way to the restaurant."

"I should go up to the Lodge."

"We could go together."

Matt tries to picture the two of them visiting first her mother and then his — weighs the obvious advantages of having another person in the room to talk to against the inevitable distraction of attention — and wonders whether it is a good idea.

"We don't have to visit together. I wasn't saying that. Just drive up there and back. Or we could swap mothers, see if they notice."

Before he can argue, she has told him she will see him in an hour and rung off.

THE POWER TO the shop has been cut off. Penelope has always turned the heat down in the winter to save on the bills. There is no point overheating a space where no customers are expected. The woolens could keep themselves warm, couldn't they? But the chill today is different, deeper. There is a finality about it. She wishes there was sun since they will have to rely on whatever light comes in through the south-facing windows, thinks about postponing the job for a brighter day. But the truck is rented, and Bernadette will soon be backing it down the alley to the loading door. They could take everything out through the front, but she knows it's important to Bernie to have this last opportunity to show off her driving skills.

She has taken down the portrait of her mother from where it has hung for nearly thirty years above the cash register, and faced it to the wall along the baseboard. She can't bear for Thora to be watching as they dismantle what's left of the work of seventy years. It's not a very good painting — nothing as good as the paintings Robin made of Penelope that summer before Matt was born — but Bernadette made it and proudly presented it to Thora when Matt was two or three, so Penelope has never had the heart to get rid of it. Until today. Perhaps she will offer it to Bernie as a memento, though she supposes that would probably be insulting.

"Good morning, boss!"

Penelope startles. Why hasn't she heard the truck? She is about to make her routine plea that Bernadette not call her boss (a plea that has always gone unheeded, even when they lived together briefly), but she supposes this one day she can let it go. *Après moi* and all that.

"At least there's less stuff to move out than there would have been in the good old days." Bernadette always tries to put a positive spin on things.

Penelope doesn't bother to point out that in the good old days they would not have had to close the business and move everything out — although, she has to admit, even in those days the risk they would have to do just that was ever present.

"I guess it's lucky after all that you recycled all that stuff into your art project ten years ago. Saves us a lot of heaving today."

Bernadette always says *your art project* as if it has quotation marks around it. She did not approve of Penelope's Robert Morris phase. Although she stopped short of calling it a waste of perfectly serviceable stock, Penelope knew that was exactly what she thought. Bernadette has always been a champion of Thora's privileging of the useful over the beautiful. Penelope's experiments with the conceptual introduced a third possibility that would never have been contemplated by her mother — or tolerated, had she still been alive at the time. Bernadette has never asked what became of the pieces from Penelope's felt exhibition. Would she rejoice that they ended up in the dump or simply see that as a further waste of useful materials?

They bring the empty boxes in from the truck. Penelope hated the idea of buying them from U-Haul, so they are an odd assortment of sizes from the liquor store and some of them are falling apart. It won't matter, she thinks, since she plans to unpack them right away at the other end, organizing their contents neatly in her workroom in the hope of a new storefront even though she knows that is impossible. It is amazing how quickly the packing of all the sweaters and socks and hats and mitts goes. Amazing and very sad. The cash register has already been sold (Bernadette loved trying out variations of a joke about getting real money for an old empty till). The mannequins and shelving are spoken for by a woman in St. Stephen.

Penelope rifles in the drawer under the counter and comes up with the paperweight her mother used for receipts when she was working. It is a metal cap about two inches in diameter with two tiny pinprick holes in its top and the remains of a cork lining inside. For years, it had smelled of gasoline and Penelope used to hide it away on the days when Thora wasn't working, which made the drawer reek dangerously. By the time her mother died, though, the scent had nearly vanished and Penelope found she couldn't bear to throw the thing out.

"She knew her own mind, your mother," Bernie says. "If she made up her mind to do something, she did it."

Penelope is tired of hearing this refrain. It always makes her feel inadequate by comparison.

"I probably shouldn't have bought the gas for her, but I had no idea what she was up to. And she was the boss's mother, still the boss too — *Bossa Emerita*. Nobody was hurt, and I think it did her a lot of good somehow. Do you remember how much better her spirits were after that old dormitory burned down?"

Penelope does remember. It took her months to make the connection, and then she had never breathed a word to anyone (not even her mother) about it. She supposes it's all right for Bernie to talk about it now, three decades later.

"Oh look. Here's one of little Matt's mythology books." Bernie has reached back farther in the drawer, having relieved Penelope of the gas cap and pocketed it in her tweed coat. "Remember how he used to sit so quietly underneath the counter or in the backroom, reading this crazy stuff and all those history books? The perfect working mom's son. And no wonder he grew up to be in museums and whatnot. Well not in museums, not like he is an artifact or anything."

"He did love history," Penelope says, hoping to cut off what will otherwise be further workshopping of the museum joke.

"You can't blame him, though, can you? For becoming obsessed with the past? I mean not knowing his father. That can be important for boys."

Penelope knows that Bernie is not referring to the mysterious and absent Jonathan Reade. She has bawled her out many times for not telling Matt about Robin, but what would have been the point? With Jonathan for a father, Matt got a tale of intrigue and espionage that fed his imagination. Her story with Robin was cliché at best. She hasn't the energy to have this discussion again. Suddenly, she hasn't the energy for anything. She plops herself down on one of the larger liquor store boxes. It squishes a little, but supports her. "Why are we bothering? Maybe we should just put it all out for the garbage."

"We're bothering because of all the sweat and tears that went into making these things. Showing respect for the makers." And then, quickly, afraid perhaps that she has let things become too heavy, Bernadette adds, "We're bothering because some of this stuff might actually come back into vogue one day and make us rich."

Penelope laughs, charitably. "But maybe it's time to let old fashions die, to be done with the past," she says, surprised by the weariness in her voice.

"Saving things isn't about being stuck on the past, boss. Not really. When you think about it, it's about looking forward — an act of faith that there will be a future, a time when a later version of us will take the stuff out and look at it again. Maybe even a time beyond that when others, strangers, will dig it out and study it."

Bernadette always was bright as a button, from the time she was a little girl, Penelope thinks. "I wasn't always very nice to you, Bernadette. Even in those years when we tried living together, when you were doing me that enormous favour of keeping me company."

"Especially in those years! There were so many rules, places I wasn't welcome, things I couldn't say."

"I was a bitch."

"No. You were the boss."

"Why did you stay?"

"The rent was right: a little cooking, a little talking, no dollars."

"I don't mean just with me in the house that time, but all these years in the shop. You're very clever. You could have done anything. Gone anywhere."

"I never wanted to leave St. Andrews. I was like your mamma that way, I suppose, only for me it was where I was born too. Like you. Mainly, though, I stuck around for the story."

"The story?"

"I wanted to see what came next."

"With Mamma?"

"At first. There was always something more to learn, something unexpected waiting around the corner."

"You wanted to see how her story ended. But she's been dead for twenty years. More." Penelope is afraid she knows what Bernadette will say next, but she is both right and wrong.

"You think I was in love with you, boss? People talked, I know they did, about us in that way. They thought we were sleeping together. Or, at least, that I wanted to."

Penelope blushes, not at the idea itself but because that had been her own reading of the situation.

"That's an easy way for people to see things. It's understandable because sex is so important to so many people."

Penelope waits for Bernadette to turn this into a joke, but she doesn't.

"That kind of attraction just never meant anything to me. The truth is, I did love you, boss. Just not like that. It was your *story* I loved. Your adventures. Waiting to see what comes next. I still do."

"You want to see how my story ends, like with Mamma?"

"I want to see how it keeps going." She bends to pick up the first box. "Now, what do you say we get this damn truck loaded and start stocking your archives?"

WHEN MATT'S HAND grazes Amanda's as they both reach for the green button at the entrance, he wonders why he hasn't suggested visiting together before. Strength in numbers; it is one of the oldest truths in the book. It is not the same visiting with Bernadette, poor Bernadette, who might at any instant be swallowed up by the Lodge, become one of them. Amanda and he are a pair of teenagers storming the gates. Seeing the two of them, the guardians wheel their chairs backward until they bump the railings that run along the wall. Amanda pauses to kiss the apple-doll forehead of one as she passes. Matt will ask her afterward who the woman was in life.

They part at the nurse's station. "Good luck," she whispers, as she gives his hand a squeeze. She is gone before he can say *you too*, but he suspects she has no need of luck.

He hears Bernadette's voice before he reaches the doorway of Penelope's room.

"It's all right, boss. All a long time ago. Your mother was ..."

Matt waits to hear what Thora was, but Penelope calls out, "Is somebody there?" He's not sure that Bernadette would have finished the sentence anyway. "Who is it out in the hall?"

It can't be a sudden fit of acute hearing. Something else. Maybe somewhere else. He steps into the room.

"Oh, Matt! I'm so glad to see you. They've put me to bed. I don't want to be in bed."

He knows his mother cannot have actually shrunk since yesterday, but she seems to take up about a quarter of the bed. "Hello, Mamma." He fumbles for her hand and kisses her forehead. She kisses the backs of his fingers and clutches on, perhaps hoping he will lift her from the mattress. "How nice that Bernadette's here. Thanks, Bernadette. Sorry to interrupt your visit."

"Bernadette was here?"

"I was getting ready to leave. She got a little agitated. Some awful story had her upset. It's hard to tell what sets it off. Anyway, she seems fine now."

Matt can't get used to talking about his mother as though she isn't in the room.

"Aren't you, boss?"

"What?"

"Fine now?"

"It's so nice to see you, Matt."

"And nice to see Bernadette."

"Bernadette was here?"

"I am just leaving, boss." She takes Penelope's other hand and shakes it back and forth rapidly. *Warmer than a handshake and cooler than a kiss. A kind of shared essential tremor*, Matt thinks. He hugs Bernadette and walks her into the hall, thanking her again for visiting.

"Can't stop out here, Matt. Who knows who has a net?" And she scurries off down the hall.

His mother's face lights up when he re-enters the room. "Matt! I've been so lonely." He doesn't bother to remind her that her last visitor is only just out the door. "There's something I wanted to talk to you about. But I can't think what. It will come to me."

"How are you feeling, Mamma?"

"Fine."

"But they have you in bed." He knows he should go and find a nurse or one of the others, ask why his mother is in bed, but he is frightened of them all. And he thinks they should really notice that he is visiting and come give him an explanation. Mostly, he is too frightened. "Is your chest worse?"

"That must be it. You could help me get up."

"I'd have to ask." He is sure there is a reason why they have her in bed. Unless there isn't. He begins to wish he had asked Amanda to visit with him. But then he would have had to visit her mother with her; that would only be fair.

"Hi Penny." Yet another caregiver he has not seen before.

His mother flinches at the familiarity, the contraction of her name that she most loathes, but Matt is glad to have his problem solved so easily. He looks at the bed.

"Our chest isn't too good today, is it dear?"

Our. Matt resists looking at the young woman's chest for confirmation.

"Doctor will be in later."

Matt notices she is holding something covered in a cloth, deduces it is a bedpan. He is about to offer to leave the room when the caregiver, *Bethany,* according to the name tag perched on her pert breast, explains. "The plumbing isn't working next door. I just have something to empty. Sorry." She vanishes into Penelope's bathroom and he hears the water running and the toilet flush. At least it got him an update of sorts.

"Did you have a nice visit with Bernadette, Mamma?"

"She needed the keys."

"The keys?"

"For the store."

"Ah."

"Or she needed me to sign something. I don't know." She rubs her forehead. "It's frightening, Matt."

He hates it most when she shows she's aware of what's happening to her, although he also knows it means he has not lost her entirely. Amanda's mother only recognizes her less than half the time. He can't imagine what that must feel like. "It's all right, Mamma. You can't remember everything."

"But I used to, didn't I? I used to pride myself on my memory."

"You just have so many more of them now. Memories. After all, when you get to be a hundred and fifty ..."

She laughs. That's good. The cough that follows is not.

"Hello, Mrs. Reade." *L'Air du Temps.*

"Amanda Williams! I like your hair like that." Matt can't tell whether his mother miraculously recognizes Amanda from forty years ago or whether Amanda has been sneaking in to visit. His mother's next words settle it, he thinks. "Did you manage to get those sweaters re-folded?"

"Everything's all set."

He admires her technique. And her bum as she bends over the bed to take Penelope's hand.

"Good visit?" he asks her, wishing immediately he hadn't.

"The usual."

"Short," he is about to say, but why would she stay any longer? Once time has been erased, one minute might as well be an hour, and the other way around. "Mamma's chest isn't too good, apparently."

Amanda sits on the bed and makes a big show of looking from one breast to the other, which sets Penelope sniggering like a rude schoolgirl, and then coughing.

"Sorry," Amanda murmurs. "I should know better."

Matt can't dismiss the phrase *die laughing*, thinks he will share it with her once they are in the car.

"You must need to get along," says Penelope when she has recovered her breath. "Where are you two living now? Isn't that stupid, I can't remember."

"We're here right now," Amanda says, her eyes locked on Matt's.

He looks away. "Amanda's daughter is having a baby, Mamma."

"Right this minute?" It has always been one of her favourite jokes.

"Well, yes, actually. Pretty much right this minute. She's in labour."

Penelope reaches out for Amanda's stomach. The way she is sitting on the bed, there is the tiniest roll. "No, that's all me, I'm afraid," Amanda laughs. "It's my daughter who is having the baby."

"A daughter?"

"They don't know. They didn't want to know."

"I'd have wanted to know. Maybe it's a good thing I didn't."

Matt thinks this is a joke.

"He turned out all right," Amanda laughs.

"Mostly. Do you have children, dear?"

"A daughter. And she's about to have a baby too. I'll be a grandmother."

"Oh dear," Penelope says, and closes her eyes.

When it's clear that she is not going to open them again, Amanda gets up carefully and makes a walking motion with her index and middle fingers. Matt stoops to pick up something that has fallen from the bed when she got up. It is some kind of needle-felted creature. He remembers his grandmother making sheep. This is something quite different. Not quite a man. Not quite a bear. A face that looks like a wolf, he thinks, as he tucks it back under the sheet next to his sleeping mother.

As he is backing the car out of the space overlooking the bay, Amanda's phone rings.

"Mike? Yes?" She might be answering a business call judging by her tone. Then, "It's a girl!" She leans across and kisses Matt's cheek before returning to the phone. He doesn't know why it makes him feel so good.

Sagas

PENELOPE STARES AT the weird little woolen man. How has he gotten here? She remembers her mother making him — not long before she died it must have been — remembers the savage thrusts of her barbed needle as it tortured the fibres, broke them down so they would melt together. She had never before seen her mother work with actual hatred. Occasionally they both lost heart in their work, even said they hated what they did, but never the wool itself. This creature would have been one of the last things Thora made. She didn't do much needle felting, just as she didn't make very many felted pictures — claimed they lay outside their *mandat*, which was to make useful things that were also beautiful. She would actually quote Horace as she lectured her four-year-old daughter. Penelope only knew it was Horace much later when she encountered his ideas about the *dulce* and the *utile* at university. Felted pictures and woolly three-dimensional creatures were merely decorative. They only satisfied the *dulce*, Thora would say, the beautiful, and not the useful. Penelope used to pretend to confuse *dulce* with dulse and ask her mother why everything they made had to include seaweed.

The woolen man, like so much of what Thora produced toward the end, was useless, and certainly not very *dulce* either. They could never have sold him in the shop, unless as an invidious way to frighten children into behaving: a kind of felted *Struwwelpeter*. She wonders where that old book has gotten to, remembers how Matt used to shiver when she read to him about the scissors man who comes to cut off the thumbs of boys who will not stop sucking them, or about what happens to children who play with matches. Someone has just had a baby. If she could find the book, she could give it as a present. She'll ask her mother to help her look when she gets home.

Nils. That's what her mother named this lump of felt. By then he was no longer referred to, on the rare occasions he was mentioned at all, as Uncle Nils. He was just plain Nils, and it was always pronounced with a sneer. There are no photographs to compare the figure with, but Penelope finds it hard to believe that the real Nils so nearly resembled a wolf. Or that his genitals could have been as disproportionately large as Thora has made them appear under the traditional *bunad* knee pants in which she has dressed the figure. Thora used to scoff at the invention of the *bunad*, the would-be folk costume of Norway. Penelope is quite sure that Nils or Uncle Nils would never have worn the stuff. Certainly not while he was working at the sardine factory. He did work there for a while — she is sure of that — until something put a stop to it.

MOST OF THE women she works with in the packing room think there is nothing wrong with what Nils has done. He has simply seen an opportunity where others might not have. He didn't create the circumstances, and it's not his fault if some people are greedy and stupid, a bad combination that surely begs for comeuppance.

His plan dates back to shortly after the two of them first arrived. They were brother and sister by day, and — when they could find a place — something more at night. Now, only the charade of siblinghood remains. There is no real reason to maintain even that, apart from habit. By day and night nearly from the time they arrived, Nils was intrigued by the widespread obsession developing around the Norse sagas. Several of them had recently been translated into English. Copies were circulating up and down the coast on both sides of the border. At the picnics that were arranged for the newly arrived workers and their families, he would lecture Thora and others about the craze; and in the narrow alleys along Water Street or the loft of an empty barn after they had made the beast with two backs, he would whisper to her how the fabled journeys to Vinland would be the making of him. People were desperate to believe that the place they lived in had a long history, to experience that tingle in the back of the neck that suggested that people from an older world had been there before them. They were mad for Vikings, didn't care about the Passamaquoddy who were there long, long before. They'd give anything for evidence. He had found a copy of *The Saga of Erik the Red*. She was quite sure he had stolen it. They used to laugh at the translations of the names, the coupling of a name with an attribute: Thorfinn the Skullcleaver, Eyolf the Foul, and his favourite — Thorbjorg the Ship-breasted (whatever the hell that was).

Thora is glad that Nils abandoned her months before he acted on the plan. His affections had shifted elsewhere. That is what he said, and he made sure everybody could see enough to believe it was true. She wonders, though, whether he left her because he was afraid she might have betrayed him. As she thinks she would have.

Morris McCann was about as plump a pigeon as someone like Nils could hope to snare. He was rich, everyone knew that, and that was crucial. But rich men can be cautious and skeptical. That is often how they get rich and stay that way. McCann's road to riches, though, was paved with enthusiasms and risks. Discretion was not his long suit. When Nils discovered the factory boss's passion for the sagas it was like a gift from heaven. You could smell the money. He could hardly refuse.

McCann is by no means alone in his determination to believe that the Vikings travelled as far as Passamaquoddy Bay. There are those who argue that it helps make sense of Champlain's arrival at Saint Croix Island. A particular combination of winds and currents, they say, must have driven both lost explorers to exactly the same destination, a few hundred years apart. Others point to odd fragments of metal found in shell middens that are thought to predate Champlain by hundreds of years. McCann's own take on it is, ironically, related to his professional role. He is an enthusiastic proponent of the follow-the-fish theory. Why wouldn't the Vikings have pursued the herring wherever they ran? Thora is amazed at his ability to overlook the fact that they have certainly not been running well in these waters for the past couple of years.

Nils has never said where he got the coin. It must have come over with him from Norway, although he did not mention its existence until several weeks after their arrival in St. Andrews — once he had learned quite a bit about saga fever. She supposes he was afraid she might wheedle him to sell it for food or clothing or any of the dozens of things that might have made their emigration more comfortable. He has shown it to her only once and she didn't pay much attention. She remembers thinking it didn't look like a coin at all. It was far from round, thanks to a large bite out of one quadrant, and dark grey in colour, not at all shiny. On one side there was a cross, while the other was a mass of wavy lines that, if you looked hard enough, suggested some kind of monster.

Morris McCann had apparently had no difficulty recognizing it as a Norse coin, though he failed to see that the actual monster in this case was the man presenting it to him.

The set-up was painstaking. It was a side of Nils she had not often seen: patience, subtlety, finesse. He and a collaborator whose name was Eyolf — the actually Foul — staged a number of cryptic conversations about a surprising find they had made while walking the rocky coastline. They arranged to be overheard in the men's dining hall, at the saloon in the Kennedy Hotel, in the canning room, and, finally, when they judged the time was just right, on the gravel walkway directly below McCann's office window. Meanwhile, a young woman named Hedvig, whom everyone knew to be Nils's current lady friend, gossiped freely about the promises her lover was making to her about a future of fame and fortune.

By the time McCann made contact with Nils, half the packing room — and the whole canning room — knew what it was about, although she thinks only she and Hedvig and Eyolf knew the whole truth. It is not hard to imagine how things unfolded from there. Nils would have shown the coin to the boss and, after some demurral, admitted to conducting explorations along the shore. Fifty dollars (pocket change for McCann) would have bought a description of the rough location of his dig. Then they would have talked him out of a further hundred for them to do some further explorations, strictly on the quiet. The problem, Nils would have said, was the man who currently owned the property. They didn't exactly have his permission to be there. He might be willing to sell the land, of course, but he would be suspicious if someone well-to-do and established like McCann approached him. He might inflate the price. And so McCann had handed over another three hundred dollars. Nils would purchase the piece of shoreline in question under the pretext of starting a small sardine cannery. Even Thora had to admire that touch. What McCann needn't know was that Nils had no idea who actually owned the piece of shoreline in question, and had no intention of finding out.

She does not know whether Hedvig or Eyolf was the one to betray Nils. Perhaps both. In Hedvig's case it would have been jealousy. Nils had no concept of fidelity. She doesn't know what Eyolf's cut of the proceeds was meant to be, but suspects he may have seen an opportunity for even more money from McCann for the information that he was being swindled. The boss's pride was well known at the factory.

They are finishing canning a batch of clams when McCann storms onto the third floor. She doesn't remember ever seeing him up here. Nils knocks over a stack of empty cans at the sound of the boss's voice. Sardine cans — the kind McCann made his money on — wouldn't roll, but these cans are for clams, so they do, right to the door. She imagines Nils wishes he were in one of them. The regular thump of the foot pedal on the machine that Eyolf uses to cut the lids continues for five more beats and then stops. There is silence in the packing room too. It would be hard to say whether out of respect or anticipation.

"Did you think I wouldn't find out?"

Thora shivers. It is the same phrase she used with Nils months ago about the girl he had bedded two women before Hedvig. She watches Nils's hand reach for the soldering iron that is heating at the little forge on the canning table, wonders whether McCann has any idea of the man's temper. *Don't back a bear into a corner*, she wants to tell the boss. Nils has two choices. He can pretend not to know what McCann is talking about or he can brazen it out. Neither is ideal in front of witnesses.

"Is there something wrong, sir?"

"You know bloody well what's wrong."

"The herring are not running?" Thora can't tell whether Nils is intentionally poking at McCann's theories about the Vikings following the fish.

"I'll have my money back."

Nils lifts the soldering iron as McCann takes a step toward him. "You paid me for services rendered. You wanted to know the place that Eyolf here and I were talking about, and I told you. You wanted us to look for Viking relics there, and we did." He is obviously banking on McCann's not wanting to admit to the subterfuge of the land-purchase scheme.

"You said you'd found that penny along the shore."

"I showed you a Norse coin. I told you we had found some interesting things along the shore. You made the connection. You wanted to make the connection."

"You conniving Norwegian bastard."

Everyone has been trying to become wall tile since McCann's arrival, but at this insult to their country, several of the men in the canning room and the women in the packing room take a step in. It is the only time she ever sees McCann hesitate. Then he picks up one of the can lids that Eyolf has stamped out and passes it over to Nils.

Nils places the lid on the can of clams standing on the table in front of him. His hand shakes a little and the metal makes a little percussive tune. Then he solders around the top and plunges the tin in the boiling water bath that they use to kill the germs. Everyone watches the tin — aware that it means something, but not sure what.

"You have sealed your fate, my friend, as surely as you just sealed that can," says McCann, and he turns on his heel and heads for the stairs.

The next day, Nils's station in the canning room is empty. The rumours fly. McCann has fired him (almost certainly true).

McCann has had him killed (frighteningly plausible). He has taken his money and run (predictable if you really know Nils). At the moment, she doesn't care which is true.

PENELOPE TOSSES THE strange, felted man across the room. Her mother had a different story about the disappearance of Uncle Nils, she thinks. But she likes this one just as well.

Body Archive

THE ORGANIZING OF the workroom has been halted for nearly two weeks, since the baby was born. Amanda has continued to come for lunch many days, but then she has hurried off on grandmotherly duties, first to the hospital in Saint John and now to Carolyn's house in Chamcook. Matt finds he doesn't mind. This is no doubt due to a combination of sharing in her excitement and embracing the excuse for further delay.

He has been using the idle time in the afternoons to visit longer with Penelope. The mornings are devoted to research. Normally, the Charlotte County Archives are only open in the afternoons, but he has managed to talk the part-time archivist out of a key so that he doesn't have to work under her curious gaze. He feels a little ashamed of using his big-city museum connection to intimidate the woman but knows it was the right thing to do.

The archives are themselves a kind of historic site in their own right, with shelf after shelf of microfilmed community newspapers and the mammoth machines, roughly the size of Smart cars, that are needed to read them. Matt doesn't know of anywhere else that still has as many as two working hand-cranked reel-to-reel readers. In one corner of the single room is a small collection of published histories of the county, diligently labelled according to the Dewey Decimal system in case one can't spare the two minutes it would take to scan the five shelves by eye. Steel shelving along one peeling wall houses unpublished family histories in manila files, with a finding aid bound in a water-stained Duo-Tang folder that reminds him of his school days in St. Andrews. He has thought about taking photos of the place, sending them to Ingrid to ask what she thinks Derrida might say.

If he came to laugh, though, he has found he has stayed to revel. The squeak of scrolling through the microfilms of newspapers in the otherwise silent building spirits him back to the earliest days of his MA work, and he allows himself now, as he did then, to read the columns that are peripheral to the focus of his research. As he does so, he recognizes that the thrust of the enterprise has begun to change anyway. It has become more of a tentative groping around — the gentle, expectant discovery of a new lover, rather than the conquest he had envisioned. Connections occur to him that he knows would not pass any test of scholarly rigour but are nevertheless — or perhaps, therefore — all the more persuasive. He supposes that it can all loosely be linked intellectually to the subject of model villages, in the sense that the town is itself one, but the lines he is drawing are far more intuitive, visceral, impossible to explain.

Afternoons with his mother have become, in a way he can't quite identify, an extension of the morning's work. He finds, once they have gotten the social niceties of the weather and the decor of her room out of the way, that she drifts farther and farther afield, the encroaching plaque increasingly playing hob with her synapses. She will embark on long and very detailed reminiscences, only to recount the exact same events entirely differently the next day. She shifts easily from her own self to, seemingly, becoming her mother without apparent notice, casting him in a series of shifting roles for which he has had no rehearsal. He supposes that stories Thora told her have become, through repetition over the years, as real to her as her own memories. Sometimes, when he tries to lead her down a lane of memory he has trusted for decades, she will happily accompany him, marvelling at his powers of recollection. Other times, she darts down a side path or looks blankly at him as though he is making it all up out of whole cloth.

"I'll start to tell her an old family story, something I grew up with, and it will be like it never happened," he tells Amanda one day.

"Maybe it didn't. Is there any more soup? I feel like I'm eating for three somehow these days. How's her cold?"

"She sounds dreadful. Half the time, though, she doesn't seem to remember she's sick."

"There are advantages to the disease."

He ladles the last of the pea soup into her bowl, starts to fill her wine glass.

"Better not. If I have any more I won't want to move from this spot."

"Is that a problem?"

"Not a problem. Definitely not a problem." She puts her hand on his forearm. "But I've got to pick up diapers for Carolyn. Not having diapers, now that is a problem. We'll see you for supper at Carolyn's? Six o'clock? She'll try to feed the baby and put her down — God that sounds like what a vet does to your dog — put her to sleep, and then we can have a civilized supper. Ha! We'll see how that goes."

Matt thinks that she is going to say something about how he must remember how it was, trying to have a baby and a life at the same time, but she catches herself. He wishes he could get his mother to reminisce about what it was like to raise him, but he knows there is no longer any sure way of steering her there.

Penelope has asked him about Grandfather Arnold's candlesticks. She is convinced they are missing, that one of the helpers at the Lodge has made away with them. That was the phrase she used, straight out of a Victorian novel, he thought. He tried to assure her that the candlesticks were fine — and polished — in her house, but that announcement led down paths he regretted. Finally, he promised to produce them on his next visit. And so, he appears at the entrance to the Lodge holding aloft two Georgian candelabra. The guardians shrink back, seeing in him, he supposes, a Loyalist ghost, or perhaps the Angel of Death.

"Has the power gone out?" his mother asks when he walks through the door to her room.

"I just wanted to show you," he begins and then realizes there is no point referring to yesterday's conversation. "I thought you might like to have these here. Grandfather Arnold's candlesticks." He knows he can't actually leave them, that if he does they will certainly disappear just the way she has already imagined they did. "While I visit, you know."

"Is Pappa coming to visit?"

"No Mamma. I don't think so. Not today."

"It wasn't his fault. How he treated Mamma. He couldn't help the way he was. None of us can, of course. My mother blamed the war, the wars, and maybe that was it."

"He was a hero."

"Neurasthenia, they called it. That's a big word. A cold word."

"What do you mean when you say it wasn't his fault, how he treated Mamma?"

"Have you come from Linkscrest?"

Matt knows this is the old name for the large house at the edge of the golf course. It's part of the marine sciences operation now. He was reading about it this morning at the archives. In the second war it was a convalescent home for a while. The second war; not the first.

"Have you seen my Norwegian flyer?"

"Uncle Nils?"

"Good God, no."

"My father was a flyer." But Jonathan Reade was RAF, not Norwegian. "Was he wounded?" He can't believe he wouldn't have known about that.

"Who?"

He wonders whether he can steer her back to her own father.

"Have I always had those candlesticks?"

"Yes. Not here."

"Who polishes them?"

"I did, Mamma. They belonged to my grandfather, didn't they?"

"At one point, I suppose. My mother hated those things. But she rescued them."

"Rescued?"

"He would pawn things, she told me. To buy drink. Luckily, it was a small town. The man would give him just enough for a bottle and then send a note around to my mother and she'd come and collect them. She ended up paying for the drink both ways. Cash and bruises."

"He hurt her?"

"Not always. In the end, he went away. Somewhere they could help him. Try to help him."

"To Linkscrest?" Matt knows that is impossible — wrong war.

"They didn't help him. He fell from a window at the Royal Victoria three months later."

"Jesus."

"I helped out there, you know, at Linkscrest. During the war. It was mostly very sad."

Matt knows he should pause to mourn his grandfather (nearly a hundred years too late), but right now he wants to know more about someone his mother apparently knew much better. "Is that where you met your Norwegian flyer?"

"Is it? Nielsen, I think his name was. Or Helmer. No, Cooper. A flyer or a sailor. A sailor, I think. Did I tell you about the winter my mother spent on a boat in Chamcook Harbour?"

"It must have been awful working at the convalescent home. Depressing."

"They were all quite rough. Soldiers. You had to be careful around them. They mostly wanted one thing."

And with that she drops off to sleep. Matt sits for five minutes staring at the candlesticks before he picks them up and tiptoes out of the room. At the nurse's station, he turns and heads down the hall to look in on Amanda's mother who calls him Florence Nightingale, which is more sign of presence than he has expected.

SUPPER AT CAROLYN'S is chaos. Carolyn's husband, Mike, whom Matt has never met, is positively surly at first. Matt hopes it's from lack of sleep, but fears Mike is pissed off that Amanda has dumped Jim the Lobsterman. There is nothing any new boyfriend could offer that would rival free lobster. Carolyn spends the first hour upstairs trying to settle the baby while the chicken dries out and Amanda and Matt drink more wine than they should. Mike keeps pace with them in beer. Carolyn, who is probably the one most in need, has nothing alcoholic and has managed to spill her Ribena down the front of her already stained shirt.

Matt tells the story of Amanda's mother mistaking him for Florence Nightingale, which nobody finds as interesting as he did. Then Carolyn asks him to tell them about his research. He doesn't see the trap at first and rehearses for them the outline of the proposal he made to the museum and what he has been able to find out about the sardine town, and his impressions of the local archives.

"And the idea is to produce a book or an exhibition of some kind?" Mike asks.

"I know it all sounds a little confused right now, a little unlikely, but yes."

"Here?"

Matt hears the trap snap. "Um. Well, no. Probably not. In Toronto, I suppose."

"Oh." Carolyn doesn't need to say more. In that single syllable she manages to pack volumes of disappointment and disapproval. Matt waits for Amanda to say something, to explain to her daughter how things are between her and Matt. That they are old friends who are helping one another through some things right now, and that there are no expectations either way. No plans for a future. And then he realizes he doesn't want her to say any of that. The baby cries before he can reframe his answer. The nervous parents run off together to tend to her. Amanda smiles and begins to clear the dishes. When Matt stands to help her, she puts things down with a clatter and twines her arms around his neck. She tastes of wine and *L'Air du Temps*.

Human Deaccessioning

THERE IS NO point telling his mother he has decided to stay. While it is a big decision for him, it will mean nothing to her either way. Half the time when he visits the Lodge she thinks he has come directly from Toronto. Half the time she thinks they are both still living in Birch Hall. With Thora. Bernadette claims to be pleased by his decision, although he senses that she remains wary of Amanda. The Director took the news exactly according to the administrative handbook, mentioning the Employee Assistance Program if Matt needed someone to talk to, feeling him out as to whether he would be looking for paid leave or unpaid, without indicating whether either was a real possibility. Even when Matt finally admitted that he supposed he was in fact resigning, the other man was careful not to leap, told Matt to think about it for a while and then to put something in writing if that was what he really wanted. Matt could imagine the Director's whoop of glee as soon as he hung up the phone.

The phone call with Jennifer is a miracle of brevity. He is glad that he decided he couldn't really afford to fly back to have the conversation.

"I think I am going to stay here."

"Okay. Um. Okay. Actually, Matt, I've met someone."

"You've —"

"I'm sorry. I should have let you know. I wasn't sure how to tell you. It's all pretty awkward. Someone you know."

Matt mentally thumbs through a deck of remembered faces of Jennifer's colleagues at faculty parties.

"It's Phillip."

The Director. The next words are out of his mouth before he can stop them. "A case of human deaccessioning, then. Not exactly by the book."

"What?"

"Nothing. I am glad you are happy. You are happy?"

"Very. How's your mother?"

Matt knows she doesn't care. "Well, you know. Still some glimpses of her, here and there."

"Matt, I've got a class in half an hour."

"Of course. Go. Go."

He hangs up. Neither of them says goodbye.

The days when his mother recognizes what is happening to her are the worst. She will suddenly catch herself in a false detail or realize she can't call something up. He tries to tell her it doesn't matter, that lots of things are definitely worth forgetting, that we place way too much value on memory. When she becomes really distraught, he tries Bertrand Russell's hypothesis on her.

"Russell had an interesting idea."

"The mathematician?" She can still recall so many things in a flash.

"Exactly. He proposed that we, and the world we live in, came to exist only five minutes ago, and that it merely appears that everything is much older. Rings in trees, rust on cars — they're all just tricks to make us believe in a past that never existed."

"Roman ruins?"

"Yup. A hoax."

"Shell middens, piles of rubble, old newspapers, boxes of letters, portraits —"

"As long as the paint is dry."

"So it doesn't matter that I don't remember things. Anything older than five minutes ago didn't really happen."

He thinks it is good that she has taken to the idea so heartily. "That's what Russell says we can't logically refute."

"Bullshit." But her eyes say *thanks for trying.*

Amanda comes to Penelope's room to collect him. The car is already packed. They are going to the Redclyffe for a couple of nights. No gin. He wants to remember every minute this time.

Felt

SHE SUPPOSES HER mother would be horrified. Disappointed, at the very least. The work is neither what she would consider beautiful nor useful. It would kill her to see what Penelope is doing — if she hadn't been dead for ten years already. She has never forgiven Thora for that, for leaving her so soon. It was one thing to joke about her allotted three score and ten, but something else altogether to adhere so literally to it. But that was Thora. She could accomplish anything she set her mind to. If she told her heart to stop, it would stop. No doubt there was supposed to be a lesson in it somewhere for Penelope about willpower and control and self-reliance. It seemed a cruel but certain way of keeping her memory fresh.

She smooths the panel of embroidered felt with the palms of her hands, reading the scene like Braille. Stupid to be flattening it, knowing what she will do next. Force of habit. Muscle memory. Perhaps a gesture of love — at least tenderness — for the wrinkled flesh, sutured with embroidery floss.

Bernadette is burning with curiosity about the new project. Her fault. She should never have banned Bernie from the workroom. It wasn't as though she ever really came in anyway, but the interdict has awakened her nosey nature. Eventually Penelope will show her. If the experiments work out. Eventually, Matt will see them too, everyone will. There will be a show, with an opening, and people will come and look and ponder and make positive noises or none at all. It is what she has thought she has wanted for twenty years — an exhibition. She wants to show something that will make people talk and wonder. Who knows whether there will be any money in it? That's less important, although God knows the shop is struggling and Matt's tuition is certainly not paying itself.

She uses paper to mock up each piece, although you can't get the proper drape, obviously. The folds are too crisp, certain angles are impossible, and it won't lie the right way over the armature. But paper is useful for conceptualizing, and there is a lot of that needed for this work. *Too much*, her mother would say, and *You're overthinking*. She sketches the scenes on a strip of paper and then bends and folds it to explore the potential for obscuring details. *Because what is hidden is what gives the piece its energy.* She imagines viewers craning their necks, crouching, even turning upside down, to try to see what lurks in the crevices and canyons, the *sulci* — she likes that word she read the other day — that she will create with the draped felt.

She has learned that an armature is essential. While the finished piece must look as though it simply happened, that effect can't be achieved by just letting things look after themselves. You have to head off a viewer who says *it just looks like the artist dropped it*. Dowelling and clips and tacks can do a certain amount, but it has been most satisfying working with steel pipes. She loves to browse in the hardware store, examining the fittings and dreaming of what she can do with the tees and elbows and crosses. At first, Bernadette thought there must be something wrong with the plumbing in the house.

Her early attempts were too rigid. She sees that so easily now that it makes her wonder why she couldn't then. One of the first looked like an elaborate table napkin in a fine restaurant. Its folds were so tight there was no way they would invite you to try to see into them. Another, as she tried to open up the view, ended up looking like the top of a pair of overalls, or the bandolier waistband on some skirt she remembers seeing somewhere. The felt needs to drape — to swoop — for the work to be effective.

The piece she is working on will hang on two sets of transverse crossbars branching off from either side of a central stem. A single shorter pipe thrusts out to the front from a tee midway between the crossbars. Naked, it could be an eccentric display rack for the shop. Draped, it will evoke a human form, with the fabric suggesting the ridges of delicate collarbones and the swell of breasts flanked by the secret caves of armpits. The deep, secret folds created by the way the felt flows over the shorter pipe will suggest something that reminds her of Georgia O'Keeffe. And the furrows in the brain. *Sulci.*

For all of this, she has her mother to thank. She knows this in the same way as she knows her mother would disapprove of the direction she has taken. From the beginning of Handworks, Thora insisted that the hooked rugs and the decorations on her precious handbags reflect what their maker saw, how they lived. In the fifties and again toward the end of her life, she carried the principle to an extreme, producing those intensely personal essays in rag and felt — mats and bags that spoke about her own very particular tortured inner landscape. At the time, Penelope dismissed that work as self-indulgent, impenetrable. Now, in her sixties herself, she thinks she has begun to understand. She has certainly begun to emulate. And so, she has embroidered on the felt some of the stories of her life, of her mother's life, of Matt's. And she has plotted carefully which elements of which stories will be exposed and which obscured — knowing, too, that a slightly different draping of the felt could change the understanding of the entire saga. She runs her fingers over Jonathan and Robin, picks at a stray thread coming off what she has imagined of Mr. McCann, and about her father, wonders about ripping out scenes from each of the wars and replacing them with something more hopeful, though she is not sure what. Finally, however, she decides it is as finished as it will ever be and she sets to work shaping the soft cloth over the cold steel pipes, flesh on bones.

"Boss? Can I come in?"

Bernadette should know by now she is not welcome in the workroom. But how to tell her *no* directly again? She has been such a devoted worker, such a faithful companion. Penelope looks into the face of the old woman in the doorway and is relieved. This hag is not Bernadette. And then she sees that, of course, it is. She looks down at the wool in her lap. Knitted, not felted; an old lady's lap rug, not an exhibition piece, not even her work. And not the workroom. Somewhere else.

"I hate it here," she says to the crone-Bernadette.

"I know, boss. It's not home, but it is a good place, the best place for you."

"Not *here*." She gestures to the sterile room that is — unaccountably — decorated with some fragments recognizable from her life. "Here." She rests the heels of her hands on her temples. "Here. Here."

"I know, boss."

But she really doesn't. Nobody can.

Acknowledgements

This book would not have been possible without the support of a Creation Grant from artsnb (The New Brunswick Arts Board) in 2018.

It would have been less plausible without work on memory by such writers as Matthew Frise, Daniel Schachter, Greg O'Brien, Annette Markham, Lise Aagaard Knudsen, Ian Farr and the essayists he collected, Frances Yates, and even Montaigne.

Its fictions rely on the firm roots of genuine historical research and writing by such Charlotte County people as David Sullivan, Ronald and Diana Rees, Kenneth Leslie, Willa Walker, and John Gilman, as well as the many people who told me stories or pointed me somewhere when they found out I was writing a book set in St. Andrews. More general historical background on the Commonwealth Air Training program and the base at Pennfield Ridge was provided by F.J. Hatch and G. Chris Larsen. Every one of the many distortions of these diligent historical researches is my own.

What little understanding I may have been able to bring to what Penelope and Matt are going through is thanks to events of so called real life.

Heartfelt thanks to Marc Côté for the wonderful opportunity of a Cormorant reunion, to the talented team of Sarah Cooper, Sarah Jensen, and Barry Jowett for nurturing this book through to publication, to Marijke Friesen for the stunning cover (by which I hope the book might be judged) and typesetting, and to Attila Burki and Gillian Rodgerson for their sharp eyes and excellent questions.

Finally, thanks to Sheila, always.

Mark Blagrave lives and writes on the ancestral and unceded territory of the Peskotomuhkati people, covered by the "Treaties of Peace and Friendship" which Mi'kmaq, Wəlastəkwiyik, and Peskotomuhkati Peoples first signed with the British Crown in 1726. The treaties did not deal with surrender of lands and resources. They recognized Indigenous title and established rules for what was to be an ongoing relationship of peace, friendship, and mutual respect between nations for two very different modes of life and land use. All settlers, including recent arrivals, are governed by these treaties and have a responsibility to consider what it means to acknowledge the history and legacy of colonialism, and to embrace treaty responsibilities now and into the future.

We acknowledge the sacred land on which Cormorant Books operates. It has been a site of human activity for 15,000 years. This land is the territory of the Huron-Wendat and Petun First Nations, the Seneca, and most recently, the Mississaugas of the Credit River. The territory was the subject of the Dish With One Spoon Wampum Belt Covenant, an agreement between the Iroquois Confederacy and Confederacy of the Ojibway and allied nations to peaceably share and steward the resources around the Great Lakes. Today, the meeting place of Toronto is still home to many Indigenous people from across Turtle Island. We are grateful to have the opportunity to work in the community, on this territory.

We are also mindful of broken covenants and the need to strive to make right with all our relations.